The

DANGEROUS YEARS

He was a moderately successful screen writer
of unchallenging, grade B movies. He was
an indifferently faithful husband to a dom-
ineering wife. He was preparing an up-
status move to a wealthy neighborhood.
And he was vaguely worried about his
recent tendency to put on weight.

There was nothing really wrong, and nothing
quite right in this middle-aged limbo of
Philip Fleming.

When green-eyed Peggy Degen walked into
Fleming's house the emptiness was filled
with the most violent emotion he had ever
known. He was obsessed by a simple,
blinding need to have this beautiful wom-
an. . . .

•

The author of *The Chapman Report* boldly
brings a hushed subject to light, and turns
the full scrutiny of his talented pen on a
hidden, unnamed fear.

The
SINS
of
PHILIP
FLEMING

by Irving Wallace

A S I G N E T B O O K

Published by THE NEW AMERICAN LIBRARY

In an earlier book, *The Fabulous Originals,* I contended
that most fictional characters in novels are inspired by
real-life prototypes. I still believe this. But I want to amend it.
I was referring to other people's novels. Not my own. This book
and the people in it are entirely products of my imagination.

SIGNET TRADEMARK REG. U.S. PATENT OFF. AND FOREIGN COUNTRIES
REGISTERED TRADEMARK—MARCA REGISTRADA
HECHO EN CHICAGO, U.S.A.

SIGNET BOOKS are published by
The New American Library, Inc.
1301 Avenue of the Americas, New York, New York 10019

FIRST PRINTING, AUGUST, 1961

PRINTED IN THE UNITED STATES OF AMERICA

FOR

Esther and Harry

"Monsieur Rapture, an exceedingly nervous, artistic and narrow-minded man, told me at Messina that not only at the beginning but also at every subsequent meeting he had always been troubled in this way. And yet I should imagine him to have been a very normal man . . ."

STENDHAL: *On Love*

1

Saturday Night

IT ALL BEGAN with a casual kiss in the hallway that led to the bedroom. What happened afterward lasted a week. It seemed a year. It was hell.

When they first bought the bungalow on Ridgewood Lane six years before, Philip Fleming used to enjoy taking his breakfast and lunches in the kitchen. From the dinette table, the view through the big picture window was incomparable. Years ago, when he and Helen had driven from Paris to Rome on their honeymoon, hugging the mountains, above the clouds, between Rapallo and Spezia, he had seen what he then believed was the most breathtaking sight on earth. But when they had moved into Ridgewood Lane, he knew that only a name-conscious snob would deny that the mass of alabaster buildings, small in the sun, stretching from West Hollywood across Los Angeles, was any less beautiful.

But that was six years before. Philip had long ceased to gaze consciously out of the window and revel in this view that was his own. He was aware of it today. More and more, he realized, he was seeing and enjoying less and less. Perhaps this was because now, more often, he was looking inward.

It was an empty Friday afternoon, early, and he was sitting at the kitchen table, alone, near the big window, eating the lunch he had made and absently reading a biography of Ruskin. He enjoyed being alone. There were no demands. Once a child came into the house, privacy was at a premium. But Danny was playing at the Cochrans down the block. Helen was at the hairdresser. And he had fifteen minutes more by himself.

He had promised Bill Markson that he would be on time. Bill was slight, and bald, and unstable as a weather vane, and Bill had a time fetish. Bill considered time as something personal and his own, and if you did not respect it, if you were not on time, it meant you did not care enough, you did not like him. Actually, he liked Bill very much. Mostly because Bill liked him, and was comfortable to be with, and because his anecdotes were so interminable that one did not have to listen very hard.

When Bill had telephoned earlier to invite him to the races, he had accepted eagerly. He was still unwinding from his last studio job, and he did not feel like work. Faced with a typewriter on a weekday, uninstructed and unassigned, he would have to face himself. He was in no mood for that. But now he was sorry he was going. The long bumper-to-bumper drive to the track was tiresome, and the endless wait between races was boring. What he liked most about the races was the exhilarating moment when the animals broke from the starting gate, and, moments later, the flashing crowded excitement when they strained around the first turn. Once, too, he had liked the betting. The Klondike aspect of it appealed to him: the possibility that one could become rich all at once, in a lump, and gratify his every fantasy. But he was too conservative to wager much on longshots, and all the promise came to nothing. It just was not worth the endless standing around.

He glanced at the clock. Five minutes. Hastily, he finished his coffee, set the bookmark in Ruskin, and went into the bedroom for a sports coat. From the closet he could see the patch of front lawn, surrounded by the low hedge and shaded by the leafy Chinese elm, and the large sign next to the brick wall reading: "FOR SALE. DO NOT DISTURB OCCUPANTS. CALL BURDOCK REALTY." The sign irritated him faintly, and down many layers it made him angry with Helen. The large new house on Windsor in The Briars had been her idea. She was positive that they would have no difficulty selling this one. They had taken a long escrow on the Windsor house, just to be certain. After four months they had not sold this one, and soon he would have to go into the new house with a burdensome down payment. Being saddled with two houses meant going to the bank. He hated the thought. Even more, he hated the daily rejection of this house which so thoroughly reflected his taste and possessions.

He slipped into his coat, scooped wallet and keys off the dressing table, and hastened to the front door. His hand was on the knob when the telephone rang. If he answered it, he might be late and have to face Bill's agitated censure. If he did not answer it, he would worry the entire day about who it might have been. He answered the telephone.

"Hello."

"Mr. Fleming?" The voice on the other end was a bird call. "Mrs. Burdock, Girl Realtor. How are you today?"

"In a hurry."

Her voice flattened. "Oh, I hope you're not going out. Is Mrs. Fleming at home?"

"I'm alone."

"Mr. Fleming, I was just going to show the house. I have a wonderful prospect. She's right here with me."

He was discouraged about the house, but he knew that he could not pass up a prospect. "Well—how long'll it take you to get here?"

"I'm in the neighborhood. I was just showing Mrs. Degen several listings—when I realized you have just exactly what she's looking for. We can be there in a minute."

"All right. But try to make it fast."

He hung up, then lifted the receiver again and dialed Bill Markson.

"Bill? This is Philip. Look, I was just going out the door when that real estate biddy called. She's bringing someone over any minute. It won't be long."

"Aw, nuts, Phil, we'll miss the first race."

"We'll make it."

"Ted's over here with a real sleeper in the first. Make it snappy."

"Okay, I promise."

He dropped the receiver in the cradle and critically surveyed the living room. It seemed in order. Danny's baseball game was open on the coffee table. Hastily, he gathered together dice, scoreboard, playing board, miniature figures, and packed them in their multicolored box. He started for Danny's room, then suddenly halted and detoured to the bookshelves. He removed two books. The illustrated Miro biography he dropped casually on the hi-fi. The Kafka he placed on the coffee table. This stage dressing always embarrassed him a little, but he justified it by telling himself that a house should look lived in and cultured. You never knew who might show up. Sometimes little things made the difference.

He was in Danny's room, stuffing the baseball game into a shelf already clogged with games, when the doorbell sounded. He held back long enough to find his pipe, quickly fill and light it—somehow, a man with a going pipe never seemed anxious—and then he went to the door.

The too familiar, elongated face of Mrs. Burdock—she looks like her mother was frightened by a Modigliani, he told Helen after first meeting her—wearing its strained professional smile, greeted him. Behind her stood two women. The more striking of the pair was tall, or rather gave the impression of being tall, and was willowy. Her hair, cut short in the Italian manner, was dark, in marked contrast to her light green eyes and flawless white complexion. Her nose was small, tilted, freckled. Her lips were generous, and deep red. Philip stared past Mrs. Burdock at the young, serious face. He felt that he had seen it before. And at once he remembered where. In a book about Marie Duplessis, the young French courtesan who had inspired the creation of Camille. A fragment of the description of Marie Duplessis sped through his mind, and he measured it against the waiting young woman: "tall, very slight, with black hair and a pink and white complexion. Her head was small; she had long enameled eyes, like a Japanese woman's, but they were sparkling and alert. Her lips were ruddier than the cherry, her teeth were the prettiest in the world; she looked like a little figure made of Dresden china."

He hardly heard Mrs. Burdock's starling voice. "Mrs. Peggy Degen—Mr. Philip Fleming. And this is Mrs. Degen's friend—" He forced himself to glance at the more mature woman beside Mrs. Degen. He saw a confused mass of brown hair piled on top of a broad-featured, heavy face. Her expensive, fitted suit was wrong for her dumpy figure, and he knew that she tore all the new diets from the women's magazines. "—Mrs. Dora Stafford."

"Please come in."

He stood aside as Mrs. Burdock marched into the house, followed by Mrs. Stafford and Mrs. Degen. As Mrs. Degen passed, she left behind the scent of a delicate French perfume. It evoked the picture of a narrow glass shop in the Place Vendome and girls in pairs strolling beneath the trees of the Champs Elysées. Marie Duplessis. He closed the door.

Mrs. Burdock stood in the center of the room and waved her hand grandly. "Isn't it tremendous? It's absolutely made for entertaining."

Peggy Degen viewed the room wordlessly. Philip did not move. He watched her. She was shorter than he, after all. And quite young. Perhaps twenty-six. She was wearing a taut black sweater that bared her shoulders, and accentuated her small but firmly pointed breasts. A full brown cotton skirt, broadly belted, emphasized her tiny waist. Her carriage was magnificent.

She turned suddenly and caught him staring at her.

"It's very nice of you to let us come, Mr. Fleming. I know you're in a hurry."

"No—no—not at all."

"I would have made it another time—but I just have to settle on a place this weekend."

"I'm glad you came. Take all the time you want." He wanted to say more, but he did not know what to say. "Mrs. Burdock'll tell you—the drapes go with the place. And the rugs are new." This was foolish. He stopped. "Well—if you'll excuse me—"

He felt awkward crossing the living room. He felt that she was watching him. When he reached the hall, he glanced back. She had moved to the hi-fi. She was picking up the Miro book.

He sat before the typewriter in his crowded study and felt vaguely disturbed. He could hear the murmur of the women's voices as they passed from living room to dining room. He had an urge to be with them. He fiddled with his pencil. Mrs. Peggy Degen. He wondered if she were married to someone in the studios. Perhaps he had even met her before. But that was unlikely. He would have remembered. Peggy Degen. There was a clean, crisp quality about her that he found attractive. That, and the Japanese eyes and the way one side of her mouth curved, as if she were privy to a secret about him.

Fleetingly, he wondered how he had appeared to her. Not that she had even noticed him. He twisted in his chair and peered into the mirror on the far wall. He had a full shock of black hair, touched prematurely with gray at the temples, but much admired by the majority of his male contemporaries who desperately combed their surviving strands over their bald domes and hopefully let their sideburns grow. Other men's wives were always telling Helen that he had a sad face. It was the trick about his eyes, he knew. They were heavy-lidded, brown, and myopic. He rarely wore his glasses away from his desk, and this gave him a fixed, yet melancholy squint that women thought interesting. His nose was straight, and it pleased him. His physical problem in recent years was weight. He was five feet eleven, and he weighed one hundred and eighty-five pounds. This moment, he wished he were ten or fifteen pounds lighter. He did not want to be stocky. He wanted to be angularly handsome, as the boys always wrote. He wished Peggy Degen had seen him that way.

He heard footsteps from the kitchen, coming along the hall. He turned quickly to his desk, pretending to work over a scratch pad.

"Oh, I'm sorry—"

He looked up. It was Peggy Degen in the doorway, alone.

"—I didn't know you were working."

He grinned. "I wasn't. I was just pretending—so it wouldn't seem I was hovering."

"If you've got someplace to go—"

"No, really—"

"Mrs. Burdock is taking Dora—Mrs. Stafford—through the kitchen, cupboard by cupboard. I'll trust Dora on that. I'm blank on kitchens."

"What does your husband do for meals?"

"I don't have a husband. He was in an auto accident over a year ago."

"I'm sorry."

"Not at all. It's hard to explain, but—it seems a million years ago."

He was watching her mouth as she spoke. Her lips were the most perfectly formed that he had ever seen. Or perhaps it was the eyes that made the lips beautiful. A pale green-eyed brunette.

He was suddenly aware of what she had been saying, and he was momentarily at a loss for the correct words with which to continue. "Were you—were you married very long?" he asked.

"No." Then she went on hastily, "Anyway, there was always a maid—so I didn't have to cook. I suppose I should learn."

"Not necessarily. Cooking is a specialty. Being decorative is another."

"I thought that went out the door with Nora Helmer."

"Nora Helmer?"

"Ibsen's doll wife."

He looked at her carefully. "If Ibsen wrote a sequel today, I think he'd have Nora come back. She'd have had her belly full of equality and independence. She might be happy to settle for the ornamental status. Don't you think so?"

"I'm not sure."

"Take my advice. Avoid dishpan hands. Stay exactly as you are.'

She laughed, pleased. Then she was serious. "Mrs. Burdock says you're a famous writer."

He was embarrassed. "Mrs. Burdock belongs to the school where all cars are sleek, all homes elegant, all writers famous. I hate to let Mrs. Burdock down—but I'm not famous."

"But you are a writer?"

"Yes. In a way. I—I work for the studios." He was desperately anxious that she have a good opinion of him. "I used to do a lot of magazine work. I was a foreign correspondent for a while. And—once I even wrote a book."

"I thought I'd seen your name somewhere—"

"Not on the book. Only two thousand four hundred people saw that."

"What was it called?"

"Byron's Circle."

"A biography?"

"Sort of—about Byron's friends—and women. You know. Jackson, the heavyweight champion who used to spar with him. That sort."

"Who else?"

"Well—Dr. John Polidori, his personal physician when he went to Europe. William Fletcher, his valet. Lady Caroline Lamb—"

" 'Mad, bad, and dangerous to know,' " she quoted.

"That's right. Do you know the other line she added to her journal?"

Peggy Degen shook her head. He hesitated, then went on. " 'That beautiful pale face is my fate.' "

"She turned a fine phrase."

"That's the sickening thing about writing—how many amateurs are talented at it. Most discouraging."

"I'd like to read your book some day."

"A copy goes with the house."

Neither of them wanted to end this. She made the effort to continue. "And besides that—you were a correspondent?"

He nodded.

"How could you give up working abroad to come here?"

"I've been asking myself that for years. I know the truth, of course. Money. I don't know what you know about writers, Mrs. Degen—but that garret bit went out with let-'em-eat-cake."

She smiled. "I know a good deal about writers, Mr. Fleming. My husband was a literary agent in New York. He moved out here to take a better job, just before he was killed." She paused. "I've always been in awe of writers."

It was imperative that she know all about him. "Of course, I've been making notes on another book—" The familiarity of this apology embarrassed him. "I suppose you've heard that before, too."

"I hope you do another one, I really do."

"I will." For a moment, he believed it as he never had before.

She inspected the study. "This is a nice room for books. I could use something like this. I've got shelves of books."

He knew this would be so.

She pointed to the nearest bookcase. "Including Stendahl."

"That's a surprise."

"Why?"

"Well—he's a cult in France—he's just never caught on here."

"That's right." She thought about it a moment. "It's because he's too involved and complex as a person. All gray and gray and shadings, and no black and white. Americans don't like that. I mean, most don't."

"I'll be honest with you. I've read his novels, but I'm more interested in him than in his fiction. Most of that stuff down there is journals, letters, biographies. I feel the same way about Byron and Rossetti. The man, not the work."

She considered it. "You know, I think I feel the same way. I've often thought about it when I help Steve sort his baseball cards. He's my son. I read the backs of the cards avidly. Ask me about the Black Sox of 1919 or the time Rogers Hornsby hit .424 or the way Tinker and Evers and Chance never spoke to each other off the field, and I'm fascinated. But the game itself leaves me cold. I like the people and the things more than the game."

He was enchanted. She made a move toward the door. "I'd better find out what's happening in the kitchen."

He did not want to be left here alone. "Would you like to have me show you the rest of the house?"

"I don't want to bother you. Mrs. Burdock—"

"I'm better for you than Mrs. Burdock. I'll show you where the glass is cracked and the vent is broken—"

She smiled. "Show me."

He led her up the hall to Danny's room. They stood inside the door. He suddenly did not like the enormous clutter of toys and games.

"We never throw anything away," he said. "We've still got his first rattle." She was too smart for that. "No, that's not it," he added. "I buy too much. It's cheaper than giving time. I'm afraid I'm not the best of fathers."

She was nice. "We're all too busy," she said. She studied the room. "It's perfect for Steve. He's four. How old is your son?"

"Seven."

"May I see the master bedroom?"

"Of course."

He took her arm to direct her toward the bedroom. The physical contact sent a wave of warmth through him. He released her quickly. They walked into the wide, sunlit bedroom.

She stood beside the oversized bed. "This must be fun," she said teasingly.

He did not know what to say. If he said yes, it was fun, that implied that it was fun to have sexual relations with his wife. That would be disloyal to Peggy Degen. Worse, it might indicate that he was happy with what he had. If he said no, it was not fun, that implied some secret rejection of sex.

"I had it made special. I like to turn over in bed without rolling off."

"I covet it. We all spend so much time in bed, it should be made the most comfortable thing in the house. You'll have to tell me where you had it made."

"Any time."

She stepped over to the first closet and opened it. It was Helen's closet. A profusion of sweaters, blouses, skirts burst upon them.

"Your wife and I seem to have similar taste in clothes."

He wanted to disassociate her from Helen. "Not really. You don't know Helen." He quickly pointed off. "There are two other closets—"

She crossed the room, examined them briefly, then stood momentarily at the opposite side of the bed. She gazed down at the silver-framed portrait of Helen. It had been taken a half-dozen years before, just after Danny, when Helen's hair was still light blonde. The photographer's lens had diffused her sharper features.

"Is this your wife?"

"Yes."

"She's very pretty."

"I'll tell her you said so."

Mrs. Burdock rushed excitedly into the room. "Oh, here you are," she said to Peggy Degen. "Mrs. Stafford's simply out of her mind about the back yard. She says it's perfect for your boy—"

Mrs. Degen started forward obediently. "I must see it."

"Did Mr. Fleming show you this side of the house?"

"He was the perfect host. It's lovely."

Mrs. Burdock wagged her finger at Philip. "You're getting too good at my business, Mr. Fleming, I won't split the commission, you know."

"A case of scotch will be enough."

Mrs. Burdock had Peggy Degen by the arm. "Your boy and his friends will positively live in the yard. It's absolutely Eden." Peggy Degen threw a pained glance at Philip. He acknowledged it with a grimace. For a moment, he felt very close to her.

After the women had gone into the yard, he paced restlessly in the bedroom, the cold pipe in his mouth. He thought about Peggy Degen and her husband, who was dead. She did not seem to be a widow in a real widow way. Of course, she had said that she had not been married long. He wondered how long. He calculated. Her son was four. She had probably been married five years ago. She had said that she had lost her husband over a year ago. That meant that she had been married to him three years and some months. He did not know what difference it made. Except that it was good to know that she had not been married a long time.

He started for the living room. From the study he looked out into the back yard, bright in the early summer sun. He could see the three women gathered about the bird bath. Mrs. Burdock was talking. Then Mrs. Stafford. Peggy Degen had her back to him. Suddenly, he wondered what she would look like in bra and shorts. He wondered what she would look like without the bra, then without the shorts. He broke it off and went into the living room.

In five minutes, they were back in the house. He could hear them. Mrs. Burdock returned first, almost on the run, breathless and beaming. "She wants it," she whispered fiercely to Philip. "She wants to buy it." Peggy Degen came in with Mrs. Stafford. They appeared to have been arguing. He heard the last of what Mrs. Stafford was saying. "—can't be that impulsive, Peggy."

Mrs. Burdock turned to them. "I've just told Mr. Fleming."

Peggy Degen looked at him. "I understand you'll take thirty-five thousand."

Mrs. Burdock tried to explain to him. "I told Mrs. Degen you had been offered that once, and turned it down—but you might reconsider."

Philip hesitated. "Well, we'd been asking forty-two, and came down to forty, but—" He had promised Helen that he would not go below thirty-eight thousand dollars. Now it seemed wrong to haggle about a mere three thousand dollars. He did not want to discuss money with Peggy Degen. How could he disagree with her? And he wanted her to have his house. It was suddenly terribly important that she have the house. Somehow, he felt, this would draw them close together. They would have to see each other again. "—I suppose I might settle for thirty-five thousand, if you could meet the down payment."

She nodded. "I can . . . There's only one other thing, Mr. Fleming. It would have to be a short escrow. I have to have occupancy in a week. I haven't got a place to live."

"That might be possible. We already have another house. We can move into it any time." But he knew that he had better proceed carefully. There was always Helen to face. "The only problem is my wife. She'll be doing most of the moving. I'd better find out if she can manage it."

"When would you know?"

"She's at the hairdresser." He looked at his wrist watch. "She should be back in an hour. Would you care to wait?"

Mrs. Burdock clapped her hands. "I've got a better idea." She took Peggy Degen's arm. "Why don't the three of us go to my office and get the papers ready? Then we can have some coffee—and, by that time, it'll be an hour."

Peggy Degen was agreeable. "That sounds fine." She turned to Mrs. Stafford. "Have you got the time, Dora?"

"Of course. Irwin can manage the shop."

Peggy Degen extended her hand to Philip. "We'll be back in an hour. I hope you can convince your wife." He took her hand, and her clasp felt private and intimate. "I'll convince her. I like doing business with you."

She smiled. "And I—with you."

After they had left, he moved to the living room window and watched them cross the brick walk to Mrs. Burdock's canary yellow convertible. They stood grouped in front of the car for perhaps a minute. Then Mrs. Burdock strode around the car to get behind the wheel. Mrs. Stafford opened the nearest door and clumsily slid in. Then, Peggy Degen got in. For a moment, as she sat back, her legs were apart, one in the car, one out of it. Her skirt was above her knees. When she drew her leg into the car, before shutting the door, Philip suddenly fastened on the image that had been in and out of his head for a half-hour.

Peggy Degen lay on her back, on the oversized bed, naked. He came to the edge of the bed and kneeled beside her. Smiling, she raised her arms and beckoned him. He joined her, tenderness succumbing to desire.

He turned sharply from the window. With difficulty, he crossed the room. He retrieved his pipe. His hand was trembling. He began to fill it.

It was insane, these fantasies, this hot churning within. The whole thing was insane. He would leave a detailed note for Helen about the deal, and let her see Peggy Degen alone, and he would go to the races. He went to the telephone and dialed Bill.

But even as he dialed the image came back.

"Bill? This is Philip. I'm sorry I've held you up—but I can't make it. We're closing the deal on the house today . . . I've got to be here."

A half-hour passed.

The study was filled with thick blue smoke. He had paced about the room without rest—drawing and puffing on his pipe, luxuriating in the image of Peggy Degen. Now, for the first time since she had left, the image was beginning to recede, to become too elusive to hold in focus, as the time approached for the return of Helen. He tried to prepare himself for Helen. As always—his favorite sport—he could write the scene. She would come in from the hairdresser with her hair freshly bleached, too tightly curled, and in some way too hard and short. She would ask him what he thought. He would say that he thought it was cut too short. She would be annoyed and remind him that women were wearing their hair this way, that it was the latest thing. He would say, wearily, that he thought it would be fine once she combed it out. She would soften, and brush-kiss him on the cheek, and say that she only wanted to look pretty for him. He would say that she looked pretty enough without help from the hairdresser. She would start for the shower—she showered two or three times a day—and he would stop her with his news. Helen, he would say, the house is sold.

After the first reaction of excitement, there would be anger. Her Dutch sense of thrift, a private preserve of her mind that had been intensified by those years when she had been an eighteen-dollar-a-week file clerk, would be outraged. And the ultimatum to move within a week would spin her into an hysterical outburst of resistance. She would rage, and he would reason. He would win because he knew her most primitive fears. Until she had gone to the analyst, and learned that her basic need was the emotional need to be wanted and loved, she had measured all security by the digits in their savings account. This intangible lump of money, in some hidden vault, was still her safe barrier against all terrors. Analysis had modified but not eliminated her financial insecurity. Philip had but to point out that this barrier would be threatened if he could not sell the house because of this difference of three thousand dollars between her bottom price and the offer, or because of her inability to help him pack odds and ends into cartons within a week. With the burden of two houses, and no buyer for the first, the lump of money would go down and down, and the face of terror would again be visible. He would win. But only after a fight.

They had fought bitterly the night before. It was past midnight, and he was reading, and finishing his fourth brandy in the living room, when he saw the lamp light blink off in the bedroom. He closed his book, returned his snifter to the portable bar, and went into the bedroom. He undressed quickly, dropped his clothes on the chair, and crawled into bed beside Helen.

She was in a pink nightgown, coiled, her back to him.

"Hello, honey." He moved his hand across her arm and cupped it around her full breast. "I love you."

Angrily she pulled his hand away. "You're drunk."

He felt put upon. "I'm not drunk. For God's sake, what's wrong with you? I'm not drunk a bit."

She turned on her back and peered up at him in the darkness. "How many have you had?"

"One—maybe two."

"I bet."

"You want me to get it notarized?"

"I just don't want you to drink. I don't want to feel you have to drink to come to bed with me."

"That has nothing to do with it. God, someone would think I was a goddamn alcoholic—"

"I'm not saying that. I'm saying just one night come to me sober."

"All right—"

"That's what you promised last night and the night before, and a month ago, and two months—"

"Damn it, will you give me a chance!"

They brooded in silence, in the darkness, and spoke nothing. He looked at her. She lay rigidly, staring up at the ceiling. One strap of her nightgown had slipped off her shoulder, and her ample breast was exposed. Anger was dissipated by mounting passion. He stretched out next to her and slid his hand over her thigh. She grabbed his wrist and thrust his hand away.

He was angry again. "Is that the way you feel?"

"That's the way I feel."

She sat up, fixing the strap on her shoulder, reached over and turned on the lamp light. They both blinked in the sudden light. He drew back and sat up.

"I don't like to make love when we're fighting," she said.

"Neither do I. But if that were a criterion we'd never make love."

"Don't say that. It sounds awful."

"It's true. We're always fighting."

"We're not. Only at night. If you loved me more—"

"I want you. Doesn't that show I love you?"

"There's more to love than that. You've said it yourself. A man can get excited by almost any woman and make love to her—but not love her. There's more to love."

"Don't lecture me."

She was in despair. "You want another child. You're always insisting. You make me the heavy. How can we have another child when you don't know how to take care of the one we have? And it's not just being a good father. It's being a husband—a grown man—behaving like a man—"

Here we go, he thought. Castration, castration. That goddamn analyst. He sat up, legs crossed, not listening, as she went on. Sometimes, after a while, it drained out of her, and the stimulus of the cross talk and disagreement made her want him, and then they were together, blotting out the anger in a fusion of ardor, forgetting the old words with soft words of love, and the morning would be good. More often, though, she would go on, and he only half listening, and then he would stop her on some particularly bitter, hurting shaft, and strike back, and this would go back and forth, back and forth, until finally both were tired of it. She would rise and go into the bathroom for a seconal. He would go into the living room for another drink. They would sleep apart, and deeply, and unnaturally. Last night, he remembered, was like that.

He looked at his watch. Helen would be home in fifteen minutes. He began to cough, choked by the smoke, and after coughing himself out, he walked into the living room. He moved restlessly about. He stared at the Kafka and the Miro, and disliking himself, picked up both books and returned them to their shelves. He sat down on the sofa, filled his pipe, lit it, hoisted his feet on the coffee table, and let his thoughts dart, from here to there, across the years of his marriage.

How falsely portrayed, in most novels and plays, and in almost all movies, were troubled marriages. In fiction, usually, a single reason was given for a marriage that did not work. As a writer he understood the necessity of this simplification. A single reason for discord could be dramatized better than many and could be better understood by audiences of varied sensitivity and comprehension. Yet, how untrue these pictures of the marital state. His own marriage worked, but not well. It had good days, lovely, wondrous days, and shattering black days. But when it was bad, it was bad not for a single reason but for a dozen reasons. They were so many, and often so indirectly related to immediate discord, that he often had difficulty in associating them with any quarrel.

In the studios there was a cliché, as phony as the producers who persistently repeated it, that if you could not tell the story you wanted to tell in one sentence, it was not worth making as a movie. "Give it to me in one sentence, kid," they would say. "If you can't, you haven't got it yet." This was the rankest nonsense. He liked to picture Charles Dickens sitting in a producer's office groping to compress his latest novel into one sterile, meaningless, pretentious sentence. Yet, the cliché was appealing because it was challenging. Often he tried to apply it to the ten years of his marriage. Not a sentence, but a hundred sentences, give or take a few. How had he and Helen become so permanently embattled?

He supposed that he had met and married Helen simply because he had once decided to spend one day in the unlikely Republic of Andorra. He was quite young at the time. He had been living in the Midwest with his parents, and had already published *Byron's Circle,* the product of months of happy hours in metropolitan libraries. The book had hardly been noticed. In desperation, he began to write articles for national magazines. He was successful at once. He continued to write for them, traveling to Tokyo and Hong Kong, and home again, and then to Paris and Madrid. It was in Spain that he heard about Andorra, the 191-square-mile independent state in the eastern Pyrenees. This hilly democracy, whose principal industry was smuggling, appealed immediately to his sense of the bizarre. He took a train to Barcelona, and a terrible old bus to Encamp, and spent a day in the thumbnail nation, and then returned to Barcelona to write his article. It was cover-lined in a national weekly. It was read and enjoyed by many, but especially by a producer in a Hollywood studio, who was planning a romantic musical set in some mythical Anthony Hope type kingdom. Within a month, Philip Fleming was in Hollywood.

He was nearing the end of his screenplay on Ruritania, when the producer's office called to inform him that a studio publicist would be visiting him after lunch. The studio was preparing a press book on the picture, and it was thought that Philip's visit to Andorra might make a colorful tie-in. At one-thirty that afternoon, when Philip returned from the din of community lunch, he found Helen Tillman lounging in his office, smoking a cigarette.

He was impressed at once. Her hair was blonde and long, and she was continually brushing it out of her eyes when she bent over her notebook. Her eyes were blue and quick, and her features regular and definite. She was a small girl in her early twenties. Her full breasts strained at her tight gray suit. Her hips were broad and female. Her legs were short but perfect. She was quick, and bright, and she laughed nicely and had an eye for the absurd and a small way of being defensively sarcastic.

Philip found that she had been in Los Angeles no longer than he. Her father was a struggling bookie in Newark. She had escaped to an office job with a garment firm in Manhattan. But she was too good for that. She soon had a minor publicity job with the studio's home office on Forty-fourth Street, and her copy was so distinguished that she was transferred to the publicity department in Hollywood. That was only four months ago. She lived alone in a modern apartment on Sunset Boulevard.

She was enchanted by Philip's romantic visit to Andorra, and his travels, and his book, and his melancholy eyes. She was an aggressive listener, and questioner, and it was four o'clock before she forced herself to leave and return to her desk. When she left, Philip asked if he might see her again. She was agreeable.

He called for her two nights later. They went to dinner in a pseudo-French restaurant, and walked to a nightclub to drink and dance, then returned to her apartment at midnight. She remarked that the roof was used as a patio, and showed him the way to the roof. They stood high above the city, their arms encircling each other, gazing down at the flickering lights below. He took her to him, and kissed her lips and neck and felt an overpowering urge to kiss her breasts. When she asked him what was the matter, he told her bluntly. She was wearing a thin, clinging, low-cut cocktail dress. Without a word, she slipped down the shoulder straps, reached back and unfastened her brassière. The result was strange. Her large, young breasts, freed, almost cascaded into him. He had his hands under her loose bra, and her warm, fleshy breasts in them. He kissed them again and again and felt her breath on his neck. He told her that he wanted to go to bed with her, and with a certain reluctance she said no. He persisted, but she was adamant. At last she covered her breasts and fastened her bra. She would not, despite his earnest pleading, let him into her apartment.

She saw him regularly after that. They spent hours on the humid roof. They would talk and embrace and he would kiss her abundant breasts, but she maintained the strength to keep him from carrying their petting any further. After three months, he had left the studio, and abandoned all notions of returning East because of his growing obsession with putting Helen to bed, and had written an original screen treatment and sold it for a large sum, when finally he asked Helen to marry him.

It was a hot August evening, and they had been out drinking to celebrate his sale, and they were at the door of her apartment when he proposed. She stared at him, her drained face very serious, and then without answering him she unlocked the door and went inside. He followed her, shutting the door behind him. The single room of the bachelor apartment was small and new. She stood beside the bed, her back to him. He went to her, and turned her around.

"You haven't answered me."

Her voice was sharp. "You know I want to marry you."

"Then say it—say yes—"

"How do you know we'll get along?"

"How do I know? We've been together—we know each other—"

"We haven't made love."

"That's not my fault, honey."

"How do you know you'll like me?"

"I know. I've got to."

She stared at him, then suddenly moved into his arms. Her voice was small and tight. "Let's find out."

He reached to the wall, turned off the light, and then slowly began to undress her. She stood, not helping him, not moving. When she was in her white nylon panties, and nothing else, he bent her back onto the bed. She lay very still, her head turned to him on the pillow. By the time he had removed his shirt and trousers his excitement had become so compelling that he did not know if he could contain himself.

She closed her eyes as he climbed onto the bed beside her and began kissing the vast white mounds of her breasts. Instantly, he was aware of the rapid pick-up of her breathing, and then of the shortness of his own breath.

She spoke once. "Phil," she said, "I—I've never—I don't know what to do—"

"I'll help you," he said. "I'll help you. I love you. Helen. I want you forever."

It lasted several minutes, intense and high-strung and punctuated with burning commitments of passion, and then it was done. She covered her eyes, and wept, and then he cried, and then their naked bodies pressed together in a long embrace. She wanted to know if he still loved her, and he said that he loved her more than ever. They discussed when they would be married, and where they would honeymoon, and what they would do when they found a home. After a while they got out of bed, and partially dressed themselves, and then she made coffee. They sat across from each other, immensely relieved, each considereing the other happily and possessively. They talked for hours, without pretense or strain, and then they returned to her bed to sleep in each other's arms. With dawn, he woke, and this woke her, and wordlessly and naturally they made love again.

Now, ten years later, in the living room, waiting for Helen, he realized that it had all been more pleasant than he usually remembered. Where, then, had it gone wrong? Or had it been wrong from the beginning?

In sorting it all out, in the years since, he had been able to discover two illogical resentments. First, she had forced him to marry too soon. In so doirg, he felt that he had abandoned his parents. All their lives, his mother and father had suffered economically. Together, they worked in their own little dry goods store, forever indebted and reduced to middle-class necessities. They had sponsored his writing career through the long apprentice years, and never asked for anything. But somehow, he knew, they expected his help when he could help. Then, at the very moment when he had made his first large sums of money, when he could share with them and lift them from poverty, he had married. Now, what was his own was also his wife's. He could not share completely with his parents. He could only donate from time to time. This he did lavishly, without any complaint from Helen, but he knew that it was not enough to satisfy his subconscious feeling of obligation. And so the guilt lasted through the early years of their marriage.

The other resentment concerned his sex life. He felt he had married too early, and he felt cheated. He had had some experience with women before Helen, but not enough to satisfy him. Once, in Paris, in an outdoor café, he had met a buxom, sloe-eyed young girl, half Arab, half French, and had traveled to the Left Bank with her and slept with her every night for a week. That had been good. Once, in New York, there had been a nurse staying at the same hotel; and in Los Angeles, just before Helen, there had been a yellow-haired starlet who appeared to have stepped out of a Petty calendar. The starlet, who had been in too few films, dwelt with a wealthy, somewhat deaf aunt. He would visit their apartment hotel suite often. Since the starlet was vocal when engaged in intercourse, all lovemaking had to be deferred until late at night, after the elderly aunt had removed her hearing aid and gone to bed. Then, Philip remembered with nostalgia, the starlet would sit on his lap, facing him. Never once did her aunt awaken.

But these memories, looking back on them now, were too few. It was a constant irritant to Philip that, after he had money and stature as a studio writer, and an endless galaxy of attractive women available to him, he was yet unable to experience the delights most men knew, because he had married too early. Of course, many of his married friends still managed an occasional affair on the side. In ten years, Philip had not once been unfaithful to Helen. Opportunities had been frequent. But not once had he accepted a chance. He told himself that the effort was too exhausting, the dangers too many, the involvement too complex. He did not tell himself that he was afraid.

Seven years before, Danny had come. He had wanted Danny, and was proud to have him, but his resentments increased. He felt trapped by the mature necessity to support a family. He hated the unreal, manufactured studio screenplays, the daily attendance by grown men to child's play. He felt a growing dullness toward Helen. With her need to devote more time to their son, she had less time for his work. She rarely asked him what he was writing—or hoping to write. And he had tired of her in bed, though he would never admit it to himself. She was, for the most, he realized, a passive receiver of love. She gave little, generated little. She seemed to feel that it was sufficient that she was there. Merely to offer herself seemed enough of giving. For one brief period, after she had begun to visit an analyst once a week to check growing cycles of depression, she seemed to have attained a new attitude toward sex. She became extremely aggressive, and doggedly worked at love play, and tried to display more passion in her reactions, and took to speaking four-letter words more and more in bed. But the novelty of this new freedom disappeared with time, and she fell back into her old passive pattern.

Philip could no longer remember exactly when he began to drink. The habit had started with a single scotch after returning from the studio, and before dinner, and a brandy at night before bedtime. Now, it was three scotches before dinner, and four or five brandies at night. During the day he rarely drank. And during the night he made love to Helen less frequently now, and was too constantly absorbed in his frustrations and plans to write a book and escape, to devote good time to Danny. Helen was unhappy with him, and he was unhappy with himself. He wanted to get away, and he could not. Inconsistently, he wanted more children, a large family (the vision of Franklin D. Roosevelt, surrounded by his great brood every Christmas, reading aloud from Dickens' *Christmas Carol*, was always with him), but Helen resisted. It was Helen who had argued for the new house on Windsor. She felt the house would give them a charge, and keep them busy. The house gave her a charge, and kept her busy. For himself, he felt only frustrated and cheated.

The footsteps on the walk, the key in the front door, made him sit up. Glancing at his watch, he saw that Helen was ten minutes late. He emptied his pipe, filled it, and waited. Helen came through the front door. Her hair was bleached in tight curls, and cut short. His annoyance was immediate.

She was surprised to see him. "I thought you were going to the races?"

"I thought so, too—but I had to wait for you."

"Had to? Why?"

"The house—I sold it."

"You what?"

"Sold it."

"Oh, Philip, how wonderful!" She ran to him, hugged him, kissed him. "I told you it would happen."

"Mrs. Burdock brought a woman. She liked it. And that was that."

"You couldn't have had better news." Suddenly she halted. Her voice was anxious. "How much?"

He braced himself. "Thirty-five thousand."

"Philip—no! How could you? You know perfectly well —you told me you wouldn't—we agreed—"

He lit his pipe and calmly listened. He was ready.

He had won, of course. When it came to rejecting the offer completely, and undertaking both houses without prospect of selling the older, Helen capitulated. But not gracefully. She said that she was too annoyed to wait around and discuss the debacle with the Degen woman and Mrs. Burdock. She would leave the details to him. She left to pick up Danny at the Cochrans.

He stood before the living room window looking out on the street, and dreading Peggy Degen's return. He had made her, in his mind, more than she was or ever could be, and he knew that on a second meeting he would be disappointed. But when Mrs. Burdock's convertible pulled up, and he watched Peggy Degen follow Mrs. Burdock and Mrs. Stafford up the walk, and when he opened the front door to let her in once more, he realized that he would never be disappointed by her.

She was in the room, and she was more than he had seen the first time and had so fondly remembered. Her green eyes, almost mocking, and her full lips, curled in the half-smile, were all promise and sensuality. When he invited her to sit and she walked across the room to the sofa, she walked with padding feline grace, her long legs moving and crossing beneath her rustling skirt, until the thought of them brought a tightness to his throat.

Sitting, searching for a cigarette in her purse, she glanced up at him. Her look was open and serious, and because he thought that she wanted only to talk business, he was suddenly embarrassed. He was embarrassed because he had, in the hour past, been so intimate and profane with her—in the image in his mind—and without her knowledge. And yet, returning her gaze, trying to read her eyes, he wondered if she had not thought of him after she left. In Mrs. Burdock's convertible, in the realty office, in the café over coffee, had she only half listened to the other two while her mind wandered to some private image of him? He had read somewhere, in clinical detail, that women did not have the same sexual fantasies as men. Or, rather, that women were stimulated by factors quite different from those that stimulated men. Nevertheless, he felt less embarrassed. He sensed that she reciprocated his interest. If this were true, she must have thought about him. He felt better about the whole thing: he had a right to his image.

"Is Mrs. Fleming here?" Mrs. Burdock was asking.

"No," he said, "she had to pick up our boy. But we discussed it."

Mrs. Burdock tried to read his face. Peggy Degen waited calmly.

He turned to Peggy Degen. "I won't say she was happy with the price," he said lightly. "But I turned on my charm."

"Thank you," said Peggy Degen.

"Thirty-five thousand is agreeable. And we can make it a short escrow. We'll be out next Friday."

"That's wonderful," said Peggy Degen.

Mrs. Burdock beamed. "Well, everybody should be happy." She dug into her mammoth tweed purse. "I have Mrs. Degen's check. And all the papers. Can we use the dining room table?"

"Of course."

Mrs. Stafford touched Peggy Degen's arm. "I'm pleased if you are, Peggy."

"Oh, I am."

"Irwin and I will help you move. We'll close the store—"

"I wouldn't have that." She looked up at Philip. "Mrs. Stafford and her husband own the Pegasus Book Shop in Beverly Hills."

He thought that he remembered the narrow, gaudy little store, next to an expensive men's tailor shop. It was avant garde. There was always an abstract print, an E. E. Cummings, an Ezra Pound, an unreadable book by an angry young man, or an overpriced, overprecious quarterly in the window. The kind of shop where young men with reddish beards discuss Sartre, and where Pearl Buck and Yerby are dirty words. He looked at Dora Stafford more closely now.

"Well, then we won't close the shop," Mrs. Stafford was saying to Peggy Degen. "We'll get someone in. But we insist on helping break a few of your old pieces."

Mrs. Burdock had the papers. "I'll just get everything ready." She went into the dining room. Philip's eyes were on Peggy Degen. He wanted to speak to her. Mrs. Stafford saw this. Without a word she followed Mrs. Burdock into the dining room. Peggy Degen made no move to leave the room. She found a cigarette. Philip hastened to light it, carefully shielding the sudden flame so that it would not singe her long eyelashes.

She inhaled. "Thank you."

He sat beside her. "I hope you'll be as happy in this house as I've been."

"Have you been happy here?"

"With the house, yes," he said carefully.

She glanced about. "If you enjoyed it, I'm sure I will." Her eyes met his. "I think our tastes are the same. Will you be moving far from here?"

"The Briars," he said. "About twenty minutes."

Suddenly she said, "I'm glad your wife wasn't here."

"Why?"

"When I meet a man, and like him—I felt this even when I was married—I like to think of him just that way. A wife changes it. She fusses over him, or babies him, or runs him down, or—oh, I dont know. Forget it. It doesn't make any sense."

"I understand," he said.

"Anyway it's been fun today, talking to you. I'm really thrilled to have your house. Somehow I feel like celebrating."

He nodded gravely. "We should celebrate, both of us. We had to sell. You had to buy. And two such lovely people—"

"That's what I mean."

"It's not even like business. If this is business, to hell with art."

"Let's have a party," she said.

"A party?"

"A houseleaving housewarming. I'll do it, but we can do it jointly."

"When?"

Her face was Christmas morning. "Next Friday—no, we'll all be too tired—Saturday—next Saturday night. After dinner. You and your wife come. Bring some of your friends. I'll invite a few of mine. We'll celebrate right here."

The prospect was exhilarating.

"I'll bring the scotch," he said.

"And I will, too."

He extended his hand. "It's a date."

She took it solemnly. "A date."

Mrs. Burdock's voice was rising from the dining room. "The papers are ready!"

He rose, indicated the dining room with a mock bow. "After you—Peggy."

"Thank you—Philip."

He held out his arm. She took it. They went into the dining room.

He did not see her again until late Monday morning.

She was seated on a green leather chair in the escrow department of the bank, her slender fingers toying with an unlit cigarette as she listened to Mrs. Burdock, when they came in. She was wearing a printed jersey sport dress, something light purple and blue.

"Hello," he said. "This is my wife—Peggy Degen—Helen Fleming."

The two nodded courteously and acknowledged the introduction.

"I do appreciate your letting me in early," said Peggy Degen to Helen. "I was in a terrible spot. Steve—he's my son—we were being evicted from a rental—the apartment house had been sold, and the new landlord wants to move in—and I just couldn't seem to find the right place."

Helen was friendly. "I'm glad you liked our house." She studied Peggy Degen. "I don't know—I—I expected you to be a much older woman."

"Is that what Mr. Fleming told you?" Peggy Degen asked, flashing Philip a quick mocking smile.

Philip protested seriously. "I did nothing of the kind."

"No," said Helen. "But he mentioned that you were a widow. I think that threw me off. Well, I think you'll be pleased. It's a house for young people." She took Philip's hand possessively. "At least, we think so."

Philip wished she had not taken his hand. He freed himself. "Well, should we get the business over with?"

Mrs. Burdock was at the railing, speaking to a stiff young man in horn-rimmed glasses. She returned to them. "It'll be just a minute. They can't guarantee clearing the title by Friday—"

"I've told you, it doesn't matter for my part," said Peggy Degen.

"Well, it'll be just a minute." Mrs. Burdock hurried back to the railing to wait, like a perched blue jay.

Peggy Degen sat reposefully, looking at the activity in the bank. Helen watched her, then moved and sat in the chair next to her.

"Philip tells me you're having a party—"

"Well, I think we meant to do it together—"

Philip interrupted, somewhat annoyed with Helen. "I told you," he said to his wife, "it's going to be a joint celebration. The old order giving way to the new. I've already invited the Marksons."

"And I've invited two couples," said Peggy Degen.

Helen had objected to the party when he had mentioned it. She did not know Mrs. Degen. She did not know her friends. She would be busy with the new house, and exhausted, and she did not want to go back to the old house. But he had insisted. It was a spontaneous plan, and it would be relaxing for both of them. Helen had given in grudgingly, on the condition that they did not stay late. Now she said to Peggy Degen, "I was just afraid we might all be so tired—"

"We can make it a pajama party," said Peggy Degen cheerfully.

Helen laughed. "All right. It'll be fun." She glanced away. Mrs. Burdock was still waiting. Helen found her purse. "I think I'd like to go to the ladies' room. Would you care to join me, Mrs. Degen?" Peggy Degen followed Helen into the corridor. Philip wished that she had remained.

Later, after the escrow formalities had been completed, and they were driving up Sunset, he asked Helen what she and Peggy Degen had talked about.

"What do you mean?"

"When you both went to the bathroom."

"Oh. Nothing much. She's got a little boy. We've got a little boy. That kind of talk. She seems nice."

"Yes."

"She's very young to be widowed. She told me she's going to be twenty-seven next month."

Twenty-seven, he thought. Thirty-five. Eight years.

"She's very pretty," Helen was saying. "Don't you think so?"

The trap. Helen had no aesthetic, impersonal interest in beauty.

"Well—if you like that type." He smiled at his wife. "Personally, I'm blonde-prone."

Helen ignored this. "She's got a magnificent body," she went on.

"How do you know?"

"I was in the bathroom with her, silly. Flat belly, narrow hips, and those legs—"

"I didn't notice."

"I'm surprised she hasn't remarried."

"I'm sure she does all right."

"I suppose." She was peering through the window.

"Philip, isn't that expensive lamp store along here somewhere? I'd love to stop by for a few minutes."

"Just tell me when we get there."

Flat belly. Narrow hips. Legs. Long legs. Gradually, the image filled his mind. He drove in silence. He felt warm and alive. He had a secret.

It was the week of cartons. Finding them. Filling them. And the best part of the week was that each day, Saturday drew closer. No hour had passed without some vision of Peggy Degen in his mind. The absurdity of his daydream devotion troubled him once or twice. He had seen the girl only three times, and then briefly. He knew nothing of her. Most of all, he had no proof that she had any interest in him, aside from his role as owner of the house. Yet, she had seemed attentive to him. And the party. After all, she had suggested it. Was it merely because she was alone and lonely and wanted company? Or was it her method of bringing them together once more? If the latter, then what? He would not allow himself to think beyond that point in a realistic way. The image, that kept him in perpetual heat, was one thing. It was a Mohammedan's dream of Heaven and could be enjoyed as such. But as to reality: he bent to his cartons.

He hardly thought of work at all, until just before dinner on Wednesday, when Nathaniel Horn telephoned. Nathaniel Horn was Philip's motion picture agent. He was actually much more. He was a true friend of Philip's, and an honest critic of his work. Horn had a loose representation arrangement with Philip's New York agent, and the two agents shared commissions on all clients delivered from the East.

Professions or trades, Philip often reflected, leave their mark on the men in them. Most doctors look like doctors should look, and lumberjacks like lumberjacks, and agents, of course, like agents. The reason for this, probably, was that most men grooming for a profession have an idealized portrait of how a member of that profession should look. They then mold themselves after their prototype. Nathaniel Horn was the exception to the rule. He appeared to be anything but an agent. The typical Hollywood agent falls into one of two broad categories: he is either a cigar-chomper, hard-talking but secretly sentimental and all heart, with office under his hat, the basic ulcer, and a single Big Name client; or he is a serious, dapper young man, cut out with the same cookie cutter as his competitors, a crew haircut, black knit tie, dark Dacron suit, and a steady supply of erotic jokes and gossip, and who is employed by some vast, cheerless talent factory. Horn fell into neither group. He was that rarity: a literate, sophisticated nonconformist who did not pimp.

Horn was a tall slender man with flat brown hair, tired, baggy eyes, and a bony but attractive face. He was a graduate of Harvard, Harry's Bar, and Polly Adler's social club of recent memory. He had read Proust in the original French. He was happily married to a splendid woman, a former actress, and they had four normal children. He vacationed regularly at a fishing resort in Mexico, and his passion was pugilism.

Now his clipped voice was reassuring. "Phil, old boy, what have you done with a whole week?"

"Gotten rich. We sold the house."

"Wonderful! Did you get your price?"

"Roughly. I've been up to my ass in packing. What's going on around town?"

"It's slow. But I think I've got something for you."

"Really?"

"Herman Ritter wants you."

"No kidding?"

Philip was impressed. Herman Ritter was the top producer at Master Pictures. Ritter, a red-faced gnome addicted to first editions, sports cars, and outsized blondes, had left UFA and National Socialism to become a Hollywood producer. His first film, a vigorous celluloid biography of Victor Hugo, had been an award-winning classic and had made his reputation. With his overnight success, and motion picture business booming, Ritter had been offered a long-term contract at six thousand dollars a week by the heads of Master Pictures. Ritter had hired a battery of attorneys to make the contract foolproof, and then he had signed it. But with the ascendancy of television, and the recession in movie business, the studio heads found Ritter's salary top-heavy. They tried to make him take a cut, but he resisted with Teutonic doggedness. Then they schemed to break his contract. A favorite story about this effort, probably apocryphal, concerned the time the studio heads made Ritter work as a tourist guide. They had combed his contract and learned that they had the right to employ him in any capacity. Ritter, it was said, smilingly undertook the assignment. With Germanic thoroughness, he spent his mornings and afternoons guiding bands of out-of-town visitors through the studio stages and laboratories. On one such occasion, one of the tourists, accompanied by his family, proved to be an Eastern banker involved in the studio's financing. Pleased with his guide's intimate knowledge of the lot, the banker complimented Ritter at the end of the tour. "I'm going up front and let them know that you deserve a raise, my good man," said the banker. "Tell me, what are you paid?" "Six thousand dollars a week," said Ritter.

He had been producing ever since. The prospect of working for such a man was exciting to Philip.

"What's the assignment, Nat?"

"A Western."

Philip groaned.

"Look, Phil, I know—but they're not giving Ritter anything better—and that's all there is. Anyway, he wants you."

"But another Western—"

"Okay, no Acadmy Award. At least, it's a thousand a week and a decent man to work for. You've got a new house, haven't you?"

"Don't brainwash me."

"You know better than that. Think about it tonight, Phil, and then we'll hash it over tomorrow. Come in around eleven. Matter of fact, there's something else I want to discuss with you."

"All right, Nat. Tomorrow."

The following morning, at five minutes to eleven, Philip parked his sedan before the office building with the colonial façade where Horn kept his Beverly Hills suite. Philip stopped briefly at the stationer's to buy the trade papers, then climbed the stairs to the second floor. Viola, Horn's cute secretary, was out. The door to Horn's inner office was open. Horn was tilted back in his swivel chair, drinking a Coke from a paper cup and reading the sports section of the airmail edition of the *New York Times*. He sat up as Philip came in.

"Hi, Phil. Just reading about last night's fight. Did you see that Mexican kid taking a beating on television?"

"No, I was packing dishes. But you can count ten over me too, if I take another Western. What's it about?"

"Ritter didn't tell me much. Some lousy book with one idea. I think it's called *The Rusty Star*. Something like that." Horn screwed up his face, trying to remember. "Anyway, this Midwest family, the daughter's the heroine, is heading for California in two wagons—"

"Sounds new," said Philip bitterly.

"—and they come across an ambushed, burning stagecoach. Only one survivor. A wounded man with a badge, a sheriff, handcuffed to his dead prisoner—"

Philip held up his hand. "Only it turns out after a while that the survivor is not really the sheriff, but actually the prisoner, a guy wanted for murder. As soon as he recovers, he expects to run for it. But the way the family treats him, especially the girl, makes him change his mind. He decides to clear up the crime of which he's been wrongly accused. Close?"

Horn laughed. "Something like that. Look, I've heard worse."

"Isn't there anything else around?"

"Not much. Well, one other possibility I wanted to mention. A certain producer, who shall be nameless—"

"Who?"

"Not yet, Phil. Anyway, he's a big independent. He telephoned yesterday. He's playing around with a biographical idea, and he's looking for the right man. He wants Ernie Ives—someone in the two- to three-thousand dollar class— so I'm sending Ives in. But I also put in a pitch for you."

"What's it about?"

"I'd rather not say yet. I don't want to get your hopes up. But I have an idea it's much better than any Western."

"You think I have a chance?"

"I don't know. I gave him something of yours to read. But don't think about it. Think about Ritter."

"When does Ritter have to know?"

"Early next week's the latest." He wheeled his chair around and regarded Philip with concern. "Look, Phil, I know how you feel about all this hack junk. I'm with you. I've told you that a hundred times before. If I knew you could afford it, I'd be the first to say to hell with Westerns and melodramas and all that crap. I'd say go down to La Jolla and write another book—or a play—do what you should be doing. But you haven't got the money. And there are no patrons around."

"Why haven't I got the money? A grand a week for how many years—where does it go?"

"You don't know. That's where it goes."

"It just doesn't make sense."

"All I know is that you've got your overhead. So I have to do my job. And my job's to see that you make a living."

Philip shoved himself out of the chair with resignation. "All right. Unless something comes up—we'll take the Western."

He drove slowly through Beverly Hills headed for home.

But, at the second intersection, instead of going straight ahead, he turned to his left. He did not know why he made the turn. Possibly, it was that he was not ready to return home yet. Or, possibly, it was that he wanted to see some-one.

There was a vacant parking place near the Pegasus Book Shop, and he took it. He stretched to see himself in his rear-view mirror, then, digging into his pocket for change, opened the door. He was inserting his second nickel in the parking meter, when he saw a matronly young woman top-heavy under a mop of brown hair emerge from the book-store.

He moved hurriedly to intercept her. "Good morning, Mrs. Stafford."

Dora Stafford looked up without immediate recognition. Then, she smiled. "Mr. Fleming. What are you doing on our reservation?"

"I was just coming in to browse."

"God knows, we can use every customer we get. My hus-band's in there. He'll help you."

"Are you going to lunch?"

"Just a hamburger at the corner. If you don't mind ptomaine, why don't you join me?"

"That's what I've been fishing for," he said with a grin.

"Come along. I haven't got all day."

They talked about the book business as they found a cramped booth, ordered hamburgers medium well with cof-fee, and then discussed a current best-seller. She told him some pointed, amusing stories about authors who appeared weekly to wet-nurse their latest publications. She spoke easi-ly, with lusty abandon, and he had difficulty in matching her. His own conversation was labored and stiff.

As they finished their hamburgers and received refills on their coffee, Dora Stafford suddenly looked up and said, "Okay, Phil—I'm going to call you Phil—we've had enough of this periphery nonsense. I've got ten minutes, so let's stop wasting time. Why are you here?"

"Because—"

She cut him short. "That's a rhetorical question. I know why you're here. Not because you're interested in an old bag like me, or in Irwin, or in any damn bookstore. You want to talk about Peggy."

"Whatever gives you that idea?"

"The look on your face the day we walked into your liv-ing room. Like you'd just set eyes on Nell Gwynn or Agnes

Sorel. I've seen that look a hundred times—on a hundred men who've met her."

"It wasn't conscious—"

"You looked like you wanted to eat her." She considered. "Maybe she wouldn't object." She laughed raucously.

Philip felt disturbed. "You seem to be saying she has a lot of men after her."

"Well, what do you think?"

He didn't know what to think. But he had to find out. "Has she?"

"I should be so lucky. They drone around her like bees around honey. They did even when she was married."

"I'm not surprised. She's attractive." He hesitated. "Does she see many of them?"

Dora Stafford grinned. "You mean, does she crawl into the hay with them? I don't think so. Maybe one or two. But I wouldn't even be sure of that. Peggy isn't exactly the confiding type—at least not about her bed habits." She sipped her coffee. "It's those damn eyes of hers. The built-in boudoir look. They make everyone think she wants to hop right into the hay. They give the wrong impression—I think. She's too cerebral for real promiscuity."

He lit her cigarette. He tried to be casual. "What was her husband like?"

"Bernie? A nervous little runt. Oh, kind of good-looking in his way, but too anxious about his work. I bet he didn't sleep with her more than once a month. Always running. Run, run. He wanted to be a big success." She thought about him. "He must have been lousy in the sack."

"Why did she marry him?"

"Who knows? Why does anybody do anything? She was a kid. Still is. Her old man's a high powered lobbying muck-a-muck in Washington. Her mother's big on the social circuit. And one of her brothers's a diplomat. She wanted out. So she went to New York to write—"

"I didn't know that."

"She couldn't write her name. Finally, she signed on with some publicity agent and ran into Bernie Degen. Her name was Peggy Laughlin."

"What did she do after he died?"

"Well, we all tried to keep her busy—cheered up—and she didn't mind being alone. She's a great reader. Horace and Rachel Trubey are her best friends. They're gems. Nauseating normal. He's the travel editor of that big California magazine—"

"Oh, yes—"

"They've been good for her. They took her along on their last vacation, with her kid and theirs. Well, she's on her feet now. She has all this insurance money, and she wanted to buy a house—and hello, here we are."

Philip rubbed his pipe with his thumb. "Do you think she'll get married again?"

"It's in the deck. Peggy's no career girl. She was put together to be taken care of and enjoyed."

His heart quickened at the last. He wanted to know everything about Peggy. Everything. He could not know enough. Dora Stafford was continuing.

"Some day someone'll come along—"

"Anyone now?"

"A few. No big passions. She can have as many as she wants—but like she told me—its more tiring pushing them off her, than turning the page of a book alone. Oh, there's one that's kind of serious. A young bachelor—Jake Cahill —he went to school with her husband. He's an economist. Runs around the country for one of those secret government projects. Always making cost estimates on some damn thing or other. Whatever it is, it can't be good for people. He's a deadly serious one, and his pipe doesn't fit. I never understand a word he's saying. It's Sanskrit. And I'm smart. Maybe I'm not being fair to him. Actually, Jake's interested in everything. When he's in town, he takes her to concerts and on picnics. I suppose he'd be good for her, though I think he's kind of dull."

She suddenly stopped and looked at Philip. "You plan to see her again?" she asked.

"Well, at the party day after tomorrow—"

"You know what I mean."

"I'm not sure I do. I'm married—"

"Don't be a horse's ass. So you're married." She considered something a moment, then spoke. "She likes you."

He could not disguise the quickness of his question. "Did she say so?"

"No. She wouldn't. She never does. But the way she doesn't want to talk about you, and keeps bringing you up, reveals more than she realizes." She grinned at him. "It'd be worth a try, Phil. Peggy's got a lot there. She won't be saving it forever."

The move from Ridgewood Lane to Windsor was achieved with minimum bickering, and some exertion, and at once it was Saturday night.

Philip and Helen were driving east on Sunset Boulevard.

He had his foot down on the accelerator hard because they were already half an hour late, and he had looked forward to this party so long.

"This is going to be the craziest party," Helen was saying.

She sat in the front seat beside him, her mink stole casually topping a pink cocktail dress. Bill and Betty Markson were in the back. Bill was humming a university football song loudly. Betty, a plain, somewhat dazed blonde, was trying to quiet him. "Please, Bill, I can't hear a word Helen's saying." She looked helplessly at Helen. "He's in his manic phase. Stocks went up." Bill stopped his humming. "What were you saying?" Betty asked Helen.

"I said it's going to be the craziest party. We don't know a soul."

Philip frowned. "We know Peggy Degen."

"She's the girl who bought our house," Helen explained to Betty. "She's very pretty."

"Say now!" exclaimed Bill, coming to life again in the back seat. "You been keeping something from me, Phil?"

"I put you down for one dance."

"Pretty, eh? Well, I could use a change of scenery—"

"Beast," said Betty. "All men are animals," she added to Helen cheerfully.

Bill resumed his humming. Philip drove faster.

Ten minutes later, they were at the door, waiting. The door opened. She stood there, a highball in one hand, slowly blinking at him in the way people do when they have been drinking. Her Italian haircut was ravishing, and it gave her a curiously abandoned Bohemian appearance. She was wearing a snug, black, semiformal dress, rather short and youthful. Exposed by its off-the-shoulder décolletage, her shoulder bones protruded slightly, and her skin was white velvet.

She held up her drink gaily. "Welcome to my favorite landowner," she said. She nodded at Helen. "Hello, Helen. Take a look at your house."

"I miss it already," Helen said and went inside.

Philip indicated Bill and Betty. "Two of my best friends —Bill and Betty Markson—Peggy Degen," he said.

They acknowledged the introduction. Betty went through the door. Peggy followed her. Bill gripped Philip's arm. "Say now," he whispered appreciatively. They went into the living room.

The room seemed full, and it appeared strange with someone else's furniture in it. Peggy's pieces were traditional, with some antiques, and the whole impression of the

room was darker, more formal, but handsome. He recognized Dora Stafford and waved to her.

"Let me introduce you all," Peggy was saying. "Then
you'd better make some drinks, Philip. You're co-host, remember."

"I remember."

The introductions went by in a blur. The slight man with
the bulging eyes next to Dora Stafford was her husband,
Irwin. The other couple was Horace and Rachel Trubey.
Philip remembered that they were Peggy's best friends,
and that he was the travel editor or writer or something.
Horace Trubey wore a crew haircut and skimpy suit and a
perpetual smile. Rachel Trubey was a rather large, sallow,
direct young woman.

"I'm mixing," Horace said. "What'll you have?"

"My God, I left my half of the party in the car," Philip
remembered. "I've brought enough to float Alcoholics
Anonymous. Make mine scotch and water. And generous." He wanted to catch up with Peggy. He watched her
leading Helen and Betty to the bedroom. He hastened outside.

When he returned, wheezing under the carton heavy with
drinks and snacks, everyone was crowded about the coffee
table, and the buzz of conversation was steady. Peggy was
sitting between Horace and Bill.

"Can I help you?" she asked Philip.

"I'll manage."

"Your drink's in the kitchen" Horace called after him.

An hour passed, and he had his third drink in his hand,
as he moved from one group to the other. The party was
special fun. He supposed that actually it was like most
parties, no better, no worse, with the usual deadening talk
about the banality of television and some hostile anecdotes
directed toward analysts, but somehow it seemed special fun.

He stood over Horace, Bill, Betty, and Helen, listening to
Horace discuss Paris. "It should be converted into an international park," Horace was saying. "Some day I'm going
to write an article on that. All the nations of the world
should chip in and build a huge grilled fence around Paris,
and the trades people and shops and institutions inside
should be supported by a world-wide fund. And people from
all over would pay to get into Paris, and enjoy themselves,
and recharge. Paris should not be subjected to the rules and
mores that govern ordinary cities. Economic crisis. Capital
versus labor. Politics. Housing problems. All that rot. Paris
should be preserved as a playground for all mankind, the

City of the Sun, Shangri-La, exempt from war and worka-
day cares. Paris Preserved—that's my crusade."

Everyone enjoyed this, and Philip liked Horace very
much. Helen said to Horace, "You sound just like Phil."

Horace looked up. "You can join my committee, Phil."

Philip smiled. "I've been secretly in your pay for years.
I've always been an agent for Paris Preserved. Christ, what
a place."

The talk resumed. He felt someone looking at him. He
turned his head. His eyes met Peggy's. She was seated between Dora and Rachel. Irwin was on the arm of the sofa,
listening to Dora.

Peggy suddenly rose. "Excuse me." She took the tray of
canapés off the coffee table.

He moved toward her. "Can I help you?"

"Have some."

He took some cheese things. They were a few feet away
from the others.

"Dora said you had lunch with her." Her voice was low.
"Do you do this often?"

"I wanted to ask her all about you."

"Oh, sure—"

"I did."

"I'm the best person to ask about me."

"I was shy. But I'll remember that."

She moved off toward the group around Horace, and
passed the canapés. Everyone was too busy talking. She
set the tray back on the coffee table, and then, without
glancing at Philip, she started toward the hallway.

He stepped to the coffee table, selected a bacon wrapped
olive, nibbled at it. He looked up. She was standing un-
steadily in the hallway leading to the bedroom. She was
staring directly at him. When he saw her, she quickly looked
away and walked down the hall, out of sight.

He set his drink on the table, and said loudly to Bill,
"Watch my drink—I've got to go to the boys' room."

He crossed the living room, intending to go to the bathroom, but hoping to see her. When he entered the hallway,
he saw her. She was in the dim area between bathroom
and bedroom, leaning back against the wall, drink in hand,
watching him. He went to her.

"I thought you might be going to look in on your son,"
he said. "I wanted to see him."

"He's staying with friends tonight," she said.

She regarded him silently, and he met her eyes. Her eyes
were lucid green. The corners of her mouth lifted in a

partial smile. "You're charming everyone," she said. "Dora and Rachel love you."

"I haven't spoken a word."

"Of course you have."

"Maybe you'll invite me to all your parties?"

Her face was the face of an earnest child. "I'd like to, very much."

His eyes were on her smooth red lips as she spoke. His heart hammered furiously.

"Why did I have to meet you now?" she asked, petulantly. "I love you."

"Well," he said lightly, "I love you, too."

She considered him solemnly. "Aren't you going to kiss me?" she asked.

Without waiting for his reply, she straightened, lifted one hand, cool from the drink, to his cheek, and pressed her full lips to his. Her mouth was moist and warm, and he felt it to the base of his spine.

"There," she said, pulling away.

She turned and walked down the hall and into the living room.

He stood unmoving. She's drunk, he told himself. A casual kiss in the hallway. Hell, everyone kisses everyone these days. Everywhere. But you don't feel it that way. He went into the bathroom and stood before the wash basin. He studied his face in the mirror, twisted the faucet, washed the lipstick off his mouth with cold water. He dried on the fancy guest towel, and went back to his drink.

It was near midnight now. He felt high and wonderful, and he was addressing a group consisting of Horace, Rachel, and Irwin.

"I'll tell you what's wrong," he was saying. "The whole educational system, that's what. If I owned a college, I'd make them teach our kids to be little bastards—"

"Not that they aren't already," Horace interrupted.

Rachel giggled appreciatively. Philip went on earnestly. "I mean real bastards. That's what's wrong with our schools. They teach kids love thy neighbor, and do a good turn, and be honest, and unselfish, and do unto others—and then they go out in the cold world and act absolutely opposite to survive—they've got to compete, not cooperate—to lie, cheat, stab in the back, fight everybody and everything to get ahead. What they were taught to do and what they must do are always at war. So you have a neurotic society. In my college, there would be courses in 'How To Make the Boss's Wife Happy,' 'How To Screw Friends and Win Promotions,' 'How To Lie To Your Wife And Get Away With It.' Et cetera. I guarantee you, my graduating class would be the most normal one in history."

"Hear, hear," said Horace.

"I want to enroll," said Betty.

Irwin began to expound his own ideas about higher education. Philip glanced at the other group. He had wanted to be with them, but he had not wanted to be obvious. Helen was very observant. Helen's back was to him now. Bill was relating some studio gossip. Peggy was in a deep leather chair, facing him from across the coffee table. She was listening to Bill with a half-listening, set smile.

He tried to watch her. He did not want to stare. Several times, he moved his head toward Irwin's conversation, nodding but not hearing. He looked at her again. Her legs were together and sideways. They were extraordinarily long, and the stockings sheer. The skirt came tight and high to her knees. Now, as she smiled more broadly at an anecdote Bill was relating, she settled deeper into the chair, and then, in an automatic feminine gesture, she reached forward to lift her skirt and cross her legs. He saw the moment of crossing. For an instant he saw the stocking inside her leg, beneath her dress, and the flash of white thigh.

She was smoothing her dress down when she lifted her eyes toward him, knowing that he was looking at her and wanting him to know that she knew. Her face said nothing. It was absurdly young and angelic. She seemed to catch her breath, and her small breasts rose and fell. She turned her attention back to Bill. The moment Bill was done, she reached for her glass. "I'll be right back." She went past Philip into the kitchen.

His eyes followed her. He peered down at his drink, and finished it hastily. "I can stand a refill," he said to no one in particular. Helen heard him. "Honey, can you get me some ice?" He accepted her glass and went into the kitchen.

She was inside, backed against the sink, arms crossed, waiting. He set the two glasses down and walked over to her.

"How did you know I'd come after you?" he asked.

"Because you knew I'd be waiting."

They stared at each other silently a moment. He saw that she was breathing faster than normally, and he felt the tightening in his chest. He leaned forward, and without taking her, he pressed his mouth to hers. The quivering was in her lips, and a hunger, and he was encompassed by a sensation that he had not known for years. He broke off to catch his breath. Her eyes did not leave his. Her lips were half parted. She closed her eyes. He bent over her and found her mouth again. Their tongues touched. He grasped her limp arms hard, as his mouth left hers. They stared at each other.

Suddenly she shook her head helplessly. "Why are you married? Or did I ask that before?"

He released her arms. "It works the other way around, too."

"Does it?"

"Every time I look at you I wish we'd met years ago."

"Well—we didn't."

"We've met now. That's something."

"I suppose it is," she agreed.

He had never before spoken to another woman this way, except banteringly and safely. Now, he felt compelled to speak what was in him. He knew that she would accept it for what it was. He felt an engulfing, passionate need to be with her, as close to her as her own body. He felt heady and reckless.

"I want to see you again, Peggy."

Her eyes held on his. "All right."

"When?"

"Any time. Tomorrow—tomorrow night."

He did not think what tomorrow was or what he would be doing or if it would be possible. "I'll be here."

She brushed past him toward the door, hesitated, half-turned. "I love you," she said soberly. She went out.

2

Sunday Night

THE SHOWER beat down upon him.

He did not bother to soap himself. He stood there, on the wet tiles, absorbing the cold needles of water. He had never felt more alive.

He had awakened all at once, this late Sunday morning, without a hangover and with a pinched sense of excitement. The shower did not dispel it. He tried to remember when he had last had this same feeling of adventure.

A night dim in memory, when he had not slept until dawn because his father was taking him, the next day, to Chicago to see Babe Ruth for the first time. That was one of the times. A blazing noon in Mexico when he had straddled a hard snow ridge, and lifted his goggles to squint, from the summit of the great mountain, through the wispy clouds at the moss green landscape seventeen thousand feet below. That was another time. A noisy first evening in Paris, in a smoky jazz cave off the Boulevard St. Germaine, when he had admired the exquisite tan animal figure of the bare-breasted mulatto featured dancer and had later danced with her when she wore a shimmering white sequin formal with nothing underneath. He had been invited to her apartment. That was yet another time.

But all were hazy in the long ago, and tonight was now.

He turned the shower faucet tight until the dripping stopped, and then stepped out on the maroon bath mat. He pulled an enormous white towel off the rack and dried himself slowly. He wanted to savor his aloneness, and his private thoughts, before the day began and the Sunday routine swept him away in an unceasing torrent of chatter and activity.

Wherever his mind turned, there waited Peggy Degen. Sometimes, she wore the snug black dress with the décolletage. Sometimes she wore only the bottom half of the dress and held her breasts in her hands and smiled at him. Sometimes she wore nothing and lay on the bed inviting him.

She had said, "Tomorrow—tomorrow night."

He had said, "I'll be here."

She had said, "I love you."

He remembered the first kiss in the hallway leading to the bedroom. Her little face as he caught her looking at him. Her smile. Her long legs crossing and the glimpse of her white inner thigh. Her green eyes staring up at him, closing, and her lips, opening. Her darting tongue.

"It was a marvelous party," she had said at the door. "I know I'm going to be happy in this house." Helen had murmured her thanks for the evening and turned to leave, but he had lingered to take Peggy's hand. "Good night, Philip," she had said softly. Her hand was cool. "Good luck," he had said, and smiled. "I'll see you soon." And he had left.

Tonight, he would stand before the same door. Alone. Waiting. And she would open it. And he would have her to himself. No Mrs. Burdock. No Dora Stafford. No Helen. He would step inside, and she would close the door, and he would turn to her.

I love you.

"Phil! Are you dressed?" It was Helen's agitated voice outside the door.

"In a minute—"

"Well, hurry up. I want you to talk to your son. He won't eat. I've done all the arguing I'm going to do."

"Coming right out."

He draped the towel on the bathtub and hastily began to dress. Once, he glanced at the ivory bathroom clock. It read ten-thirty-two. Nine more hours, he told himself.

The walk from the spacious master bedroom, across the deep gray rug, to the kitchen was a long one. For the first time since they had moved into the new house, he was aware of its size. Coming out of the short corridor into a longer corridor, he was brought face to face with the study. Inside the effect of disarray created by the cartons of books, still not placed on the shelves, was heightened by several of Danny's games littered about the television set. He had not put them away the evening before. Philip reminded himself to speak to the boy about responsibility and neatness. The study was still darkened against the sun. Philip picked his way across it, pulled the drapes, and the brilliant sunlight flooded in. Outside, beyond the circular drive, the expanse of front lawn fringed by trees and bushes gave him a quick pride in ownership and his station. Yasnaya Polyana, he thought. Count Leo Nikolayevich Tolstoi is going to breakfast.

He continued through the one-story house, past the wide living room with its broad window (like an enormous glass lens holding the shining patio, and pink rose garden, and rolling carpet of back yard in focus), and entered the kitchen.

"And a good, good morning, mates," he said cheerfully.

Helen looked up from the stove where she was scrambling eggs. "You talk to him," she said.

"Hi, Pop," called Danny, from the table where he was beginning to read the comic section of the Sunday paper.

"Hi, yourself." He sat down across from Danny, sipped his orange juice, and contemplated his son. Danny was normal height for his age, but delicate and small-boned. Philip hoped that he would not remain delicate. Philip did not want him to become one of those fragile and breakable adults who mature inwardly but shrink from all outer violence. Danny had shaggy, hazel hair—it was as if the hereditary hormones had been unable to decide between Helen's blond hair and his own dark hair, and feebly compromised —and a tentative, pale face. He had his father's melancholy eyes, and much was made of them by relatives and friends. He also had a persistent tic beneath his left eye, that came and went, and it irritated Philip. This morning the tic was absent.

Philip finished his orange juice and made his gesture to maintain parental harmony. "Why aren't you eating?" he asked Danny accusingly.

"I don't feel like it." The boy ducked his head to avoid his father's stern gaze.

"Only animals do just what they feel like doing."

Peggy Degen drifted into his mind. Firmly, he turned her away.

"If you want muscles," he continued, "and want to become a ball player, you've got to eat. Now, finish that cereal."

"I don't care if I'm a ball player," said Danny.

Hey there, thought Philip, that's un-American. What is this kid going to be—a mush-headed, near-sighted bookworm?

Helen arrived with the eggs. "I told him if he doesn't eat, he can't go to the movies next Saturday."

"You heard your mother," Philip said to Danny.

Danny whined. "Can't I eat twice as much for lunch?"

"No," said Helen.

"Eat your cereal," said Philip.

"Aw, awright." He dragged the soggy cereal back before him and began to dig at it with a spoon.

Philip ate his egg in silence. After a while, he said to Danny, "When you're through, I want you to go into the study and pick up your games."

"Can't I do it after I play with them some more?"

"All right." Philip granted the compromise for peace. He was sure it did not matter anyway. Peggy had slipped into his mind again.

Danny cleaned his bowl, swung off the chair, and headed for the study. Helen came to the table balancing two cups of coffee. She set one before Philip and the other at the place beside him. "He just wants to be told what to do," she said.

"I know," he said, blowing at the steaming coffee. "Strong father image."

"Go ahead. Make fun."

She moved to the kitchen door, closed it, returned to the table and sat down.

"I've been waiting to talk to you alone."

"Let's finish breakfast first."

Helen's tone was firm. "No."

He drank his coffee and waited.

"I discussed Danny with Dr. Wolf," she said at last.

Dr. Julius Wolf was Helen's analyst. Eighty dollars a month. When Helen had first gone to him, she had been terrified by the couch and the idea of free association. She had heard of psychotherapy and had said that was what she wanted. And so, once a week since, she sat in a chair opposite Dr. Wolf and asked questions, and argued, and crucified her parents (who would have been bewildered) and castigated Philip and continued to hate herself. He had met Dr. Wolf once, at the analyst's request, when Helen had first started visiting him. He remembered Dr. Wolf as a bald, bespectacled, smiling man, with a moon face, and an affection for marathon sentences. He had been charming and open and the soul of consideration before Dr. Wolf, in a conscious effort to prove that he was not the ogre that Helen had probably made him out. But, later, he felt that Dr. Wolf had probably seen through this and had been amused by him. After that, Philip did not like Dr. Wolf. He never liked people who thought themselves superior to his superiority or who laughed at him. At first, Helen defied his antagonism, but long since she had made her truce and ceased to speak of Dr. Wolf in Philip's presence.

"What's there to discuss about Danny?" he wanted to know. "Haven't you told him enough about Danny?"

"Yes. From time to time. When it came up. But I've been so worried—so Thursday, we just talked about Danny."

"A kid doesn't eat his cereal. Twenty bucks down the drain."

"Stop it. I can't stand it when you're being stupid."

"All right, I'm being stupid. You talked about Danny."

"Dr. Wolf thinks Danny needs help. He recommended a friend of his—a child psychiatrist—Dr. Robert Edling."

Philip glared at her with real anger.

"I'm not letting you put a helpless kid on the couch. Are you crazy?"

"How can a man be a writer and yet be so insensitive?"

"I'm not letting any seven-year-old child of mine go to a head shrinker. That'd be a fine memory he'd have of his golden youth—I remember mama, papa, and my analyst."

"Phil—please—this is important. They don't put him on a couch. He's too little. The analyst takes out toys and clay and things, and sits on the floor and plays games with him. He finds out what's bothering the child. That's all there is to it."

"I bet."

"Dr. Wolf says that Danny needs help." Before he could interrupt, she went on. "I know how you feel about Dr. Wolf. But he is an M.D., he is a psychiatrist, he's trained to know when something is wrong. He knows our situation—"

"Your version."

"My version," she conceded. "He's smart enough to see through me and know your side, too."

"Oh, yeah—"

"He doesn't think it's serious. He thinks Dr. Edling will get to the root of it right away."

"The root of what?" he demanded with exasperation.

Her eyes were pleading. "Phil—Danny's not behaving like

a normal boy. I don't mean little things, eating, that nonsense. I mean important things. When we had trouble with school, you said wait till summer vacation. He'll love camp. Well, you see how he loves camp. We were lucky to get him into the bus once in three weeks. The other children love camp. They go without arguing. They have fun. He won't go at all. He's afraid. He doesn't know what fun is."

Philip felt disturbed and suddenly unsure. "All boys aren't the same—"

"They've got to be in some ways. If he didn't want to swim or play ball or ride a bike or any one of those things, I'd say that's all right. But not to want to do anything! To be afraid of everything! He won't go out to play. He sticks to his room. And he whines and clings. My God, I can't go to the bathroom without him holding on to me as if he'll never see me again."

"It's a phase," said Philip doggedly, but weakening. "He's a little insecure—we've been fighting—I've been too busy, maybe—and the moving—"

"Phil, he's troubled," Helen said flatly. "He needs help, and I'm going to see that he gets it. I've made an appointment with Dr. Edling." She faced him, all defiant motherhood.

"Great. Then why bother to consult me?"

"Because Dr. Wolf said that child psychiatrists often want to see the parents, too. Dr. Edling's going to see me. He might want to see you."

It was disagreeable, true, but not immediate. Philip felt that he could afford to be cooperative. "If he wants to see me, I'll see him."

"I'm taking Danny in at noon tomorrow."

"You might be surprised at how normal he is."

"I hope so. Dr. Edling's going to talk to him. Then he wants to talk to me—"

The kitchen door opened. It was Danny.

"I picked up the games," he said to Philip.

"Good boy."

Danny came to Philip and leaned against his knee. "What are you going to do today, Daddy?"

"I don't know. Since it's a nice day, maybe we'll start out by sitting on the new patio and reading the funny papers. You want me to read them to you?"

"And how!"

"After that, we'll see. Maybe we'll visit the Barlows—you can play with Liz and Tony. Would you like that?"

"If you would," said Danny.

Philip gathered up the thick Sunday paper and started for the patio, Danny trailing after him. He wheeled the lounges next to one another and settled on the warm pad of the bigger one, while Danny crawled on the other and waited expectantly. He held the comics sideways toward Danny, and read the words in the balloons aloud, as Danny's eyes devoured each strip. In half an hour, they were done.

"That was fun," Danny said, falling back happily.

"When I was a boy, the comics had silly jokes in them. Now they're too serious—"

"I like them."

"Well, that's all that matters."

He suggested to Danny that he bring his pirate ship and schooner outside and have a war, while he finished the papers. Danny was obliging. Philip sorted out the Sunday paper in the same pattern he had followed for years. News section. Sports. Theatrical and books. Magazine section. The rest, he discarded.

Danny had a simulated sea battle on the grass, and Philip read through the paper. When he had finished, it was afternoon. His face felt hot, and his mind felt unenlightened. He sat up, collected the papers in a neat stack, and absently gazed at the boy's rubber figures falling off the vessels. He wondered about Peggy Degen's son, whom he still had not seen, and he thought of Peggy Degen.

Sooner or later, he must plan a way to leave the house after dinner. Normally, going out alone presented no problem. Helen trusted him completely. He would say that he felt restless, and go for an hour's drive alone, and she would barely look up when he returned. He would say that he wanted to visit the out-of-town newsstand, and that would be an hour or two with the driving, or visit Bill Markson, and that was often all evening, and Helen rarely objected or questioned him after. But this evening was different. He was afraid that she might be suspicious and regard his announcement as unusual. Moreover, he did not want to limit his going to an hour or two. He wanted as much time as possible. Bill Markson would be the best reason for being out. But what if Helen had occasion to telephone there? He could say that he was meeting Bill in Beverly Hills for a drink. But what if Helen called Betty and learned that Bill was home? Further, it required making a fellow conspirator of Bill, and he was not ready for that yet.

"Well, what do you think of the patio?" It was Helen at the dining room screen door. "Isn't it a dream?"

He would work something out in his mind before dinner-time.

"Great. It'll be sensational for barbecues."

"I was just thinking that. . . . Danny, let me put some sun lotion on you."

Danny shook his head and continued to play.

Helen came outside and inhaled her private air. "I can't tell you how pleased I am with this house. Are you going to the Barlows today?"

"I think so. I'll call Sam up. Want to come along?"

"There's too much to do. I'd better stay with the unpacking. I haven't found the linens yet, and the kitchen—"

"I don't have to go out. Do you want me to help?"

"No. I think I can do better with Danny out of the way."

"Well, we won't be long." He got up and stretched. "I'll call Sam."

He went inside and telephoned Sam Barlow. He asked Sam what they were doing, and Sam said that they were doing nothing and invited him to bring Danny over. He told Sam that he and Danny would drop by for a little while after lunch. He hung up, and was pleased with the arrangement. About once a month, he or the Barlows visited like this, informally, and for the children. The eldest Barlow child, Liz, the adopted one, was just a little older than Danny and complacent as a vegetable. Danny liked the Barlow boy, Tony, too, because he was younger and smaller than Danny, and could be pushed around. Sam Barlow was another attraction. He was an older man than Philip, but he would lower himself to the floor and play with the children, earnestly, seriously, with an absorption that Philip envied, and Philip guessed that Danny believed in him and felt safe with him. Liz Barlow had started the second grade with Danny, and Helen had met the Barlows several times at PTAs. Eventually, this led to an invitation to dinner, and now, through their children, they were friends.

After lunch Philip, with Danny in the front seat beside him, drove through the crowded beach traffic toward Bel-Air, where the Barlows lived in an expensive two-story hilltop house. Philip and Danny played beaver from the moment they turned onto Sunset Boulevard. Philip played casually, for his mind was elsewhere, but Danny played with a dedicated passion. "Beaver!" shouted Danny, tugging Philip's arm.

"Look out," said Philip. "Don't pull my arm. You'll get us into an accident."

"Beaver—beaver," chanted Danny, pointing to the station wagon that was approaching.

Philip supposed every seven-year-old boy played beaver. It was not a game calculated to encourage driving safely. To play it successfully, one had to take one's eyes off the road. Sighting and identifying station wagons was the object of the sport. Each new station wagon was a beaver. Each beaver was a point.

"I'm leading eight to one!" shouted Danny.

"I'll catch up with you yet," said Philip, pleased with his son's normal exuberance, and surer than ever that he was not fodder for Dr. Robert Edling.

Danny settled back to scan the fruitful horizon. Philip thought again of the Barlows.

Sam Barlow was short, and fat, and financially successful. He was physically unattractive. His head was too small, his eyes too narrow, and his hair was a stiff brush of gray. He had no neck. His barrel body sat on squat legs. But his speech was soft and gentle. Occasionally, he made a wry quip, most often against himself. And he was a gracious listener. Those who met him the first time were repelled by his physique. Once they spent more time with him, they found his warm personality attractive and the physique seemed to vanish.

This was the only explanation of Tina. For Tina was twenty years Sam's junior. Tina was beautiful. She could have done better. Yet, after a long engagement, she must have overlooked his physical appearance because of his personality. That was the only explanation, that and his wealth.

Sam was that phenomenon of a commercial era, a chain store dentist, a man who applied techniques of mass production to medicine. Sam owned eight flourishing offices, scattered throughout the Los Angeles area, and in them he installed eager young graduates of dentistry schools. He paid them high salaries and gave them bonuses. Despite the wounded outcries of the medical associations, Sam advertised his dental parlors, published signed endorsements of his painless extractions, served aching patients on a discount basis, and publicized a pay-as-you-go plan. Sam, himself, had not drilled a tooth in years. He managed the organization.

Wholesale dentistry had paid for the hilltop house, with its kidney-shaped swimming pool, in exclusive Bel Air. And it had paid for Tina.

Tina Barlow was Philip's favorite other man's wife. Sometimes, after parties, Philip and Helen discussed the mates of their friends. It made for fascinating pillow talk. Which of the wives, Helen liked to ask, would Philip prefer to sleep with? He knew the game by heart and played it well. He would look thoughtful, and think, and then say that none of them really appealed to him that way. Helen would beam, and press him. Wasn't there one, just one, who was physically attractive? He would consider. Well, several were attractive, he would say, that is, in a technical sense. Betty Markson was attractive. And Greta Unger. And Marie Valetti. But sleep with them? No, thank you. Those were the good nights with Helen.

Actually, he never thought of sleeping with the wife of a close friend. The relationship automatically neutered them. The overtones were incestuous. Wives of acquaintances were fair game, but wives of friends, never. Tina Barlow was the exception.

She was thirty-two, and junoesque. Her hair was a soft copper-red, and she wore it sleeked back and bunned most of the time. Her complexion was fair, an English pink. Her large and round eyes gave her the appearance of a startled virgin. Her nose was classical, her mouth sensuous. On her right cheek, like a slash, was a long dimple that showed when she smiled. Her body was a full woman's body, with large breasts, a long fleshy torso, and big female hips. Everything about her was provocative: her glance, her walk, her speech.

He tried, now, to visualize her beside Peggy Degen. It was difficult. Both held sex promise, but differently. Tina was less subtle and less fragile. Tina was a woman. Peggy was a girl. Now, he wanted Peggy. But, for all of the year before, ever since he had first laid eyes on her, he had wanted Tina. Here, too, there was a difference. His desire for Peggy was sudden, sharp, deep, obsessive. His old desire for Tina had been an easy, relaxed, daydreaming, fleeting and contemplative thing. It lacked staying power. But it had been there, until Peggy. And Tina had sensed it, and, in a way, provoked it and played upon it. Her gambit with him rarely varied: direct declarations of passion, lightly and publicly proclaimed; constant and frank admiration of his person; persistent but indefinite invitations to enjoy her companionship. He collaborated in this love banter. But beyond a kiss or squeeze at a party, he made no move. He was not a practiced seducer or lover. The complexity of an affair with the wife of a good friend appalled him. With Tina, he could control himself. With Peggy, he could act only as he felt.

They had reached the asphalt parking area before the

Barlow carport. "Ten to one," Danny was saying. "I really beat you."

Philip slammed the car door in feigned anger. "I'll trounce you on the way home," he said.

Tina was waiting. "I heard you drive up," she called out. She stood, framed in the doorway, smiling. She was wearing a skin-tight, light blue swim suit. The skirt was pulled several inches above her crotch. She leaned against the doorway, her pink flesh legs crossed.

"Did your ears burn last night?" she asked as he approached with Danny.

"What time?"

"Three in the morning. I dreamt about you. It was enough to give Sam grounds for divorce in any state—and you should have seen our state."

"I'm glad *you* had a good time," he said with a mock disgruntled air.

He kissed her cheek, and she pressed his hand warmly. Then she looked down at Danny and tousled his head. "How's my Danny boy today?"

"Good."

"Liz and Tony are in the pool with their father. Do you want to go swimming?"

"No," said Danny.

"Go ahead and watch them," Philip said.

Danny ran ahead. Tina took Philip's hand and they walked leisurely through the spacious, modern house toward the pool. She glanced at Philip.

"Where's Helen?"

"Moving furniture. We just got into the new place."

"Already? I thought it was going to be next month."

"All very sudden. We found a buyer."

"When are we invited?"

"Soon," he said.

"I hope so. I was beginning to think you didn't love me, Mr. Fleming."

"I love you very much, Mrs. Barlow. You, me, and Sam are my favorite triangle."

"Quadrangle. Helen."

"All right, Helen."

They had reached the bar, and he could see Sam floating in the pool, like an exhausted porpoise, with the children splashing around him. Danny was at the edge of the pool, clapping his hands at them.

"Want to go in?" she asked.

"I didn't bring my trunks."

"Who needs trunks? I'll take off my suit if it'll make you feel better."

"This I want to see."

"This I want you to see," she said, sliding her hand provocatively down her thigh.

She went outside. Philip followed her.

"Hi, Sam."

Sam waved. "Get yourself a drink, Phil."

"Later."

He watched Tina walk to the pool. The swim suit covered only part of her buttocks, and the protruding flesh rolled as she moved to the diving board. It was a delightful sight, Philip thought. Women are a delightful sight, he amended.

He settled lazily into a deep wicker chair, stuck his feet out, and relaxed in the shade, drawing on his pipe. Tina stood poised on the board. Voluptuous was the word in Philip's mind. She dove gracefully, and swam across the pool in strong, definite strokes. Sam continued to float. Not a porpoise, Philip decided, but a distended lifebuoy. Liz and Tony waded about in the shallow end, squealing as they threw a wet ball to Danny, who circled the pool and happily threw it back.

Philip observed the scene contentedly, and then he surveyed the setting. Remote and idyllic, he thought. The patio and pool had been set into a thick cliff, high above all worldly cares and curious eyes. To the left, behind the diving board, were two freshly painted white cabanas. Across the pool was a six foot wooden fence, built to contain the children but actually decorative with its lush clinging vine and white roses. Bending off to the right were the rows of orange poppies.

For the briefest interval, the raucous voices of the children and the splashing of the water were shut out. Philip felt detached from any commitment with his fellows excepting Peggy, who was detached with him, and thinking of her, he thought of tonight. What excuse would he make to leave the house for the entire evening? He considered Sam. The voices and the splashing increased in volume. Could he enlist Sam? He tried to gauge Sam's reaction. Sam never told off-color stories, and he laughed uneasily when someone else told them. To make Sam a confederate in an enterprise that might involve infidelity might make Sam unhappy. He was sure that Sam would oblige. But reluctantly. Who else was there? He reeled off a parade of acquaintances. Acquaintances were safer than friends. There used to be the studio gang that he played poker with once a month.

But they had not played since last Christmas. Still, he could pretend the poker game had been revived. Well, that would be the desperation measure, if he could invent nothing better.

The Barlows cavorted in and about the pool for three-quarters of an hour. Tina climbed out of the water first and waddled, toes out like a ballet dancer, dripping, to the nearest white cabana. A few minutes later Sam lifted the children out of the water and led them into the second cabana. Danny reurned to Philip.

"I think you ought to take swimming lessons again," Philip said.

"I don't like them," Danny said.

"You're missing a lot of fun."

"I don't care."

Philip rose, and moved restlessly into the bar, Danny tagging right behind him. Philip took a cork and played catch with Danny, until Sam, sheathed in enormous blue denims, appeared with Liz and Tony. "Come on, Danny," he said, "Liz has a new game. Let's find it." He started out with the children, then called over his shoulder to Philip. "Just opened a new bottle of scotch, Phil."

Philip glanced at his watch. It was three-thirty. A little early, but he felt jumpy. He walked around to the back of the bar, as Tina, wearing a polka-dot halter that covered all but the tops of her lavish breasts, and tight white shorts, came in.

"Make one for me, too," she said. "Be right back."

He set up two glasses, opened the refrigerator and tugged free the small tray of cubes. He cracked them loose. Through the archway he could see Sam enter the living room, carrying a cardboard box. Sam sat on the floor, and the children surrounded him.

Philip absorbed himself in the ritual of preparing the drinks. He dropped three cubes into each glass. He found the scotch at the edge of the bar, measured out a jigger to each glass, then added a half-jigger more to each.

He was about to reach for the water, when he felt a hand stroke the inside of his leg. He started, half turned and looked down. Tina was crouched behind the bar, playfully rubbing the inside of his leg with one hand, as she opened the cupboard below to search for a bottle of tonic. Alarmed, he looked off through the archway. Sam was explaining the new game to his children and Danny.

Philip quickly crouched beside Tina.

She smiled. "You have nice legs."

"So have you."

"No kidding, Phil, why don't you drop by sometime during the week?"

"You might be sorry. I might take you up on it."

"I want you to."

"Sam wouldn't like it very much."

"Sam's away at work all day. It gets awfully lonely. We could have a swim—talk—"

"I can do that with my wife."

"I can do a lot of things better than your wife."

He tried to keep it light. "Now I'm interested."

She stared at him seriously. Suddenly she took his face in her hands and, lips parted, kissed him. It was exactly what Peggy had done last night in the hallway. "If you want the rest—come and get it," she whispered. She grabbed the bottle of tonic, stood up, and busily began to open it. He remained kneeling beside her thighs. He lifted his eyes to the high line of her abbreviated white shorts. He had an impulse to slip his hand under her shorts. He wondered how she would react. Instead, teasingly, he ran his fingers up her bare leg, as she had done to him.

She did not stir or look down at him, as she continued to pour the tonic. It was almost a dare. He drummed his fingers higher. Still she did not move. He stopped. He rose to his feet. She did not look at him. "Chicken," she said. He tried to read her face. "Next time, I won't be," he said.

He poured water in his drink, and left the bar to join Sam and the children.

When he arrived home with Danny, having sustained another crushing defeat at beaver by a score of eight to three on the way, Helen was in the kitchen writing a note to him. Now, she tore it up.

"I was just leaving a message for you," she said. "I was going out to the market. Nathaniel Horn called."

"Oh? What did he want?"

"He didn't say. He wanted you to call back."

"Something about that Western, I suppose."

"I'll take Danny to the market," she said. "How were Sam and Tina?"

"As usual. She asked when we're inviting them over. She wants to see the house."

"We've got to straighten up first." She shook her head. "What a mess—"

"It looks fine to me. Have you been unpacking all the time?"

"Steadily, grimly," she said. "I'm bushed. The junk that collects! You just have no idea. What are we still doing with your old army uniform and helmet? And why Christmas cards eight years old and a thousand National Geographics? And shoes that we haven't worn since our honeymoon? I'm going to be ruthless. I'm going to load up those Salvation trucks until they scream uncle, and then I swear, never again." She looked about. "Where's Danny?"

"Bathroom."

"How was he?"

"Just fine. Played with the kids. No problem."

"Did he go swimming?"

Philip frowned. "He didn't feel like it. I didn't push him."

"Next year this time he'll be swimming. You'll see."

She went to find Danny. There was a brief, indistinct argument. After being promised a candy bar and a comic book, Danny appeared, followed by Helen. They went out the service entrance to the garage. Philip made his way to the portable bar in the dining room and poured himself two jiggers of scotch. He carried his glass to the refrigerator, took out a plastic tray of cubes, twisted it, removed two cubes and dropped them into his drink. He then picked up the telephone in his free hand, set it on the kitchen table, and dialed Nathaniel Horn.

While the telephone buzzed, he sat down, and sipped his scotch. After a moment, the connection was made.

"Hello?" It was Nathaniel Horn's voice at the other end.

"Nat? Philip."

"I'm glad you called. Something came up about a half hour ago—"

"You mean a job?"

"Remember when you were in Thursday? I mentioned a big independent who has a biographical idea? He wanted Ernie Ives, but I told you I gave him something of yours to read?"

"I remember."

"Well, it was Alexander Selby. He got hold of me a half-hour ago. He wants to get together with you."

In the motion picture industry, the name Alexander Selby and the word Class were synonymous. Philip had met Selby several times at social and political gatherings—once, at a Democratic fund raising dinner, he remembered—and he was sure he had made no impression. Selby involved himself in only one or two pictures a year, and for these he hired the most expensive and glamorous writers. To work for Selby, one had to head the current best-seller list or have a recent successful opening on Broadway. Selby was a slender, drawling aesthete, with a chalky face, who served tea at four o'clock in his office and spoke of thematic values with the faintest hint of an English accent, the last acquired during two years spent working for J. Arthur Rank in London. It was rumored that he was homosexual, though Selby had promoted himself from assistant director to producer through an intelligent marriage to the stepdaughter of a studio president. The fruits of the marriage were a son and an independent financing deal. The son demonstrated that Selby was heterosexual, to say the least, and the independent company proved that Selby had talent for management and organization. He was not a creative producer. New and daring ideas did not spring from his head. "He has become a success," remarked a weekly news magazine, "by employing only the successful." His films were always based on costly, well-known properties. These were lavishly mounted by the foremost technical specialists in show business. They starred the guaranteed box office names (to woo these names from the major studios, Selby had been the first to offer actors and actresses partnerships in his ventures). More often than not, his pictures made considerable profits. He was often misunderstood, credited with virtues he did not possess, and criticized for failings that did not exist. It was not for selfless charity that he contributed so much of his time and fortune to the ailing and the needy, but for immortality. It was not out of vanity that he employed two sets of press agents to serve him (and telephone him daily), but out of loneliness. This unsure and self-cultivated Croesus rarely hired the uncertified Philip Flemings of his industry, and this was what puzzled Philip.

"What in the devil would he want with me?" Philip asked Nathaniel Horn. "I haven't had a best-seller lately—"

"You wrote *Byron's Circle*," Horn said simply.

"Don't tell me he's heard about it?"

"He read it last night. I gave him my copy—"

"But why?"

"Because the big biographical picture he's planning—it concerns Lady Caroline Lamb—"

Philip's voice reflected his astonishment. "A picture on Caroline Lamb?"

"Three million dollars' worth of picture to be shot in England. It's a setup for three of the biggest names in Hollywood and London—and from what he told me, the drama's built in—the tempestuous Lady Caroline caught between love for her husband, Lord Melbourne, future Premier—and her lover, Lord Byron, most romantic figure of his age—"

"You sound like a billboard." But at once Philip could see the finished product.

"I'm just quoting Alex. Anyway, I remembered you had a chapter in your book on Lady Caroline. I told our friend to read it. He read the chapter, then the entire book, last night. He was impressed. He wants to see you."

"Does he want to hire me?"

"I don't know, Phil. He must be interested, or he wouldn't bother to see you. All he told me was that he'd like to meet you—that he had a few notions he'd like to try out on you—"

"You think there'd be a trip in it?"

"There might be. Alex likes to do his things up right."

"Christ, wouldn't that be something?" It would be more than something, Philip knew. It would catapult him out of the Western class, the mediocre credits, into a new and exalted position in the motion picture industry. Yet, even this possibility gave Philip no surge of excitement. He recognized what it might do for him. Dollars and cents. But it was still a screenplay. One hundred and twenty to one hundred and fifty pages of dialogue and action, peppered with dissolves, to serve as the most pliable blueprint to a hundred or more men who would change it, twist it, distort it, and make it their own. It was not what he wanted, but it was what he needed.

"I've set it up for lunch," Horn was saying. "I think I'd better be on hand to break the ice. Twelve-thirty at Panaro's."

"I'll be there."

"Better spend tonight taking a little refresher on Caroline Lamb."

Tonight. Philip smiled. Tonight he would be doing better than Caroline Lamb.

"Don't worry," he told Nathaniel Horn. "I'll dazzle him."

When he hung up, he was suddenly pleased, not with the knowledge that he was to meet with Alexander Selby, but with the realization that, at last, he had a valid reason for taking the night off.

Impatiently waiting for the return of Helen, he took his scotch into the study. He poked among the cartons until he found the one on which he had printed with crayon, "Handle with care." It contained ten copies of *Byron's Circle*. He opened the carton and removed one volume. Again, even as on the first magical morning when he had received advance copies of the book from the publisher, it felt substantial and important in his hand. He moved to the rust leather chair, sank into it, setting his drink on the end table, as he turned the red and gray book over in his hand.

He began to leaf the pages until he found the chapter. Then he settled down to read. At once, it surprised him how well he had written. The genuine scholarship was reserved and easy, the style was brisk, and the approach was filled with understanding and perception.

He filed the facts in his head as he read. Lady Caroline Ponsonby Lamb. Born November 13, 1785. At twenty, in 1805, married to William Lamb, afterward Lord Melbourne. Hysterical collapse the day of the wedding. One child, an imbecile. In 1812 met Lord Byron. For a moment, he stopped filing facts to read what he had once written:

"Caroline received Byron regularly in her rooms at Melbourne House. He arrived late in the morning and stayed the day. Mostly, he talked, and she listened. Both were deeply in love, but neither moved to consummate this love. Byron proceeded warily in the early stages. If her talents were pleasing, they were, as he told her, 'unfortunately coupled with a total lack of common conduct . . . Your heart, my poor Caro (what a little volcano!), pours lava through your veins.' When she offered him her jewels to relieve his debts, he declined with a rare blooming rose and a note reading, 'Your ladyship, I am told, likes all that is new and rare—for a moment.' But this could not go on. In a few weeks, they were lovers."

He ignored facts entirely now, as he became absorbed in the torrent of words recounting the brief, passionate affair, Byron's eventual attempts to break it off, and Caroline's undisciplined behavior afterward. He read on, almost forgetting that the words had come from his mind and been set down by his pen.

He dropped the book into his lap and thought about the pretty, capricious, pathetic Caroline Lamb. How had he not seen it years before? She was the perfect pivotal figure for a dramatization. In one neurotic blonde were all the elements of box office: nobility, beauty, nonconformity, sex. Alexander Selby was a genius.

He was about to resume reading when he heard the front door open.

"Philip!" It was Helen.

Hastily he returned the book to its carton and hurried to the entry hall. Helen was loaded under two precarious packages of groceries, the key still in her fingers. He relieved her of one package, held the screen door open for Danny, who staggered in with a dozen soft drinks, and then followed them into the kitchen.

He helped her unpack. She had forgotten about Nathaniel Horn's telephone call. He had better remind her.

"I called Nat Horn back," he said, piling the crackers on the shelves.

"Anything important?" She was at the freezer in the service porch.

"Could be," he said. He waited for her to return. "Nat heard that Alex Selby was planning to do a big picture on Caroline Lamb."

"Who's Caroline Lamb?" asked Helen, rattling about for the frying pan.

This always annoyed him. "If you read my book, you'd remember. Byron's mistress."

She was immediately contrite. "Of course I remember. It's just so long ago since I read it. He's making a picture about her?"

Philip nodded. "That's right. And he read my book. He likes what I wrote."

"Are you going to get the job?"

"Too early to tell. Selby wants to see me tomorrow. Anyway, Nat's going to fill me in on the details tonight. Sort of brief me."

He waited. She was walking from the refrigerator to the stove with the butter. "Is Nat coming here tonight?"

"No, I promised to meet him in town after dinner."

She was buttering the frying pan. "Well, don't stay out too late or you'll be dead in the morning."

It was done. It had been almost too easy.

Sunday night had arrived.

He parked before the house on Ridgewood Lane, pulled the emergency brake, shut the motor, and dropped the ignition key into his pocket. He leaned across the front seat, peering through the opposite car window at the house. The lights were on in her living room. He glanced back to see if any of his old neighbors were outside. The street was empty.

Straightening, he took a last look in his rear-view mirror. His hair was in place. He had showered, shaved, and dressed with meticulous care. He was wearing his most casual and flattering outfit: dark gray sport coat and slacks, light gray shirt and blue knit tie.

He gathered the brightly wrapped gifts from the seat beside him. The bottle of Arpège he stuffed into his coat pocket. The bottles of whiskey and cognac he carried. He stepped out of the car and started up the brick walk.

He pressed the doorbell twice and waited. After a moment, he heard her footsteps. The door opened, and there she was. He had half expected that she would be smiling and would kiss him as he entered. Instead, she was serious and reserved.

"Greek bearing gifts," he said, holding up the bottles as he went inside.

"You didn't have to," she said, shutting the door.

Standing there, they were silent and awkward. He ran his eyes down her figure, and gave an exaggerated, approving nod. "Very pretty," he said. She was wearing a sheer white silk batiste blouse, which revealed her lace brassière beneath, and a form-fitting navy blue skirt. Her legs were stockingless.

She inclined her head in a curtsy. "Thank you." She indicated the chair. "Please sit down. I'm putting Steve to bed."

He waved his bottles. "I'll deposit these in the kitchen. Would you like a drink?"

"Definitely. Whatever you're having."

"Scotch?"

"Fine."

She disappeared toward Steve's room. He went into the kitchen and prepared the drinks.

When he returned to the living room, she was waiting with her son. Her own fragility, the fact that her husband had been small, had led him to expect that her boy would be as delicate as his own Danny. In his pajamas, the handsome boy was a block of granite. His hair was sandy, and his eyes and nose were his mother's.

"This is Mr. Fleming, Steve. He sold us this house."

Steve extended his hand. "How do you do."

Philip took it. "Hello, Steve." He glanced at Peggy. "You have quite a gentleman here," he said, remembering his own son's often gauche and ill-mannered meetings with friends.

"I believe in manners," Peggy said simply. "I don't believe in being too permissive. I detest progressive schools."

He was irritated. "I send Danny to a progressive school. I'm for authority, of course, but I don't like strictness for its own sake. Strictness turned out a couple lousy generations."

"You're offended," she said.

"No." But he was, and he could not conceal it.

Steve's head moved from one to the other, bewildered. Philip turned to Steve.

"How old are you, young man?"

"Four years old."

"I've got a big boy of seven. You'll have to meet him sometime."

Peggy took her son by the hand. "Time for bed. Say good night."

Steve spoke his reluctant good night, and, trotting beside his mother, he went off to bed. Philip sat in the chair and drank his scotch. Even the sharp whiskey tang did not rid him of the growing feeling of disappointment. He had not liked the trivial disagreement with Peggy. But deeper and more nagging, he knew, was the feeling that he had anticipated too much. He had expected her to greet him with arms open, to be full of warmth and exclamations of affection, returning his ardent kisses eagerly with her own. Instead, she had been withdrawn, treating him as formally as she might a stranger. Was it that she now regretted inviting him?

She returned to the living room, brushing back her hair. "What a day," she said. "Steve. Unpacking. And Dora and Irwin trying to be helpful." She picked up her drink, and sat on the sofa across the coffee table from him. "I suppose Helen is madly efficient."

"Not really. About this time each day, she looks like she had tangled with a giant twister."

"Well—did you have a good day?"

"Not especially. I was restless. I was looking forward to tonight."

She ignored this. "What will you be doing tomorrow—what will you be working on?"

"I don't know. My agent called today. Have you ever heard of Alex Selby?"

"Certainly."

"Well, he wants to do a picture on Lady Caroline Lamb—"

"Isn't that a wonderful idea!"

"I think so. Anyway, he read my book. There's a chapter in it on Caroline—or did I already tell you that? He liked it and wants to see me tomorrow."

"I hope you do it." She pointed to the volume, open and face down, on the coffee table. It was *On Love* by Stendhal. "You got me interested in Stendhal all over again. I've just started reading it. It's really poorly written and sophomoric. But it's fun. He was such a child. And there could be five volumes on what he didn't know about love."

"Who knows about love? Each person has only his own private knowledge."

"About women, then. He knew nothing about women. Only about himself."

They discussed Stendhal at length, and when they had exhausted him they had also finished their drinks. Philip went into the kitchen to mix two more. He made them doubles. When he returned, Peggy was smoking. He remembered the gift in his pocket. He found it and handed it to her without a word.

"What's this?"

"A present for you."

"You hardly know me." But she opened it and was pleased. "I take that back. Maybe you know me very well."

"I feel I do."

"I bet you'd make some mistress happy. Spoil her. You're the type."

"Maybe I would."

"Do you give your wife presents?"

"On birthdays. Also anniversaries, Mother's Day, Easter, Christmas. Oh, yes. Flag Day."

"Silly." She set the perfume down and took up her drink. She sipped it, looked up. "What did you put in here? Are you trying to get me drunk?"

"Yes."

She shrugged. "If it'll make you happy." She drank. "Did you have any trouble getting out tonight?"

He shook his head. "I'm doing research on Caroline Lamb."

"Are you?"

"In a way."

"What would Helen think? Have you done this before?"

"Never."

"I don't believe you."

"I never wanted to—seriously. You're the first one. I saw you, and I had to see you again."

She brushed her hair back. "It's either your talk or the drink—but it sounds good." Suddenly, she asked, "You're not with me because I'm a widow?"

"What do you mean?"

"A man at a cocktail party once told me that men on the make like to go out with young widows. They're the easiest."

"That's ridiculous."

"He said they've lost all sense of safety and solidity and

Continuity. Their moral armor is weakened. Besides, they need someone. They're lonely."

"I wouldn't know about that," he said.

"It's true," she said. Then she added, "Though I don't think I'm typical. I can live alone and like it."

"Dora told me you had many admirers."

"Good for Dora. I have a few."

"Anyone serious?"

"You mean, am I serious about anyone?"

"Yes."

She thought about it. "Not really. Maybe one."

"Jake Cahill?" he asked.

She seemed surprised. "Where did you hear about him?"

"Dora."

"Well—he wants to marry me, yes. I don't know. He's going to be in town the end of the week." She offered it almost as a challenge. He understood and accepted it at once. He frowned. "You mean I'll have to let him see you?"

"I'm afraid so."

"Maybe I won't allow it."

"You sound awfully possessive for a man with a wife."

"I want two wives," he said.

"I want one man," she said. She handed him her empty glass. "I'll take a refill. But don't make me drunk."

He finished his drink, and went into the kitchen with the two glasses. He dropped ice cubes into each, gave her a jigger and a half, and poured himself another double. He filled each glass with water and returned to her.

She accepted her glass and began to drink at once. He wanted to sit beside her but was not able to. He settled in his chair across from her and drank.

They conversed in fits and starts. He asked about her family, and she told him. She asked about his, and he told her what he wished to tell her. They discussed New York. They remembered some plays they had both seen. They talked about travel. Except for a trip to Cuba, she had not been out of the states. He told her about Paris. He tried to personalize it for both of them, draw her into his secret dream, but she held back.

She finished her drink. For all the liquor, she seemed strained and reserved, and he was confused.

They had been silent for almost a minute when he, at last, decided to speak his mind.

"You seem sorry you invited me," he said.

"Maybe I am."

"Why?"

"It's so damn involving. You're married. I don't know—"
Her voice thinned, trailed off.

"But still, you said I could come over."

"I couldn't help it." She seemed to hold her breath. "I
love you."

He was on his feet, impulsively, without thought. He
moved around the coffee table, as she waited tensely. Then,
kneeling on the sofa beside her, he stooped and kissed her.
At first, she merely accepted his kiss, and then, her breath
quickening, she kissed him back, groping for his arm
where the muscle had tightened, holding it desperately.

He lowered himself slowly, half on the sofa, half against
her, never taking his lips from her lips. Her arms encircled
him. One of his hands was behind her head, pressing her to
him. The other he slid down to her knees, and then under
her dress. He passed his fingers over her bare unfamiliar
thigh until he touched the edge of her lace pants. He caressed her gently, unceasingly.

Suddenly, she jerked her lips from his, and pushed his
arms away. Disheveled, she managed to stand. "Oh, what the
hell—"

He watched her. She stared down at him. "Do you want
to make love to me?"

"What do you mean?"

"Do you want to screw me?"

The word, from her high-strung child face, was incon-
gruous and shocking. Philip was no puritan, except down
deep, but the primitive implications of the word shook him
and frightened him. Her knowledge and use of the word
implied raw intercourse without romance and limitless superior experience. All this sped through his mind, as he
jumped to his feet.

"Very much," he replied, embracing her.

She freed herself. She stared at him, her lips pressed tight
with decision. "Give me a minute to get ready," she said,
almost angrily.

She went into the bathroom.

Unaccountably, he felt a chill and began to tremble. He
did not know why he was reacting this way. Wasn't this
what he had secretly wanted and hoped for? Wasn't it? He
did not know. He searched through his confusion. Then, he
knew. He had expected to go to the brink, as he had several
times before, but not over it. He had wanted other women, but
he had never once been unfaithful to Helen. It had been
good conversing with Peggy, and just now indulging in

stimulating love play, and all the time imagining an act of love so savage and tender, so perfect, so endless, that it could not exist. Now, suddenly, behind the door of the bathroom, she was stripping off her clothes, the sheer blouse, the brassière, the tight navy skirt, the lace panties. Presently she would, in utter nudity, supplant her image on the bed. He would stand before her. And the act of love would have to be perfect on his part.

Almost blindly, he found his way to the kitchen, unscrewed the cap from the bottle of scotch, and sloshed the whiskey into his glass. He did not bother about ice or water. He drank deeply, feeling the sting of the raw whiskey in his throat and chest, and wanting desperately to be lost in the safety of intoxication at once. He prayed the chill and the fear would go. But they did not.

He finished his drink and walked slowly into the hall. He heard the water running in the bathroom and imagined her mystic libations. He continued hurriedly into the darkened bedroom.

He yanked the bedspread back, and tugged the blanket free. He pulled off his tie, unbuttoned his shirt, and draped both on the chair. Then, sitting down uneasily, he unlaced his shoes, lifted them off, removed his socks, and stuffed them neatly into his shoes. He unzipped his trousers, stepped out of them, and tossed them on the chair. He hesitated, then sat on the edge of the bed, still in his shorts. He could hear the water continuing to run in the bathroom.

The suddenness of it all was what had petrified him. He had fantasied this moment every waking hour since he first laid eyes on Peggy Degen. But in his heart, not for an instant had he expected it to happen. Or was it that he had hoped it would not happen? He thought of her husband alive. Bernie Degen. Had Bernie satisfied her? Had he been well built and virile? Had he been able to sustain intercourse for long periods? And the men since? How many of them like this? How many times like this? And how good were they? What did she know? What did she expect?

He heard the bathroom door creak open. He felt the chill give way to a streaked flush that ate across his body. And then he was excited, wanting to see her loveliness, wanting to feel the warmth of her naked flesh beneath his hand.

She appeared in the open doorway, the hall light behind her, and she was wildly beautiful. All that he had hoped and imagined was true. He felt exalted that she could stand before him, privately, this way. Confusion melted before desire. The yearning brought him to his feet: to be her lover, to plumb the depth of her inner emotions, latent and invisible, and to know her response.

She was wearing a sheer pale blue nightgown, the bodice trimmed with lace and the skirt pleated downward from the waist. The hall light behind her showed through, so that he could see the tantalizing outline of her slender, tapering body, more womanly that he had imagined. "Do you like it?" she asked, holding out the skirt of the nightgown. "It's the first time I've worn it."

Before he could reply, or intercept her as he planned, she brushed past him, around to the opposite side of the bed, and sat down. She swung her legs onto the bed, and worked herself to the center, almost beneath him, and then laid her head back on the pillow. She looked at him openly.

He kneeled on the bed, and then stretched his naked body beside her own. She looked at him with a sweet, lonely look. "What you must think of me," she said.

"I love you," he assured her. "I love you with all my heart."

And he meant it with all his heart.

He kissed her hair, the glossy, soft brunette hair, and then placed little kisses down her face, across the short bridge of her nose, along her high cheekbones, reaching the mouth, and kissing around it and into it, meeting her tongue with his own. With one hand, he slipped the strap off one shoulder, and she obligingly lifted her arm to let it fall away. Her small, deep breast, one large brown nipple hard and straight, was exposed. He kissed her under the nipple, and then took it in his mouth. The delicious sensation blended with the thunder of her heart against his cheek.

With his free hand now, he reached down and began to pull up at the skirt of her flimsy nightgown. Suddenly, he felt her hands on his face. Gently, she pushed him away. Surprised, he drew back and watched her. She reached down and took the roll of nightgown in her hands. Then, forcing herself upright, she tugged it up over her head. From an elbow, he continued to observe her, feeling awe and a swelling pride of possession. Her legs were the longest he had ever seen, or so they seemed. Her belly, except for the crease at the navel, was perfectly flat.

She threw the nightgown aside, and shook her hair and held out her arms wide, and he moved into them, taking her into his arms. They were half sitting, flesh against flesh, her breasts hard against his chest, her fingers playing along his back. He tightened his embrace, and they fell back upon the pillow.

"You're wonderful," he gasped, "wonderful—"

"I love you. I'm not sorry. I want you. I need you."

"I love you more," he said.

He lowered his head, kissing her breasts again, and then moved his lips down to her navel. He caressed her urgently with his hand, and she began rotating her hips, sighing and sighing.

One of her arms suddenly covered her eyes. Her face reflected bliss and pain. "Philip," she whispered with difficulty, "Philip—now—I've got to—now—do it—"

She lifted and bent her body toward him.

He moved as if to encompass her, but suddenly realized that it was useless. The fear that had been growing, that he had pushed down but was there all the time, now reached into the pit of his stomach and clutched him. He did not have to look to know that it was useless.

He glanced at her, and her arm was still over her eyes, her lips parted. This was the moment to possess her. All of his mind wanted to possess her, and yet his body could not.

She lay there, suppliant and ready, her eyes shut, her bosom still rising and falling.

Panic held him helpless. He knew that he must act. Do something, anything, he told himself. It might help. It might help.

He rose and enfolded her, hardly feeling her thighs against his own, thinking only that it must happen, as it always had before. He pressed the dead weight of his frame upon her supple, compliant body and waited, and hoped, but nothing happened.

After a while she opened her eyes. Her forehead was puzzled. She stared at him. He did not know what to say. "I guess I'm not ready yet," he said.

"Did I do something wrong?" she asked.

"No," he said miserably.

He slid over and lay on the bed beside her. "I'm sorry," he said. "Be patient—"

He began to kiss her face again, but the passion had gone out of both of them. She accepted his kisses. But she did not return them. Bewilderment had settled upon her, and desperation upon him. He found her lips and her tongue, and gradually her ardor began to renew itself until her breathing quickened once more. He continued to caress her, but felt nothing inside himself, nothing but the familiar cold chill and a disconcerting emptiness. She was embracing him again, revived and responding. He guided her hand,

and almost reluctantly, without skill or art, she stroked him, but he felt no reaction.

After a while her hand was still. Her eyes met his, dropped briefly to his body, then turned away, and he realized that she knew. Slowly, fumbling for the blanket, she turned on her side.

With a sinking sensation of futility, mechanically and without emotion, he tried again. The love play did not stir her this time. And it stirred him not at all.

Finally, he lay on the bed staring at the ceiling, not seeing it, holding her hand tightly and hoping for a miracle. It was useless. Neither of them said a word.

After what seemed an eternity, he turned his head and peered at the luminous clock beside her bed. It was almost two o'clock in the morning. He had promised himself that he would be home by midnight. A later hour might not be easily excused by mentioning Nathaniel Horn. And a much later hour might mean serious trouble. At first he thought: to hell with Helen. He would risk everything at home, and stay the night here, until it worked. But suddenly he felt too tired of it all, and he wanted to leave this bed and the naked body that mocked him, and flee to safety.

He sat up. "It's two o'clock."

"Yes."

"I'd better get home."

She said nothing. He gazed at her briefly, wordlessly, with a curious detachment. Her magnificent body was a familiar object now, and he knew that he wanted it, but he no longer knew if he wanted it because he loved her or because he hated himself. The need for this naked object rose hotly inside him. On impulse he reached out, fumbling for her, touching her thigh. She closed her legs tightly in reproach, took his wrist, and firmly removed his hand. "I'm tired," she said coldly. She groped for the blanket and pulled it across her.

"Peggy, I'm sorry. I don't know what to say. I can't explain this."

"There's nothing to explain."

"Of course, there is," he said with annoyance. "I don't know what happened to me. It's the first time it's ever happened like this. I've slept with women." He was careful not to mention his wife. "I've always been all right."

"Maybe you drank too much," she said.

"Maybe that's it," he said without conviction. He studied the angel face. "You're beautiful, Peggy."

"You'd better go home. I want to sleep. I have to take Steve to school early tomorrow."

He did not want to lose what they had. "I love you, Peggy—I love you more than anyone in the world."

She said nothing.

He swung off the bed, and numbly he dressed himself. When he was done, he looked at her. She was on her side, her back to him. He could see the curving line of her spine in the hall light. He leaned over and kissed her hair.

"I'll call you tomorrow."

She did not reply.

"You were very good to me," he said. "I love you."

He walked through the quiet house, softly opened the door and closed it, and stepped outside. The air was cold. He made his way woodenly across the brick path to his car. He opened the door and got behind the wheel, feeling secure again within its familiar interior. It seemed years since he had left the car, arms filled with gifts, his spirits filled with excitement and hope.

Why had he come here at all?

His arms were too leaden to move. He was drained from head to toe. Not the soft and wondrous weakness after orgasm or a long job done, but the self-hating weakness of self-anger and frustration after awaking from an acrimonious fight or a suicidal drinking session or an indefinable night of mental depression. There was the deep, pushing ache inside. His heart was heavy. A cliché, he thought, but a cliché because it was exact and true. His heart was heavy.

Never, in his entire life, had he felt so ashamed.

He started the car and drove blindly home.

3

Monday Night

HELEN was one of those people who hated to awaken in the morning. She made it seem as if God and Philip had conspired to invent this monstrous calvary just for her. She always woke bit by bit, tentatively and with anxiety, and once her eyes were open she was inevitably resentful and ill-humored. Dr. Wolf had earned several hundred dollars listening to the angry details of this collusion between Nature and spouse.

It always baffled Philip that he was a part of Helen's resistance to facing a new day. She liked to blame this resistance on her marital unhappiness, which, in turn, she said, was caused by Philip's inattentiveness. "What's there to look forward to?" she would ask wearily. For himself, Philip had a simpler explanation. Helen woke reluctantly because it irritated her that he came awake so well. Most often, he rose as lively and good-natured as he would be during the best part of the day. Helen could not understand this capability, and he was sure that she hated him for it.

This morning, when he awakened, the bed beside him, mussed and empty, told him that Helen was already in the kitchen with Danny, girding herself for the endless hours ahead. The sun, filtering through the thin drapes, was on his face, and for a moment, the comfortable and familiar feeling of life ahead and secret surprises encompassed him. And then, at once, he remembered. And for the first time, fully awakened, he knew how it was with Helen.

He lay still as stone, thinking back on those night hours, on the flushing humiliation of them. He reviewed every move, every word, every thought. In the bright daylight, it was even more shameful than the night before. His mind reached to Peggy, contrite, pitying, and he wondered how she had awakened this morning. Had she lain there, on the bed he had so recently left, and been suffocated by embarrassment at her nakedness, at offering herself, at being rejected by his inadequacy? What had been in her mind this morning? What could she think of him?

He knew that he must face a decision. His instinct was not to face the situation, or her, but to turn his back upon it. He would not call her again, or see her, but rather he would push the ugly episode away, out of sight, until in time it diminished in importance.

But at last, when he got out of bed and sat heavily in his rumpled pajamas, shoving his feet into his worn bedroom slippers, he knew that he could not ignore what had happened. Reality had revised his old image, and a new image floated vividly in its place: Peggy, naked on her back, beautiful and inviting, waiting to receive his passion, and he, over her, impotent, unable to give it.

Sitting, considering his fiasco, one thing gnawed at him. She, so desired by so many males, had made a choice. She had selected him for sexual union and gratification. And he had failed her. Under like circumstances, any other man would have given her something. Perhaps not perfect, but something. Bernie Degen. Jake Cahill. Bill Markson. Even that little Irwin Stafford. Even Sam Barlow. And Kip Carster, his one actor friend, his actor friend with the improbable name and the incredible reputation—oh, how Kip would have reveled in the opportunity, and made use of it, and gratified her. Any man alive would have succeeded in some way. He had floundered utterly.

He saw clearly that it was no longer a question of merely desiring her. It was a question of proving his masculinity. This he saw, but there was something else he sensed vaguely. He sensed that, after a long journey, he had arrived at an emotional crossroads. That he had already failed with Helen he had no doubt. She persistently attacked his manliness. Not in the narrow sexual sense, but in a broader, more inclusive sense, in the sense that Freud referred to sex as something more than intercourse. Then, there was the problem of Danny, the evidence that he was performing immaturely with his son. And his career, a monument of jello. Everywhere he had vacillated, evaded, failed. Peggy was a symbol of all his failures, and if he ran from her, there would be no stopping, ever again. There, he thought. There, that ties it up in a neat package that a twelve-year-old audience can understand. "But what's the theme?" the producers always asked. "What's the point? What are we trying to say?" And somehow, you always wrapped it up for them in a neat package. "Two-thirds through the story," you said, "the hero comes face to face with this problem, symbolized by this woman. This is the moment of decision. He has two choices. To face her or run. Well, being the hero, he faces her, has the showdown, and wins and this solves his whole life, and he's able to return to his girl, and we go out on happily-ever-after music."

It was not quite that way in real life, Philip knew. Suppose he did not turn his back on the episode? Suppose he did not try to blot it out? Suppose he faced it with Peggy, and consummated their love? Would that solve everything? After the final triumph, the final spasm, would life with Helen be miraculously changed, and with Danny, and with his work? Yet, he knew that something vital would indeed be changed. What would be changed was the way he felt inside.

He trudged into the bathroom, and had a quick shower, and then absently dried himself. He observed his body in the mirror, and then he knew how he felt. It all narrowed down to the male organ, after all, right down to basic, primitive virility. He felt like a subject in one of those photographs they publish in nudist and nature magazines, where the naked men and women seem neuter because their organs have been air-brushed. He could see plainly in the mirror that he was physically intact and normal. Yet he felt neuter. What he possessed seemed as inanimate as a fossil. He felt the old sickness and shame, and he felt a lie as a man.

Wanting to hide from himself and his obsessive flagellation, he dressed hurriedly. Once fully garmented, he realized a small measure of security and escape. But walking to the kitchen, the details of the fiasco returned, and the new image of Peggy on the bed, and he knew finally that there was no escape. He would have to see her again.

Helen was at the kitchen table, in a hostess gown, reading the morning paper and drinking coffee.

"Good morning," he said. He looked around. "Where's Danny?"

"The little boy from across the street came over and introduced himself. He invited Danny to his house. Danny didn't want to go, as usual, but I forced it. I walked them both across the street and left them."

He went to the stove and poured himself a cup of coffee. He opened the breadbox, took two slices of dietetic white bread, and dropped them in the toaster.

"What can I get you?" asked Helen.

"Nothing. I'm not hungry."

She studied his face. "You look awful. Your eyes are bloodshot. Were you drinking?"

"Of course. We didn't have malteds."

"What time did you get in? I didn't hear you. I took a pill."

Relieved, he said, "I thought you heard me. Oh, it was after midnight."

"Did Nat have anything encouraging to say?"

"Not really." He suddenly remembered that he had a lunch date with Alexander Selby and Nathaniel Horn. He wondered if it would be possible to postpone it.

"Well, what did you talk about?"

"He filled me in on Alex Selby. Now there's a character." The bread popped out of the toaster. He took the hot slices and the coffee and joined Helen at the table. "Then we hashed over the whole Caroline Lamb idea. Even if I got it, it wouldn't be easy."

He reached across, fingered through her paper, and removed the sports section. He looked at it, without reading it, and wondered how he would get out tonight.

"You know I'm taking Danny to Dr. Edling today," Helen said.

"So you told me. What time?"

"Twelve noon."

"We'll be getting home at the same time. I hope he's not hard on the kid."

"How can you even think that? Children are his business."

"It's just that Danny's so sensitive—"

"Sensitive children are his business."

"All right, you win," he said, and returned to the sports section.

She was leaving to get dressed, when he said that he was driving up to the corner to buy some tobacco.

"Is there anything I can get you?"

"No."

He finished his coffee. "If there are any calls for me, I'll be right back."

The moment that she was gone, he found his gray sport coat where he had left it in the dining room the night before, felt inside the pocket for the ignition key, and then went out the service porch to the garage.

He drove the six blocks to the small, expensive, suburban shopping area. Leaving his car in the filling station with instructions to fill the tank and check the oil, he strolled to the wire-meshed glass telephone booth near the station entrance. He found several dimes, edged into the booth, deposited a coin, and dialed his old number, which Peggy had retained.

The telephone rang three times, and then, an unfamiliar voice answered. "Hello?"

"Peggy?"

"What?"

"Is this Peggy Degen?"

"This is the cleaning woman. She's went out to the store."

"Any idea when she'll be back?"

"She said in ten minutes. An' that was ten minutes ago."

"All right. I'll call back."

"Should I tell her who called?"

"Just a friend. I'll call back."

He emerged from the booth with a feeling of disappointment, and stood uncertainly at the station entrance. The neighborhood was new to him, and he examined it. The filling station squared off against a gaudier rival station across the street. Behind him he saw a neighborhood drugstore, and on the far corner a professional building with a self-service market next door. He chose the drugstore.

The drugstore was the one American institution he had always missed in Europe. Just as he missed the continental café in America. Now, if Paris and Los Angeles could be blended into one city, on Atlantis, with the temperament and mores French and the plumbing Anglo-Saxon, he would never want to travel again. He paused before a crowded showcase of toilet articles, wondering if he should buy Peggy an expensive perfume, and then thinking better of it. Browsing through the store, he scrutinized the customers. They were mostly young marrieds, with their healthy, sun-kissed daughters, and they reflected the property taxes inflicted on The Briars. Almost to a person, they were coated in the deep tans that indicated leisure, and were equipped with the rhinestone sun glasses, fashionable blouses and Bermuda shorts that indicated high income. Philip imagined that the drugstore was an imperative part of their weekly day, along with tennis lessons and bridge groups and art classes. In the recesses of their stately homes, the manual work was being silently, efficiently accomplished by starched colored maids and electric machines, and they here were the lost class, the victims of Westinghouse and the abundant life.

Philip halted before the magazine rack, thumbing several paperbacks, then devoting himself to a page-by-page examination of a new slick humor magazine that was filled with layouts of delectable redheads in G-strings. One reminded him of Tina Barlow, but all reminded him of Peggy on the bed. He thought of Tina. Had she seen his miserable performance last night, she would have been less inclined to invite his attentions. He noted the time, started out, then remembered that he had told Helen he was going to buy tobacco. He bought a tin of tobacco.

Returning to the filling station, as he packed his leather pouch with the contents of the tobacco tin, he saw that his car had been removed to a parking area. He handed the waiting attendant his credit card, watched it being stamped on the bill, signed his name.

"Mind if I leave the car a minute? I have to make a phone call."

But the attendant had already dashed off to a new customer.

Philip went inside the telephone booth. He deposited his dime, laid another in readiness on the small shelf, and dialed. While waiting, he pulled the folding door shut. It was stifling, but he wanted privacy.

"Hello?" He had not realized this about her voice before. It was low, insinuating. One knew that the speaker had to be beautiful. Usually people were of a piece, and what was promised was most likely there. Helen always noticed this about the movie actresses. They had lovely faces. But when you looked further you saw that most of them also had lovely bosoms and legs. Perhaps the perfect whole was always sought, and these were the survivors of a severe elimination.

"Peggy? Hi, this is Philip."

"Did you just call?"

"Ten minutes ago."

"Clarissa said it was some man with a nice voice. I couldn't imagine who."

"Thank Clarissa, and I don't think you're very nice. Did you just get in?"

"Yes. I've been in and out all morning. There's so much to do here."

"What are you wearing?" He had to know the way she was this minute.

She hesitated. "Well—a pink sweater—Capri pants—"

"Sounds attractive."

"I won't disagree."

It troubled him that she was not asking about him. She was replying. She was reacting. He worried that she was no longer interested. Had last night been the end?

"What are you going to do today?" he asked.

"A hundred things. You want the highlights? I'm going to pick Steve up at school. I'm going to fix lunch. Then I'll take a sun bath, and after that help Clarissa unpack my things. Then the beauty parlor. And dinner. Dull, isn't it?"

She did not mention the night.

He could let it go this way, he knew, and she would not mention it, and he would not mention it. They would ignore it, pass around it, and over it, and under it, in their little word dance, but still it would be there. Or he could bring it up frankly. The other was straining, the safe patter without recognition of reality. The truth would be torturous, but then they would have something to talk about, and they could go ahead. He took the mouthpiece of the telephone in his free hand, and bent it downward, so that he might speak more closely. The gesture gave him confidence. It was like taking courage in his hand.

"Peggy," he said, "I'm goddam sorry about last night."

"Don't be silly."

"I'm not being silly. It's on my mind. I hardly slept a wink. It's all I thought about the entire morning. I can't tell you how I feel. I've been miserable."

"It's just your male ego—"

"It's more than that," he said pleadingly. "I fell in love with you. I wanted you. I physically wanted you."

"Well, you had your conquest. That ought to make you feel good."

"You know better than that. I wanted the whole thing for us, all the way. I keep worrying what you think of me."

"You saw how I felt about you—"

"No, I mean now. I don't want you to be angry at yourself and at me."

"I'm not."

"What have you been thinking about it? Tell me what you've been thinking."

"I haven't had time to think. I've been on a merry-go-round."

"Stop it, Peggy. You know you've thought of it."

There was silence a moment. Then she spoke. Her voice was very low. "I'm sorry for you, that it didn't work."

"And for yourself?"

"I haven't done that since my husband died. So one more day didn't matter."

The last gave him a surge of hope.

The metallic voice of the operator interrupted. "That's three minutes. Deposit another ten cents, please."

He could have strangled her with his bare hands. "One second—one second—" He found the dime on the shelf and pushed it into the slot. It made a noisy, rattling descent into the box. Those damn operators, he thought, they must listen in on every word. He wondered if they did, and fleetingly lamented the opportunity he had once had, and turned down, to join several other fathers and their sons in a visit to the telephone company.

"Peggy?"

"I'm here."

"I just want you to know I feel the same way about you —the way I felt the first day I saw you—"

"I'm glad."

"I want to see you, Peggy. Can I come over tonight?"

"No, not tonight."

"Tomorrow then. What about tomorrow?"

"I don't know. I may have something—"

"Why not tonight?" he asked.

"I'm busy."

He did not believe her. "I'm coming over anyway."

"Please don't."

"I've got to. I've got to see you. I want to talk to you."

"I'm having people over."

He still did not believe her. "Then I'll wait—I'll wait until they're gone."

"No."

"I'll see you tonight, Peggy. I love you. I've got to run now." He hung up.

It was twelve twenty-five when he drove into the parking lot next door to Panaro's.

He had actually tried to postpone the meeting. The fiasco filled his mind, and Peggy, and he had told himself that he would do poorly with Alexander Selby. His only wish had been to vegetate, alone, until this evening, when he might see Peggy again and revise her estimate of him. He had telephoned Nathaniel Horn to discuss a postponement. Viola had answered, and, after the usual exchange of pleasantries, had told him that Mr. Horn was at the studios and would not be in for an hour. Philip realized that then it would be too late. He did not want to see Alexander Selby, but he also did not want to alienate him. The old survival instinct acted upon him, and he had told Viola that it was nothing really important.

He went into the restaurant. Panaro's was an intimate continental island on Wilshire Boulevard. It had opened the year before. A renowned singer had used it as a rendezvous with another man's wife, a female columnist had written French phrases of ecstasy in mentioning the decor, a sophisticated disc jockey had referred to it as his home away from home, and it was the current rage. Philip had eaten in Panaro's several times. The menu was limited and expensive, the food atrocious, but the waiters spoke with accents, and there were Matisse posters on the walls. In a year, it would be bankrupt, and some foolhardy new proprietor would try to win the fickle movie crowd back, by making it an Oriental restaurant.

The faultless maître d' with the thin moustache—he seemed familiar and a friend because he played faultless maître d's in films—peered inquiringly at Philip, and Philip asked if Mr. Horn and Mr. Selby had arrived yet. The maître d' consulted the pad in his hand and said that they had not arrived. Philip thanked him and took a seat at the bar.

He was halfway through his scotch and water, when he felt a hand on his shoulder. He turned quickly, and there was Nathaniel Horn, and behind him Alexander Selby.

"Mr. Selby—Philip Fleming."

He rose and took Selby's soft hand. The producer was slightly smaller and thinner than he had remembered, and there was an aristocratic, beaky quality about his face. His cigarette was in a long silver holder. There was an enormous monogrammed ring on one finger. His narrow, blue silk suit was impeccable.

Horn walked ahead; as they were led to their corner table, Philip was beside Selby.

Selby glanced at him. "Haven't we met before?"

"I think several times, briefly, at parties."

"I thought so. I'm dreadful with names. But faces stick."

They sat, and Philip stayed with his highball, while Horn and Selby ordered Gibsons.

"Charming restaurant," said Selby. "Reminds one of Maxim's."

"I'll take Maxim's," said Philip.

Selby smiled. "Of course."

"I saw *Including The Kitchen Sink*," Philip said to Selby. This was a pleasant domestic comedy Selby had appropriated from Broadway and converted into a two-million-dollar glossy farce. "The audience laughed so hard, I missed half the dialogue. I'll have to see it again."

Selby seemed pleased. "It's on its way to establishing a new box office record at the Music Hall," he said.

Philip found it difficult to appear astonished, since every new epic established a new box office record at the Music Hall.

"What have you got in the hopper for next year?" Nathaniel Horn asked Selby.

"Well, nothing really, except this Caroline Lamb thing. It's perfectly frightful, the sort of tripe they're passing off for dramatic plays in New York this season. And the books —I read myself blind—but I think it would be more profitable to confine myself to the juvenile lists." He turned to Philip. "I don't know what has happened to writers in America. If they knew how we hungered for material, but decent material—"

His voice trailed off, and he shook his head. Philip was tempted to ask Selby if he really thought the duty and function of the American writer was to supply stories for motion pictures, but he suppressed the temptation. Instead, he said, "Well, writing a book or a play is one thing. Writing a movie is another."

"It doesn't have to be that way," said Selby firmly. He thought about it, and then added, "I don't mean to imply that the novelist should slant for Hollywood. That would be the death of art. But, under certain circumstances, I think the novelist and the producer can work more closely, and both profit by it." He paused significantly. "I think that's why I wanted to meet you today."

"Alex has come up with an interesting notion," Horn said to Philip. "I think you'll like it."

"I'm curious," said Philip, and he waited.

Selby flicked the cigarette stub from his silver holder and pocketed the holder. He took up his Gibson, and sipped it, and then carefully set it down.

"I read your book," he said to Philip. "It was more than competent."

Philip knew that Selby was not being patronizing, and he was pleased. "I'm glad you liked it."

"I reread the Caroline Lamb chapter last night. I thought you got into her very well."

Better than he got into Peggy, he reflected bitterly, and immediately regretted the vulgarity of his reflection. He wondered if Peggy really was going to be busy this evening or if she had been trying to avoid him. She had every right to be disgusted with him. He was disgusted with himself.

"You showed compassion," Selby was saying.

"Caroline Lamb deserves it," Philip said.

"Yes." Selby washed the onion through his drink. "Have you ever thought of writing another book?"

"Many times."

"Why haven't you?"

"No patron," he replied.

Selby looked up. "I might be your patron," he said quietly.

Philip was surprised and puzzled. He had not expected this turn. He withheld question or comment.

"What I mean," said Selby, "is that I believe movies should be presold, not only to impress the audience but to impress the players you want to hire. If I go to one of the leading actresses in the industry and tell her that I want her to play Caroline Lamb, she will ask to read the book or play. When I tell her it is only an original idea, she will feel unsure. She may do it because she knows my reputation for good taste and she trusts me. On the other hand, she may not. And then I will have to settle for less. When I present the film to audiences, they too may feel uncertain. And I might have a failure." He lifted his drink. "It's a pity this is so, but it's a fact," He finished his Gibson.

Philip knew what was coming, but he waited.

"If I decide to go ahead with the project, I will want a book on it first, a novel. Do you think you can write a novel?"

"Of course I can write a novel," he said too quickly.

"It wouldn't be easy. I'm very demanding. It would have to be a good novel. Once done and published, I might help it become a best-seller. I would certainly spend a considerable sum exploiting it. When *Caro* appeared as a film— *Caro,* that is what I would call the book—it would be well known, presold. And, I assure you, we would have a well-known actress in the lead."

"Are you saying you would simply want me to write the novel?"

"Oh, no. If that were so, I would hire a prominent novelist. No. Essentially I want an experienced screenplay writer, who can also write a good book. I want the projects married. That was what I was trying to explain before. One man would research the book in London, create a novel from his research, and then translate the novel into a screenplay. It would all be part of a single deal. I think this could be quite an opportunity for you. A trip abroad. A chance to write a book again—with a patron to pay for it. And an important screen credit."

"I won't pretend," said Philip. "It sounds great."

"Nor would I interfere with the author's artistic integrity," Selby added a little pompously. "I would want to talk out the story line, of course, and approve. But after that the author would be on his own."

"In London," Philip said.

Selby nodded. "In London. I've already discussed the terms with Nat, if I decide to go ahead."

Philip glanced inquiringly at Horn.

"We've just kicked it around, roughly," said Horn. "Transportation to and from London for you and Helen, and expenses while you're working there."

"With a limit of four months," said Selby.

"Yes, four months," Horn agreed. He faced Philip again. "Five hundred a week while you write the novel. Then twenty-five thousand more if Alex decides to use the novel for a picture. And twelve hundred and fifty a week for sixteen weeks on the screenplay."

Stephen Crane, he thought, how was it when you wrote your novel?

"I'm satisfied if you are," Horn said to Philip.

Philip grinned and looked at Selby. "When do we get started?"

"That is entirely up to you, Mr. Fleming," said Selby. "One thing is holding me from a definite commitment. I'm not sure there's a third act in Caroline Lamb, and if we find there isn't, I just wouldn't want to go ahead with it."

He signaled the waiter, and they all ordered lightly. After the waiter had gone, Selby began to discuss the Caroline Lamb story, as he saw it. He continued slowly, thoughtfully, until they were served, and then through the entire lunch. He saw the first and second acts clearly. The first act would dramatize Caroline's background and character, her courtship with William Lamb, her wedding, her early married years, and would end at the point of her meeting with Lord Byron. The second act would dramatize her uninhibited affair with Byron until he deserted her for Lady Oxford, and it would end on the July night in 1813, at the ball given by Lady Heathcote, when Caroline tried to slash her wrists in Byron's presence.

"It's the third act that troubles me," Selby said with a frown, as they sat over their desserts. "Byron goes to Italy and then to Greece. But what do we have left of Caroline? Complete disintegration, that's all. She tries to recreate her Byronic romance with a series of tawdry, illicit affairs. She takes to drugs and brandy, and to being slovenly. She drives her husband off, has a mental breakdown, and in 1827, she dies."

"With William Lamb faithfully at her side," said Philip.

"True. But it's not enough. The whole last third is just too bloody downbeat. It'll bother audiences. It bothers me."

"It's difficult to tamper with facts."

"I know—I know. Still, there must be some way to make that third act as exciting as the first two."

"It would take some thinking," said Philip.

"I appreciate that," said Selby. "Now, Nat knows my problem. I've got to make a decision on my next property by the weekend. If I feel Caroline Lamb is right, I will go all out with it. But if I'm not sure, I'll have to take up the option on a play I've been holding, and then it'll have to be the play."

"You mean you want a third act from me by the weekend?"

"By Friday, I think. Oh, it needn't be worked out in detail. But just a line on it, so that I know where it's going. If it makes sense, I'll buy it. And you can apply for your passports. We'll be in business."

"Fair enough," said Philip.

After Horn had paid the check, they lingered a moment before the entrance to Panaro's. Selby reminded Philip that Friday was his deadline, and Philip promised that he would have something on or before that day. They spoke their good-bys, and Selby walked to his Bentley. The moment he was out of earshot, Horn gripped Philip's arm.

"Well, what do you think?"

"Fantastic," admitted Philip. "But that third act'll be rough."

"I've seen you lick worse," said Horn.

"Not at these stakes," said Philip.

"Well, I trust you. Now one more thing. The Western

at Master Pictures. Ritter is still holding it open, and I've been stalling, but he must have an answer by Wednesday."

"You know how I feel about the Western. I want to do this."

"Then I'd better tell Ritter—"

"No, wait." The old insecurity welled up. "If we kill that, and this thing falls through, I'm left flat on my ass."

"Well, until something else comes up."

"But you've been saying things are slow."

"They are."

"Look Nat, the new house has got me nervous. Can't you stall Ritter a little longer, until I know if I can lick this damn Caroline Lamb thing?"

"I can try. I can't guarantee it."

"Try," he said, and immediately he despised himself for his effort to hedge his bets, for his inability to decisively turn his back on what he did not want and gamble for that which he really desired most. Absently, he said good-by to Horn and went to his car.

In the old days—say, three days ago—he would have been insane with excitement over the opportunity that Alexander Selby held out to him. But now he had driven no more than two minutes from Panaro's, before he knew that he did not give a goddamn about Caroline Lamb and her third act. All that he could think about, all that he cared about, was Peggy Degen and their second act. Involuntarily, the events of the night before paraded through his mind. He felt nauseated, and wished that he had not had lunch.

When he returned home, he saw Helen, in a sunsuit, seated on a lounge in the patio, rubbing oil on her back. He removed his tie and coat in the dining room, and stepped outside to her.

"How's the Goddess of the Sun?" he asked.

She looked up and continued massaging oil into her back. "Hi." She tried to read his face. "How did it go?"

"A fabulous deal," he said.

He recounted all of it, as best he could, down to the missing third act and the Friday deadline. She listened gravely.

When he was done, she asked, "Can you do it?"

"What do you mean?"

"Satisfy Mr. Selby?"

"I don't know. This is my meat. If I can't, nobody can."

"London," she said with wonder. "Phil, you've got to do it. Think of the trip, and a paid-for book. You couldn't in-

vent anything better for yourself. You've got to start thinking of the story right away. I'll help you."

"How can you help me?"

"I'll do research. I'll listen. I'll make suggestions."

"Fine."

"Think of it—Danny in Piccadilly Circus."

He had almost forgotten about Danny. "Where is he?"
he asked suddenly.

"In the den drawing a cartoon strip. We just came back."

He remembered. Dr. Robert Edling.

"Did you take him to the psychiatrist?"

She nodded. "Two hours' worth. He had the first hour.
Then I went in."

"Well?"

"At first I didn't think we'd make it. Danny threw up in
the waiting room. What a mess."

"You mean he was scared?"

"Wouldn't you be? But the doctor was a wonder, a ma-
gician. He had Danny eating out of his hands in five minutes.
They went into the room together and I just sat and
waited."

"What did they do in there?"

"Well, I didn't see, but Dr. Edling explained it to me
after. They sat on the floor and did things with clay, and
talked, and after that they lined up little miniature space
men. Then, they played games. You know how Danny is
with games. The doctor said Danny clung to him and didn't
want to leave when the time was up. 'He wants a father,'
was what the doctor said—"

"I was waiting for that."

"Phil, I swear he said it, exactly."

"Just don't make up things and label them Dr. Edling."

"If that's what you think—"

"Oh, Christ, get off it, Helen."

She glared at him. "I knew you'd be this way."

"What way?"

"Hostile. I told the doctor you'd say I was putting the
words in his mouth—"

"Naturally. What else did you tell him?"

Helen bit her lip. "How can I talk to you, if you're not
going to be open-minded?"

"All right. I'm open-minded, wide-open, wide-minded.
Danny came out, and you went in—"

"He gave Danny some books to read, and a candy bar.
He's a very nice man. Gentle and sweet. He sat in a chair
next to a table, and I sat across from him. He told me
about Danny, and we just talked."

"What about Danny? That's what I want to know."

"Dr. Edling says he's emotionally disturbed. He can't control his inner anxieties. He's worried about me, that I'll stop loving him. He's confused about you. He needs a strong father image. Someone he can believe in and copy, someone who'll give him time—"

"I give him as much time as the other fathers give their kids."

"It's not how much time, not the quantity—it's the quality of the time spent. Danny's got to know that you're deeply interested in him. And he wants to know we love him and will protect him—"

"He knows very well we love him."

"Apparently not. Anyway, that's what Dr. Edling says, and I believe him. He says our home life has been so argumentative and unhappy, that it's rubbed off on Danny. That's why he's insecure—full of fears—"

"All right. What does the doctor intend to do about it?"

Helen studied Philip. "If you don't bite my head off, I'll tell you."

Philip contained himself with difficulty.

Helen went on. "He wants to see Danny once a week, like this, for a few months. He wants to see us, separately, from time to time."

"Starting when?"

"He'd like to meet you this week. He told me to ask you to call him."

"That's all I've got to think about this week."

"Phil, it's only for fifty minutes. What's more important?"

"You want to go to London, don't you?"

"I want Danny well."

He turned away. "Okay, I'll call him."

Her voice nagged after him. "When?"

"This week—this week—"

He had reached the screen door to the dining room, when he remembered the thing that he must not forget. He hesitated, and turned casually back to Helen.

"By the way, I almost forgot—I'm seeing Alex Selby tonight—"

"But you just saw him."

"He had to run right after lunch. He wants to kick that third act around some more. He thinks we can do it better together. I think it's worth a little time, don't you?"

"I suppose so. . . . Phil, you will see Dr. Edling?"

"Of course, honey."

He went into the house. In a few hours, he would be with Peggy.

The dinner was over, and it was Monday night.

He shaved with his safety razor, taking great care, but constantly aware of the time. It was a quarter to eight. When the last of his beard was gone, he lathered his cheeks and chin, then washed the lather off. He wet his hair and combed it back. Returning comb, shaving cup, and razor to the cabinet, his eyes fell on the after-shave lotion that Helen had given him at Christmas. He had never used it. He disapproved of men who smelled artificially of pine needles. But tonight was an occasion, and it demanded special measures. He uncapped the lotion, poured a small amount of the liquid into his palm, and passed his hand over his smooth face. He was careful not to apply too much. It might be unusual and elicit a curious comment from Helen. When the application was finished, he knew he smelled of pine needles, yet felt strangely festive.

He wanted to wear a sport shirt and had already taken one from the hanger, when he remembered that he was supposed to be seeing Alexander Selby. One did not wear a sport shirt to visit a fastidious patron. Helen would have been the first to remark on it. Quickly, Philip returned the sport shirt to the hanger, relieved that he had not blundered into arousing his wife's suspicions. He settled for a gray button-down shirt and striped blue tie.

It was ten minutes after eight when he reached the living room, where Helen was catching up with the morning papers. He bent and kissed her.

"What time will you be home?" she asked automatically.

"I don't know. Selby's a windy one. If we latch on to something, it might be a late session. Better not wait up for me."

"Try to get home early. You need the sleep. You look a wreck."

This irked him. He thought he looked rather well. "There'll be plenty of time to sleep on the boat to London."

"I was just thinking, Phil—if that London job did work out—we could get Dr. Edling to recommend someone over there for Danny."

The oddity of it conjured up an unreal picture: his son, product of a hundred television horse operas and gallons of fresh orange juice, sitting on a carpet in Harley Street with a foreign psychiatrist, modeling figures out of clay dug six thousand miles away. "We'll cross that bridge when we get to it."

He turned to go, when Helen's voice caught him.

"Is there a number you can leave, Phil?"

"I don't know Selby's number. Anyway, it's unlisted."

"Well, good luck."

He smiled. "Good luck to us."

Good luck, he thought, as he hurried through the kitchen and service porch. Good luck. Do you hear, Peggy?

He drove the winding thoroughfare at moderate speed because he did not want to devote himself to his driving but to his thoughts. The extraordinary thing that had occurred last night, he reassured himself, could not possibly happen again. Why, the law of averages was against it. When two healthy human beings desired each other, nothing could prevent their union. Surely, the stimulation of Peggy Degen would overcome any degree of intoxication, exhaustion, or psychic disturbance. Of course, it had not the night before. But then, he decided, he had been too anxious and overwrought. Tonight, he would not think about it, he would not suffocate it in his mind. Tonight, it would be simple and spontaneous. Just plain sex. Like with Helen. You were hungry. You ate. That was all there was to it. Of course, there was always the possibility that Peggy might not be in the mood. But she had not seemed in the mood last night, and then there was physical contact, and that changed her. A woman can always be put in the mood by the right man. She would know how much he loved and needed her, and she would love him.

He turned left and drove up the hill, then turned right on Ridgewood Lane. The houses that he had known so well for six years passed his window, and he wondered how many of the men were out seeing their Alexander Selbys. There were several automobiles before her house. He swung his wheel sharply and pulled into her driveway, parking directly behind her convertible in the open garage.

He went to the door, and pressed the bell. He heard her approaching, and her voice as she called off to someone, and he had a moment of panic. She opened the door and seemed not at all surprised. "Philip Fleming," she said rather loudly, obviously for the benefit of others. "This is a surprise. Won't you join the party?"

His disappointment was immediate and keen. He had been confident since their telephone conversation that she would be alone this evening. She had not lied to him, after all. "Hello, Peggy." He entered the room.

There were three of them. Horace Trubey was slouched in a pull-up chair. Dora Stafford was bending over the coffee table working a lighter. Rachel Trubey was on the sofa.

It was unlikely that any one of them would ever see his wife again, but nevertheless he had to play it safe. More than that, he must not compromise Peggy.

Horace pulled himself to his feet. "Hiya, Philip."

"Hello—hello," Philip called out to Horace and the two women. He turned to Peggy. "I'm sorry to bust in like this. I—we needed the garden hose today—and—I remembered I had left it in the garage when we moved. I happened to be driving by. I thought I'd pick it up."

He saw Dora's amused look, over the lighter, as she smiled conspiratorily at him. He remembered: It'd be worth a try, Phil. Peggy's got a lot there. She won't be saving it forever. He wondered suddenly how much Dora knew. Had Peggy confided in her? Did she know about last night's fiasco? Was she smiling at him or with him? At once, he felt certain that Peggy would not have told Dora. He tore his glance from Dora and looked at Horace and Rachel. They apparently accepted his excuse for dropping in.

"You do your own gardening?" Horace was asking. "How am I ever going to get my wife to water the lawn again?"

"The hose is for the gardener," Philip replied, with a smile. He turned to Peggy. "If you don't mind, I'll just get it—"

Horace interrupted. "And leave me marooned with these three windbags? Not on your life. Now that you're here have a drink and help me get a word in edgewise."

"Please stay," said Peggy simply.

"Well—all right," he said. "For a little while."

"I'll get you a drink."

"Never mind—"

She started for the kitchen. He watched her, and then followed her. He felt Dora's eyes on his back.

Peggy had the refrigerator open. She was trying to loosen a tray of ice cubes. He studied her briefly. She was wearing a translucent gray blouse of Italian silk, and it was open at the throat. Her charcoal skirt flared wide and revealed the ruffled petticoat beneath when she bent over. Her legs were stockingless again, and she was wearing soft gray ballet slippers. As she bent forward to remove the ice tray, he stepped quickly behind her and brushed the exposed portion of her neck with his lips.

She turned sharply, almost in anger, and glanced worriedly at the door.

"You're beautiful," he whispered. "I'm glad I came."

"Here's your ice," she said. "Mix your own drink."

She handed him the cold tray and hurried out. He prepared himself a double scotch, and then returned to the group in the living room.

Horace was in the midst of relating a story about an Indian tribe that he and Rachel had visited in South America. According to the marriage ritual of that tribe, the bride was separated from the groom immediately after the wedding and turned over to a medicine man for deflowering. Eventually, exorcised of evil spirits, she was returned somewhat used to her husband. Horace said that he liked to recount the custom, and recently he had told it to a rising young film starlet who was working for him on a travel layout. But, to Horace's surprise, the custom did not strike her at all as strange. She thought it a tribal practice long familiar to Hollywood. In the movie colony, she said (and she spoke from experience), an ambitious and attractive young actress could not be mated to career and stardom until a variety of holy men had served her in the very way the medicine man served the Indian bride.

Philip, seated across from Peggy, listened politely. From time to time, he watched her. She did not look at him. He tried to concentrate on Horace, who was now detailing some of the starlet's more lurid adventures.

Conversation about sex, Philip told himself as he scanned the intent faces of the others, always made a group more intimate. The persons present might be of different callings and persuasions, and little acquainted, but once any aspect of sex was discussed, the people present became closer and were bound in a secret union. As an occasional party host, Philip knew that any one of three elements made a gathering successful: a guest who had provocative or non-conforming opinions, who was also a reasonable listener; double whiskies served up twice before dinner; or a discussion of sex that grew out of gossip, a considered opinion, or something controversial that was recently observed or read. And, of these, the discussion of sex was the best.

Yet discussion of sex, in Peggy's presence, made Philip feel uncomfortable. But Horace, apparently, had his audience and would not be diverted from a successful subject. Philip knew that there was nothing to be done except listen and murmur occasional approval.

When, at last, Horace had finished with his memoir of the ill-used starlet, he went on to editorialize. He felt, he said strongly, that the men of power in the movie business were forcing helpless young actresses into becoming a colony of courtesans, and that these men, from producers to the lowliest agents, were monsters who behaved viciously.

Listening, Philip decided that Horace was a hopeless and unrealistic romantic.

"Of course, I'm just guessing," Horace said. He had turned to Philip. "You're the only one in this room who's in the movie business, Philip. What do you think?"

Philip had not wanted to be drawn into it, but now that he was, he had no choice but to speak his piece. "There's two sides to it, Horace," he said. "It's really a which-came-first-the-chicken-or-the-egg situation. You can say that there are no virgins in the entertainment business because the men with power take advantage of their positions. On the other hand, the women themselves give these men their disrespect toward women and sex. Consider the kind of person who becomes an actress. Isn't that the goddamnedest way to spend your days? Walking, talking, making faces, pretending, acting out make-believe in front of large groups of people? Isn't that an insane way for an adult woman to spend her life? Yet, because all the adult children watching want the same escape from reality, the rewards are fabulous. These women become worship objects, and through fame and fortune, they become powerful. The goal is so exalted, that young girls will do anything to achieve it. Knowing that their sex is desired, and therefore a useful weapon, they use it. To be crude, they lay it on the table, they say here it is, if you want it then you must do something for me. They start with minor contacts, with agents, and they work up through the hierarchy, casting directors, directors, producers, and studio heads. When, at last, they achieve fame, they can withdraw their sex bait, and be more discriminating. For the first time, they can offer it for pleasure. But, by then, the pleasure is difficult to come by, and the real meaning of love is forgotten. Believe me, Horace, the actress on the make is an aggressive human being. Hell, I remember one talent scout telling me that when he interviewed new girls for a possible contract, he always left the door of his office wide-open. Too often, these girls had tried to compromise him, offering to strip down and give themselves to him then and there, without preliminaries and special privacy, just for the most minor contract. Now, I know that your argument is valid too. If the men did not demand or expect sex, the girls would not have to offer it. But also remember that if the women did not make it the cheapest of commodities, the men might not expect it."

He paused, embarrassed at the length of his discourse, but he saw that Peggy, as well as Dora and Rachel, had been hanging on every word. "I didn't mean to unwind like this," he said apologetically.

"I'm with you," said Rachel.

"And how would you behave if you became a producer?" asked Dora.

He smiled. "My reign would be known as the Reign of Fleming the Lecher." He peered down at his watch, and rose. "Well, I'd better pick up that hose and run. Good to have seen you all again."

Peggy was on her feet. "I moved things around in the garage," she said. "I think I'd better help you."

He shook hands with Horace, bade Rachel and Dora good-by, and followed Peggy out the front door. They moved across the lawn in silence.

When they reached the garage, Peggy said, "I'm glad you came by. You made my party."

He could see that she was pleased with him, and he was pleased. "I just wanted to be near you," he said.

She turned to the garage. "Is there a garden hose or did you just say that?"

"I just said it. I didn't want to put you on the spot."

She was facing him again. "Thank you. You can be thoughtful." She held out her hand. "Good-by, Phil."

He took her hand. "I'm not going," he said.

"Oh?"

"I never intended to leave. I came here to see you alone, and I still want to see you alone. I just couldn't wait them out. It would have looked bad."

"What are you going to do?"

"Take a drive and wait until they're gone."

"It'll be too late. I still have to serve coffee."

"I don't care. I've got to see you alone."

She stared at him. "All right," she said a little breathlessly.

"I love you, Peggy. I've got to have you." He pulled her to him and kissed her soft lips. She moved her head gently, ever so gently, kissing him back. Then, with a quick smile at him, she went into the house.

He wanted to sing. He would have another chance. His old damaged ego would be repaired and whole again. Walking to his car, he inhaled the cool, sharp, grass-smelling air, and he felt alive. But once behind the wheel, he knew another scent, and it was in his memory. It was the faintly erotic and intriguing odor of talcum and flesh. He traced the remembrance to the night before.

He drove slowly down the hill and into Hollywood. He parked near Highland Avenue and walked along Hollywood Boulevard, until he reached the brightly lit racks of the

out-of-town newsstand. He poked among the magazines and
pocket books, without interest, continually glancing at his
watch, and after an hour or so he started back.

When he reached Ridgewood Lane again, he could see
that there was still one automobile in front of Peggy's house.
He drove past at ten miles an hour, leaning sideways with one
hand on the wheel, to see what he could see inside, but
he could see nothing. He assumed that the Trubeys had
departed and that Dora was still there.

He tried to make a U-turn, but the street was too narrow. He backed up, drove past the house again, and then
continued on down to Sunset Boulevard. He parked and
walked. He halted before a new Spanish nightclub, *Ear of
the Bull,* and went inside. The bar was small and dark, and
there was a great mural of Belmonte at the moment of truth.
He lifted himself atop a stool and ordered a double scotch
on the rocks. He drank, listening to the castanets in the
next room and constantly marking his watch. After twenty
minutes, feeling mildly intoxicated, he paid for his drink and
hurried back to his car.

In short minutes, he was on Ridgewood Lane again, and
this time there was no automobile before Peggy's house.
He pulled up at the curb. It was twelve-twenty. With a
mounting sense of excitement, now anticipation crowded by
apprehension, he traversed the brick walk to the door.
Somehow, he knew that it would be unlocked. He tried
the knob, and it opened. He went inside.

Peggy, legs curled under her skirt, was on the sofa, smoking a cigarette and reading. She looked up, as he turned the
lock in the door.

She laid down her book, ground out her cigarette, and
stood up, as he crossed the room to her.

"I began to think you weren't coming," she said. "I was
going to bed."

"You can go to bed now," he said.

He took her in his arms, and her hands reached around
his head and drew him closer, and they kissed. It was as
good as it had been before, feeling the red lips and the
round pressure of her breasts, and at last her thighs against
his own. The kiss was long, with passion rising, and they
came apart emptied of breath. She turned, slipping one arm
around his waist, and he encircled her waist with his arm.
Slowly, without a word, he walked her into the hall, and
through the hall, past Steve's closed door, and into her
bedroom.

When they arrived at the bed, he saw that it had been
turned back and was ready. He embraced her again, aware

of each supple projection and recession of her body fitting against his own.

"Undress me," she whispered in his ear.

He stepped back, and awkwardly, he tried to unbutton her silk blouse. She assisted him, at last, her eyes never leaving his intent face. When the blouse fell open, she wriggled out of it. He reached behind her and unclasped the brassière. It fell away. She caught it and dropped it to the floor. He made no move for a moment as his eyes devoured the sight of her. She stood in perfect repose, like an exotic Balinese dancer, her breasts quivering ever so slightly, the charcoal-skirt accentuating her nudity.

Presently, he unzipped her skirt at the side, and it descended to the floor. There remained only the powder blue nylon pants. He touched the elastic, but she held his hand and indicated his own attire. He nodded and hastily disrobed.

She sat on the bed, then swung onto it and stretched out, as he unbuttoned his shorts. He went to her. She raised her hips slightly, and he worked the last filmy concealment free.

"I'd better do something," he gasped.

"No—no—I've taken care of that—"

He rose high over her, as she shut her eyes, sighing, waiting. He thought that he could bring to completion what they had begun, and he tried, but it was impossible and wasted and frustrating. At last, he gripped her and dropped to his side, so that they were face to face. He continued to move within her clasp, but it was useless.

At last, opening her eyes and shutting them again, her free hand moved caressingly across his body, as though she were determined once and for all to bring him to the amatory pitch that she had achieved. Acutely conscious of her need and her demand, he was yet unable to respond.

After a long while, she brought her hand back over her head against the pillows.

Out of his deepening shame, he tried to liberate and satisfy her.

She pushed him away. "No," she said.

"I want you to be happy."

"No."

Propped on an elbow, miserable and alone, he looked down at her with a special pleading in his eyes. Her gaze did not meet his. She stared up at the ceiling.

There would be no more tonight, he knew. He had failed her worse than before.

Eunuch, he told himself. You goddamn, goddamn, goddamn eunuch.

4

Tuesday Night

ONCE, in his youth, in the year between high school and the university, he had spent the summer with several young friends in Colombia, and one Sunday they had undertaken to scale an eight-thousand-foot mountain. At a distance, and from the maps, it had appeared a routine task. But on the overgrown trail hemmed in by trees and sharp bramble, stifled by exhaustion and heat, he had found the task too formidable. He had decided to forego the summit, and return to the patio of his cool pension, and so had separated from the others to return to the village alone. Halfway down, soaked in perspiration, his defeated legs stiff as stilts, he had collapsed. Rising at dusk, he had lost the path through this jungle of hostile green, but knew that safety was in continuous descent. He had gone on and on, downward, sightless and uncontrolled, bumping into trees and tearing his skin on pointed thorns, and nowhere, it seemed, was there a way out. It was a small hell of blind man's buff, until, with night, he reached the foot of the mountain, and saw automobile lights flashing on a nearby highway and stumbled to safety.

Even after the many years, the hot, helpless confusion of that experience was painful in his memory. And now, this late morning, seated on his study floor surrounded by the books he had been unpacking, he remembered it again. He thought of it, he knew, because it was the way he felt this moment. The mountain was a woman, and he could not attain her, and he was lost. It was not his corporeal being that was injured, but that great part of him that was pride. The emotion he felt was no longer merely shame, but shame compounded by bewilderment. What had happened to him the second night was the shame. But why it had happened was the bewilderment.

He had told himself that he must think of Alexander Selby and reread his references on Caroline Lamb, and with this in mind (oppressed by the bewilderment), he had come directly into the study after breakfast to unpack his books. There were several Byron biographies, each containing many pages on Caroline Lamb, and these he laid aside but did not look at again. For he knew, as he continued his search, that these were not the books he really wanted. There was one other, and he steadily searched until he held it in his hand.

It was a small, slender, gray book, and he had owned it long before he had met Helen. It had been advertised in a magazine, and the price was two dollars and fifty cents. It came, at last, in a plain wrapper, and he had devoured it in a single night. Years after he had married, he had found it on a bookshelf during an intoxicated party. He had stood in the center of the room and read aloud from it, and it had been a gay joke. This morning, it was no joke at all.

He opened the book to the index, and found what he was looking for, then hastily leafed through the pages to those that he wished to read. He was dismayed to learn that the book was actually a marriage primer. This he had forgotten. Nevertheless, he continued to read on about the causes of temporary impotence: fear of inflicting pain upon the bride . . . reaction to her dislike of the marital act . . . a recollection that destroyed passion . . . deep-rooted doubts about one's virility . . . organic disease. Impatiently, he skipped ahead to the passages devoted to the cure and treatment of temporary impotence. The phrases sounded faintly clerical and old-fashioned.

There may have been some truth in the old book, Philip conceded, but it offered no acceptable cause and no practicable solution, and he threw the volume back into its carton with disgust. He gathered together the Byron biographies and took them into the kitchen.

He meant to heat the coffee and read about Caroline

Lamb, but he knew that he did not have the heart for it. He glanced at the electric clock above the stove. Helen had taken Danny to the beach, over highly vocal resistance, and she would not return for an hour. The house was a bachelor's house, and the telephone could be used as he wished. He knew that he must call Peggy Degen, but he could not define clearly what he wanted of her at this moment. It would be impossible to invite himself over a third time and force a third chance. He had no right to demand it, and even if she granted it, he feared the inevitable failure. Yet, see her he must, but to what end, he did not know.

He took the telephone and dialed her number. After a moment, her voice came on crisp and clear.

"Hello?"

"Peggy? This is Philip. How are you?"

"I don't know yet. I'm not sure I'm up."

"Are you in bed?"

"Heavens, no. I'm in the kitchen—trying to bake a cake."

This was new. He remembered, at their first meeting, she had said she could not cook. "A cake?" he repeated. "I didn't know you longed to be domestic."

"The new look. Domestic *and* intellectual."

"And desirable."

"Well, I hope so."

She did not inquire about his activity. It was the one flaw in a woman who appeared to be flawless. Was it that she was a taker, not a giver? No, he knew that was not so. Was it that her interest in him was limited? Possibly. Was it that she restrained herself from displaying proprietory interest in him, from further investing emotionally in someone she did not possess? Most likely. If she would not inquire, he would tell her what he had been doing.

"I was just reading an interesting book."

"Really? What?"

"An inquiry into the causes of temporary impotence."

There was a moment of silence. At last she spoke. "What did you learn?"

"That the whole thing can be psychological."

"How do you mean?"

"The book says have confidence and all will be well."

"I shouldn't have thought you lacked confidence."

"Maybe I do. Maybe it's hidden under heavy strata of assurance."

"I never thought of that."

Philip swallowed. "Anyway, you can see that I'm still upset. And I want to apologize."

"Please don't."

"It makes me feel better."

"I just don't like it. Now let's forget the whole thing."

He was not prepared to forget the whole thing. For that could only mean that he would have to forget Peggy. And at the moment, he desired her more than ever.

"Peggy," he said at last, "I'm not going to ask to come over tonight—"

He waited, but she said nothing.

"—because I could not stand it, if you turned me down," he continued. "I'm going to ask you something else."

"Yes?"

"I'd like to take you out for drinks and dinner."

He waited hopefully. There was the briefest silence. Then, she spoke. "How can you do that?"

"I can."

"Aren't you afraid someone might see you?"

He was dreadfully afraid, but he answered, "Not really."

"Why do you want to take a chance like that?"

"Because I want to be with you." Then, he added lightly, "Besides, I would charge the dinner up as an income tax deduction."

"How?"

"Inspiration," he said brightly.

"You make it irresistible," she said. "How can I say no?"

"Great, Peggy. I love you."

"Will it be hamburgers or dress up?"

He had not thought yet where they would go, or the kind of restaurant it might be, but he answered immediately, "Dress up."

"It sounds like fun."

"Better throw something around your shoulders. We'll go down to the beach."

"What time?"

"Oh—let's say seven-thirtyish."

"All right. I'll get a sitter for Steve."

"See you soon."

He hung up, satisfied but troubled. What pleased him was that he had managed to prolong their relationship. He had adroitly placed the nagging sex thing in the background. He considered what the evening meant. They would have a chance to become better acquainted, to be drawn closer. By taking her out publicly he was boldly demonstrating his true feeling for her. Several evenings of this would dim the failures, would revive their relationship, and when it had reached the proper romantic level again, she would be ready, even eager, to accept him in bed once more. But what troubled him was the difficulty of maintaining this secret, yet open, courtship. The basic problem was getting away from his house for dinner. He had managed successfully two evenings off, after dinner, and that had been easy, but he knew instinctively that he dared not use Nathaniel Horn or Alexander Selby again. Helen was not naturally suspicious, but she was always quick to see through anything clumsily managed. And then he remembered Bill Markson, and he knew that in Bill he had the perfect alibi.

Some months before, he and Bill had met for a series of dinners, sans wives, in Beverly Hills to discuss the possibility of a television series. The series, *White House Girl*, concerned the adventures of a young lady who was a Presidential secretary. Philip had been very keen on it, and his enthusiasm had infected Bill, but the project was soon lost in a mist of alcohol and a haze of gossip. Philip had enjoyed the good fellowship, but had mourned the waste of time. Now, suddenly, it seemed that the time had been well spent. For, those dinners with Bill had established a solid precedent. Helen had not objected to the dinners. She was fond of Bill. She could not object if he and Bill met on business again. Should it be a revival of *White House Girl*, or would it be wiser to say that he wished to test some Caroline Lamb ideas on Bill? Probably the former. The invitation should be initiated by Bill. That would make the dinner date above suspicion. Of course, Philip realized, he would have to confide in Bill. This was something that he had not planned to do. Once, a few days before, he had rejected Bill, and Sam Barlow, as conspirators. But now there was less choice. The time for such discretion was past. The situation demanded intrepid action. And chance circumstance had cast Bill perfectly.

He remembered that Bill was still working in a studio in Culver City. He telephoned him. Bill was affable as ever, but hurried. He was on his way to a story conference. Philip asked if he could make it for lunch. There was something important that he wished to discuss.

"What about here in the studio?" asked Bill. "We can eat at the writers' table."

"No," said Philip. "This is—well, sort of private."

"Private?" Philip could see Bill's eyebrows shoot up. "Okay, Phil, old boy, you've got me on the hook. Where do you want to make it?"

"What about The Little People?" This was an expensive hamburger shop in Culver City. It featured double-decker sandwiches, and onion rings, and booths. It was usually quiet during the day.

"Suits me fine. Say noon?"

"Swell, Bill."

"Remember, I'm expecting something juicy—even if you have to make it up on the way. Gotta run. See you at noon."

Philip wasted the next hour, pacing through the house, daydreaming, picking up books and putting them down. At last, anxious to be gone before Helen and Danny returned, he left early. He reached Culver City twenty minutes before noon, parked his car in the restaurant lot, and then took a slow stroll through the business section.

By noon, he was in a booth, impatiently waiting. After ten minutes, he began to have misgivings. Confiding in anyone was dangerous and imprudent. But when Bill, small and frenetic as ever in a neat linen suit, popped through the doorway, and greeted him with a warm smile, Philip decided that he was doing the right thing after all.

They ordered the double-decker hamburger sandwiches— Philip was careful to say no to the onion rings—and they spoke about their work. Bill gave a progress report on his assignment, an all-star musical, and Philip mentioned the Western that Ritter was holding up. He did not tell Bill about the Caroline Lamb possibility. He knew that Bill would react with unrestrained enthusiasm, and he was in no mood to talk it into the ground. His mind was on the evening.

The arrival of the hamburgers interrupted Bill's torrent of talk. He opened his sandwich, shook some catsup on the meat, and looked up.

"Well, Phil, old boy, what is it?"

"What do you mean?"

"You said you had something important to see me about. When somebody says they have something important to see you about, it's usually important to them, not you. I read that somewhere. All right, what's important to you?"

"I need your help."

"You mean—money?"

"No, of course not," said Philip. "In a different way. I said it was something private. I meant that, Bill. Whatever I say to you, I don't want it to get out of this room. Not even to Betty. Especially not to Betty."

Bill held up three fingers. "On my honor. In one ear, out the other."

"Well, I've got a situation." Philip hesitated. Then he went on. "There's someone I have to see for dinner tonight. I need an alibi to get out of the house. I don't want to make a production of it—but to me it's important."

Bill regarded Philip with genuine surprise. "You mean you got something going?" He shook his head. "And I always thought you were like me—a talker, not a doer."

"I'm just a talker, too. But this time, well, I shut my eyes and jumped."

"Anyone I know?"

Philip was silent, unsure if he should confide.

Suddenly, Bill's eyes widened. "Hey, you wouldn't be seeing someone about an escrow, would you?"

"Well, as a matter of fact, something like that."

"Oh, geez—why does everyone else have the luck? You know, after we got home from the party Saturday night, and I got to bed, I started thinking of her." He shook his head wistfully. "That babe's real stuff, Phil, that's the McCoy."

Philip felt pleased and proud. "That's what I thought the moment I saw her."

"Have you been out with her yet?"

"Well—yes."

Bill was a little boy peeking into the bedroom. "Did you get in there? Or is it none of my business?"

"It's none of your business."

"Boy, oh boy, that face and body—like a hundred-dollar hooker." He reflected. "Of course, she's not much in the tit department, but who needs it anyway? Phil, when you're through, just tell her you've got a friend."

"I'll tell her . . . What about tonight?"

"Tonight?" He furrowed his brow, thinking. "I don't think I've got anything on."

"Well, now you have. You're going to invite me to dinner. Panaro's. We'll talk about the television series."

"Anything for Pythias."

"Call me up around five—no, better make it four. Invite me. I'll accept. You know that means you can't stay home tonight. Helen might check with Betty. Do you mind?"

"If you do the same for me sometime. You've got me feeling damn horny. . . All right, I'll go to a movie or drop in at the Guild." He shook his head with unconcealed envy. "You lucky bastard, you sure fall into things."

"Can I help it if the women won't leave me alone?"

"Oh, sure."

"She's a nice girl, Bill."

"Nice girls also make love. What other reason is there for overpopulation?"

There seemed nothing to add. Both returned to their hamburgers, both thinking of their wives, briefly, and then of Peggy Degen.

He was driving on the Hollywood Freeway, north to the ranch that Kip Carster owned beyond Encino.

He had fully intended to return directly home after lunch with Bill Markson, but somehow, since earliest morning, he had been thinking that he must see Kip Carster. It was only after Bill had departed, and Philip had telephoned Carster and verified that he would be home the entire afternoon, that he had analyzed why he wanted to see the actor. In Philip's mind—and not in Philip's alone—Kip Carster's name was synonymous with uncomplicated sex. On the screen, Carster was Hollywood's billboard of virility. Strong, rough, yet gentle. ("You treat all whores like ladies, and all ladies like whores.") But, where many other male stars, publicized for their masculinity, were quite the opposite in real life, Carster remained consistent and undisappointing. He was an authentic primitive, and amoral as an alley cat. "Then why see him, of all people?" Philip had asked himself. What kind of masochism was this? Yet, for Philip, Carster held out a desperate promise. Had he, of all men, also once had a fiasco? If yes, then it could happen to anyone, and if it could happen to anyone, it was not so serious with Philip.

As a rule, Philip knew, actors and writers mixed poorly. Actors resented writers for their glibness and their defensive superiority (possessors of a special mystique and a creativity not conferred on lesser mortals) and despised them for their fawning lack of integrity. And writers disliked actors for their empty-headed intellectual pretentions, their elevated position and power in the industry, and their undeserved incomes. Philip was no different than his colleagues. He usually dismissed actors with a disdainful wave of his hand. ("Well, what do you expect—he's an *actor*"). In fact, Kip Carster was the only actor that Philip cultivated and enjoyed, but then Carster was only an actor by sheerest accident. In Philip's eyes, Carster should have been a handsome Polish garageman and a habitué of Muscles Beach—which, indeed, he had been before a renowned Mexican nymphomaniac discovered him, shirtless and bulging, washing a car one afternoon some years before. She had taken Carster under her wing as protégé and stallion, and recounted his prowess without inhibition at every Hollywood party. Her female and feline superiors in reputation and salary were consumed with curiosity, and soon enough Kip Carster was on his way.

Philip had written Carster's second starring film. In it, Carster played a rugged Mississippi river boat gambler. In one scene, he stripped down to swim to the steamer, and then climbed aboard to belt three heavies into the water, and the result was a box office sensation. Carster associated Philip with his success, and liked him personally, because he did not speak like a writer. And Philip appreciated Carster because he was an original, and genuine, and fun.

Now, driving to Carster's Encino ranch, he thought of the man and tried to see him through Peggy's eyes. Carster was a big man, certainly six feet three and two hundred pounds. He had the wild, torn face of Peking Man, and his whole aspect evoked dark caves and clubs and a raw new world. In his abbreviated bikini trunks, he was a magnificent creation. The untamed sunken face set on a matted barrel chest, and the brawny legs, impressed men as well as women.

Carster was neither imaginative nor clever, but he was not dumb either. He had little patience for reading, but since a celebrity must have opinions, he formed his through listening. His mind was a mammoth blotter, and it absorbed and retained fragments of a hundred other minds. Too, he was canny in a shrewd animal way, especially in matters that involved finances. His speech was salty and ribald.

In matters sexual—and these matters dominated his life —he was straightforward. He had no patience for romance or verbal love play. He felt that what he had to offer of the essential thing was enough, and his companion must decide to accept or reject it at once.

"Most guys babble too much," he liked to say. "That kicks sex right out the window. If you got to talk, all right then, talk about sex. No nonsense. The minute you bring it right out in the open, you're halfway there. I talk sometimes, when I got a real frozen one on my hands. I bring it out in the open, all the words, and then she begins to see it's not so private and mysterious, what she's got. Of course, like you know, usually I don't talk much at all. Usually, after a couple drinks or after dinner, I say, Look, baby, I want to make love to you—exactly what I say depends on the girl's class—and I say take it or leave it. Most of them take it. I heard some guy say that once you break down the whole puritan thing, the moral thing, you know, inhibitions, there's no defense and the rest is a shoo in.

Well, my batting average is pretty good. Take ten gals. I proposition all ten right off. So maybe one slaps me—she's the one that lies down the quickest, begging. A couple kind of laugh nervous, like you're kidding, but they come across. Sometimes, one tightens and you can't get to first base. Sure. But the rest of them don't even make believe. They just say yes. Out of ten, I'd say eight or nine. You do the courting kid. I'll do it my way."

The approach was apparently right. At least, for one of Kip Carster's endowments. It was a legend in Hollywood that not one of Carster's leading ladies had ever escaped seduction. One had been a grandmother. Another had been fifteen years old. A third had been happily married and with five children. And each and all had fallen prey, with varying degrees of reluctance. Once, Philip remembered, a girl he had known on magazines in the East had arrived in Hollywood with assignments to interview several motion picture stars, among them Kip Carster. When she learned that Philip knew the actor, she sought his help. Philip was less than enthusiastic. The girl was a tall blonde, in her early thirties, somewhat ingrown and bound tight and given to sarcasm. If you touched her, you just knew she would jump backward. Philip did not think she was exactly the type to interview Carster. Nevertheless, as a favor, Philip arranged it. Philip and Helen had promised to take the girl out for dinner, after the interview, and they waited and waited. At last, she appeared. The glacial look was gone. She was disheveled and still breathing heavily. Helen led her to the bathroom to give her time to regain her composure and freshen her make up. Then, the girl confessed, half-tearfully, half-proudly, what had happened. "He just said he wanted to, and I was too paralyzed to say no, and too mixed up, and, I must have been crazy, but I wanted to know what a famous movie star was like. And the next thing I knew, he was all over me." She shook her head with disbelief, and for a moment, her old sharpness returned. "You know, Helen," she said, "it's the first time I ever *really* put a story to bed."

It had been a sweltering hour's drive, when at last Philip reached the dirt road that twisted west to the rise of land on which Carster's vast sprawling ranch house was located. A Japanese houseboy showed Philip through the cool living room to the rear. Carster, shirtless and barefooted and wearing blue cotton denims, straddled a deck chair playing solitaire and drinking vodka.

He greeted Philip with a hospitable roar and a great outstretched ham of a hand.

"Just in time," he said. He shouted to his houseboy, "Yosuke, another vodka, and a scotch on ice for my friend!" He turned to Philip. "Sit down, sit down." As Philip sat, Carster gathered up his cards, laid them aside, and held up his hand for attention.

"A story," he said. "If you heard it before, don't stop me."

He proceeded to recount, with gusto and gesture, a bawdy story about a farm boy who lacked finesse and refinement in his relations with the opposite sex. Philip had heard it before—in the earlier version the farm boy had been an automobile salesman—but he did not stop Carster. When at last the actor bellowed forth the tag of the joke, he fell against the deck chair, holding his sides, laughing until he choked. Philip laughed, too, as much at Carster as at the joke. For the story had been marvelously autobiographical, and Carster did not know it.

The drinks were served, and Carster wanted to know what Philip was doing. Before Philip could tell him, Carster launched into a blue tirade against the studio. It appeared that his studio wished him to perform in a melodrama about an American airline pilot who became involved in a murder in Hong Kong. Since Carster had already done the same story in Buenos Aires and Marseilles, he had ample justification to object.

Carster admitted that what he really wished to appear in was a best-seller novel being adapted at another studio. The role suited him perfectly, and he had been requested for a loan-out. Now, he summarized the novel for Philip. The story was set against the backdrop of the Korean conflict. A sergeant in charge of a small infantry platoon had learned, just before his platoon was cut off and trapped behind enemy lines, that he would inherit a half-million dollars. Inevitably, the sergeant was faced with a dilemma: to make a run for it, at some risk, to preserve his own skin and new-found wealth; or to keep his platoon behind enemy lines, at greater risk, and forfeit the easiest avenue of escape, because there was a golden opportunity to sabotage a Red advance. The novel told the tale of the sergeant's inner conflict, and his growth, and this was the role that Carster wished to play. According to Carster, his studio had agreed that if he would first appear in the film about the airline pilot in Hong Kong, he would then be loaned out. Carster regarded this as the rankest blackmail and had point-blank refused, and now he was on suspension. In the end, of course, Philip knew, as did Carster, that he would play the role of the airline pilot as well as that of the sergeant in Korea. Meanwhile, there had to be the face-saving and costly suspension.

They sat in the sun and talked on like this, or rather Carster did, for the better part of an hour. Then Philip, becoming increasingly apprehensive about the time and Bill Markson's phone call, decided to speed things up and get to the root. He inquired about Carster's last leading lady, and at once the conversation turned to sex. Philip sat back in the afternoon's glare, shading his eyes, sipping his drink, listening, and knowing that it was as if he were listening to a truck driver read aloud from Henry Miller.

Suddenly he thought he heard his cue. He sat up and quickly interrupted. "Aw, cut it out, Kip," he said. "The way you talk, someone would think you never struck out."

"I never said that."

"I'm sure you've had failures like everyone else."

Carster fell silent, laboring his mind over this, searching back, and then he nodded. "Sure I had failures, if that's what you want to call them. Did I ever tell you about the time we were shooting that mystery picture in London, three years ago?"

Philip's heart leaped. "No, I don't think so," he said.

"Well, there was an Irish broad, built like a brick you know what." He smiled at the recollection. "I picked her up in a restaurant off Piccadilly, and after we had a few, I took her back to her apartment for a quickie. I wasn't trying very hard, but I assure you, a good time was had by all. Anyway, it turned out this Irish broad had three other boy friends—she was a mink, that one—a French count, a Czech who was with the Embassy, and a little English accountant. This is for real, Phil. She had those three guys, and they were all romancing her regular, and now there was me."

A brief look of nostalgia crossed his face. "She was a prize," he continued. "I got to admit I enjoyed her. Anyway, I went back for more. Well, once after I'd romanced her, and was sort of satisfied with myself, I asked how I stood up against her three other friends. 'You're awright,' she said. 'You're more fun than the French count.' That got my back up. 'What about the Czech and the Englishman?' Well, she just shook her head. 'Nope,' she said. Well, you know me, Phil. That flung the old challenge right in my face. So the next time I started early and wooed her all evening like she was the last dame on earth. 'Well?' I said to her afterward. She thought about it. 'Well,' she said, 'I got to admit you're more fun than the Czech.' That infuriated me. 'What about the Englishman?' 'Nope,' she said, 'not him.'"

Carster looked at Philip seriously. "Phil, I tell you, that started eating into me. I was determined to be her favorite. I just set my mind to it. I went into training. I cut down the booze and smoking, and I watched my diet. I even did some pushups. I kept away from her for a week. I kept away from all women. I wasn't leaving my best fight in the gym. I really rested for the big night. Then, I went back to her, and I made up my mind, this was it. Well, let me tell you—just let me tell you, and I don't brag—I made Casanova look like a rabbit. When it was over, I knew it was my finest hour. 'Well?' I asked her. 'What do you think?' 'I think you're wonderful,' she said. 'Am I first?' That was all I wanted to know. She just shook her head. 'Nope.' I was outraged. 'Who's first?' I wanted to know. 'The Englishman?' 'That's right,' she said, 'the Englishman.' Well, that beat me altogether. I threw in the towel. I had to know this miracle man's secret. 'How come?' I said to her. 'How come he's first?' Well, she just looked at me with those wide colleen eyes and said, 'I like him better.'"

Carster held out his hands as if to say: women. Philip laughed and believed the story, and thought that maybe it was the story of all sex.

Carster found his drink. "Anyway, there you are. You wanted a failure. I say, there you got one."

"It's a great story," said Philip, "but that's not what I meant. I meant a failure in bed, a fiasco—"

"I don't read you."

"—temporary impotence."

"Oh, that." Carster snorted. "How in the hell can that happen? You want a dame, you want her, you make her. Nobody'd have that happen except maybe a fag—"

Philip flushed. "It's happened to a lot of guys who weren't fags."

"Well, maybe if you got too drunk," Carster conceded. "Matter of fact, when I first broke into pictures, we were having a party on the set after the last day of shooting, and I got plastered good, and this producer's secretary, one of those tall uppity dames like you see in the fashion magazines, I could see she kept looking at me like I was a special exhibit. So after everybody went home, I hung around to have one for the road with her, and then I kind of took her by the elbow and asked her if she wanted to see my etchings and took her into the portable dressing room.

Well, I was too drunk to even ask her. I just backed her against the wall, and began kissing her. Well there she was and there I was, but goddamnit, you're right, Phil, for about a minute—nothing. I'd just had too much happy water. So I dragged her over to the cot, and began to concentrate on her like she was a harpsichord. Eventually, I'm happy to report, I sent her back to her shorthand wiser and fulfilled. It gave me a new respect for Carrie Nation—the demon rum is the enemy of romance. Anyway, that's as close as I ever came to fouling out."

Now fully warmed up, Carster continued to tap his rich store of memories. Philip refused a second drink, and it was twenty minutes before he could take his leave. When he reached his car, he felt depressed. He was sorry that he had come to see Kip Carster at all. He was sorry because the actor's simple animal lust made him feel small and shriveled. The fiasco seemed more disgraceful than he had remembered it.

When he reached home, it was ten minutes after four. He found Helen in the study shortening a new dress. He bent and kissed her. He wanted to ask if Bill Markson had telephoned, but he knew that he could not.

"Where's Danny?"

"In his room, as usual. Where have you been all day?"

"Oh, I went to the library, did a little research—"

"Any luck?"

"Not especially. I'll come up with something yet."

"I hope so. Were you in the library all this time?"

"No. I drove out and saw Kip Carster."

Helen frowned. "Why?"

Philip knew that she did not like Carster. As a married woman, she probably regarded Carster as a threat. His free-wheeling sexual activities made husbands envious and restless and regretful. But deep down, Philip suspected, she was probably curious about Carster and attracted to him. Philip wondered if she had ever mentioned Carster to Dr. Wolf.

"I just felt like seeing him," he said. "Picture talk."

"Did you tell him about Selby?"

Philip suddenly realized that he had not had the chance to tell Carster anything about himself. "I just mentioned it in passing. He's never worked for Selby."

"What did you talk about so long?"

"Sex," said Philip.

"I bet. That egomaniac's got nothing else on his mind."

"Is that so terrible?"

"It's not normal. I'll bet he hates women, really. He's a latent homosexual."

If Carster could only hear this, he thought. "Oh, stop it," he said.

"You men are such children. Anyone who sleeps with a dozen different women, because he's trying to prove something, he's a big hero."

"I never said he's a hero."

"Don't tell me you wouldn't like to be in his shoes."

"I'd like to have a harem also."

"Why don't you?"

"The policeman on the corner. In this case, you. I can just see you, if you found out I'd cheated."

"I've told you a hundred times it's not mere sexual infidelity that upsets a woman, it's emotional infidelity. If you told me you slept with some actress, just as a passing thing, I'd forgive you. If you told me you fell in love with her, I'd throw you out of here."

"Why is it always me?" asked Philip. "What about you for a change? Are you telling me your mind's a temple of purity twenty-four hours a day?"

"Women are different from men."

"Not that different. I've seen you look at Kip during parties. Don't tell me you wouldn't be curious, if you had the chance, and there were no consequences."

"Don't be disgusting!"

"And don't be holier than thou."

"I'm sorry I started it."

"I'm glad you're sorry." He moved to the door. "I better look in on Danny."

Before he could leave, she spoke again. "I almost forgot. Bill Markson called. He wants to talk to you."

Philip almost sagged with relief. He kept his voice casual. "I wonder what about? I'd better call him right back."

He started back into the room. He picked up the telephone and dialed Bill. Betty answered, and after a moment she put Bill on. Bill played it straight, as if Betty and Helen had bugged the telephone. He had a marvelous new idea for their television series. He wanted to discuss it right away. Was Philip free to have dinner at Panaro's tonight?

"One second, Bill," he said into the phone. "Helen's right here. Let me ask her."

He cupped his hand over the mouthpiece, as Helen looked up curiously. "Bill wants me to meet him for dinner tonight. It's about that old television series. He's got something new on it. He's busting out all over. Do you mind? Or have you got dinner on?"

"No. I was just defrosting the meat."

"I suppose I should see him."

"This'll make three nights out—"

"It's one of those weeks." He took the calculated risk. "Look if you want me to stall him, I'll stall him—"

He was depending on her unfailing insecurity. He waited.

"I guess that wouldn't be fair," she said finally.

"It might lead to something."

"Yes. You better speak to him. He'll wonder what's going on."

He took his hand off the mouthpiece. "Bill? It'll be okay. Say, about seven o'clock?"

After he hung up, Helen said, "I should think you'd spend your time better on Caroline Lamb."

"I'm doing my best. You can't force those things. Anyway, Bill sounds like something's cooking. Maybe we'll have a good session tonight."

She returned to her sewing. He walked to Danny's room. Not until he reached it, did he realize that he was whistling.

It was Tuesday night, at last. Philip was behind the wheel, and Peggy was beside him, and they were driving toward the ocean. He took his eyes briefly from the road, to glance at her with the pride of possession. She was lying back easily in the swaying seat, staring upward at nothing, smoking a cigarette. A soft white cashmere shawl covered her shoulders. She was wearing a low-cut black net dress and pointed black pumps. One leg was crossed over the other.

He brought his gaze back to the curving highway. "What are you thinking?" he asked.

"As a matter of fact, I was thinking of your wife."

He did not know what to expect. "What about her?"

"She's lucky, that's all." She paused a moment, and then continued. "I think you'd be fun to live with a long time."

"I'm not sure she thinks so."

"Why?"

"I don't know—we just don't get along."

"Is that why you pick up other women?"

He looked at her sharply. She was smiling at him teasingly.

"I don't pick up other women," he said seriously. "You were an accident. I fell in love with you."

"You don't even know me."

"Enough," he said. "For that matter, you don't know me."

"I liked your eyes," she said. "And I liked the way you talked."

"Is that all?"

"You made me feel safe."

"I'm sorry I've been such a flop," he said. "I've wanted to show you how much I love you."

"You mean making love to me?"

"Yes."

"That's not everything."

"No, but it's the main thing. All roads lead to that. If you don't have that, you have nothing."

"I thought we were getting along very well."

"There's still that," he said miserably.

They drove in silence for a short time. He heard the rustle of her skirt, and turned his head. She had curled her legs on the seat, adjusting her skirt, and she was looking at him.

"Tell me more about your wife," she said.

"Like what?"

"Is she good in bed?"

He did not know what to say. "Satisfactory," he said, at last. "She's there." But he knew that was too cruel, and he immediately went on. "She wants to be good. She's just not spontaneous. She was all knotted up when I met her. She's less that way now, but you get the feeling every move is being coached from the sidelines by her analyst."

"Maybe I'm not any better."

"I think you are. I can tell."

"Philip—"

He glanced at her. Her young face was very intent.

"—what do you want from me?"

"I'm in love with you."

"You keep saying that, but what, really? I know you want to sleep with me. I know that's important to you now, because of your ego. But what else?"

"If I'm not with you, I'm miserable. It's that simple. If I had met you when I met Helen, I'd have married you."

"If you had married me then, and met Helen now, you'd be out with her tonight."

"No."

"I think yes. But don't worry your little head about it. I'm glad I met you, I won't be sorry when it's over."

The finality of the last surprised him. He had never applied man-hour limitations to his affair with Peggy. He had vaguely thought of it as something infinite. That she foresaw an end at all was disturbing. "It won't ever be over," he said.

"Won't it? How many nights do you think you can continue like this, without your wife knowing? She's not stupid."

"I'll work it out."

"How? For a week maybe. After that it would have to come into the open. And you'd have to make a decision. I don't want it to come to that, Philip, I just don't. Fun is fun, but let's not be foolish."

"Do you love me?"

"Of course."

"I love you. Now let's forget everything else and have a good time."

They drove along the coast highway, beneath the great dark cliffs, with a stinging, cool breeze through the window reminding them of the ocean hidden in the darkness to the west. They drove past Malibu, toward Trancas, and, at last, came on the tricolor neon lights of Biarritz Court on the ocean side. Biarritz Court was a combination restaurant and motel, with a parking lot for both between. The rows of motel bungalows, each with its floral patch in front, were small and elegant. The restaurant, glassy and candle-lit, hung precariously over the water. It smelled faintly of seaweed and French sauce. Philip turned his car off the highway into the parking lot. Over the motel office, a red vacancy sign flashed on and off. From the restaurant came the muted sound of an Edith Piaf record.

Philip helped Peggy from the car and, still holding her arm, he led her inside. The large cocktail lounge was empty, except for a half-dozen people at the bar. Philip surveyed them hastily, to see if he recognized anyone, but they were all strangers. He saw that the tables were empty, and steered Peggy through them to a corner table. As they sat down, Philip could see through the archway two couples moving slowly on the tiny dance floor. The dining room beyond was only partially filled.

A waiter, small and Gallic, but without an accent, appeared at once. Philip said to him, "I have a reservation. Fleming. I'm a half-hour early, but be sure to remember."

"Definitely," said the waiter.

Philip looked at Peggy, who had thrown off her shawl. "What would you like?"

"I would like to get very drunk," she said. "I'll have what you have—but double."

Philip turned to the waiter. "Scotch and water for both of us. Doubles."

After the waiter had gone, they sat in relaxed silence,

listening to the breakers on the rocks below, and looking at each other. He dropped his eyes to the low line of her gown, to the dividing cleft at her breasts, and was tantalized.

"Are you hungry?" he asked at last.

"No. I feel just right—cozy and what the hell. The drink'll make it perfect."

The drinks came. Peggy lifted her drink.

"Vive la France," she said.

He touched his glass to hers. *"Voilà* and *oui,"* he said.

They drank steadily, speaking little, listening to the lapping of the waves, staring into the flickering candlelight and at each other. They ordered refills, and when these were served, they drank some more.

"I would say I am fairly intoxicated, Mr. Fleming," said Peggy.

"But not stiff?"

"Oh, no, not stiff."

"Good," he said.

"I always intend to ask you what you're doing—with your writing, I mean—what you're writing—but we constantly get sidetracked talking about something else. What are you doing?"

"I'm an author in search of a third act," he said.

He told her the details of the meeting with Alexander Selby, and the opportunity to write a book in Europe on Caroline Lamb, and how important the book might be and the movie, too.

"It sounds terrific," she said at last.

"Too good to be true," he said, "and that's what I'm afraid of. No third act. It's a helluva triangle, she boozing and drugged and having tawdry affairs in the country house, her husband in London, and Byron in Greece. How do you pull it all together?"

"I wish I could help you."

"Well, maybe I'll think of something."

"You must. You should do a book—and London—Paris—" She finished her drink. "Are you taking Helen?"

"I'd like to take you," he said.

"I'd like that. I've never been anywhere."

"I'd take you to a little hotel I know off the Champs Élysées. I'd show you Paris, block by block. You know what we'd do the first day?"

"No, what?"

"We'd get into bed, and we'd stay there all day and all night."

"And the second day?"

"The same."

"Wouldn't I even get to see the Eiffel Tower?"

"A month or two later, maybe."

"And I thought you loved me." She pouted.

"Well, we wouldn't be out for long. Just to see the Eiffel Tower and buy *Time Magazine*."

"I think I'd like Fleming's Paris."

"Oh, yes, you would—you would—"

She held up her glass. He summoned the waiter. He ordered a third round of doubles. They went on talking about their Paris. When the waiter came with the drinks, he said that their table was ready. Philip looked at Peggy. She capped her hands over her glass. "Let's stay with this." He waved the waiter off. "Later," he said.

He turned back to Peggy. "Now then, what were we talking about?"

"Something in the Cluny Museum."

"Oh, yes, the chastity belt."

"You mean they're for real?"

"Certainly. The crusaders didn't trust the wives they left behind. So they had locksmiths make these belts. There was a lock, of course, and only the husband had the key. The Parisians say Henry II made Catherine de Medici wear the one in the Cluny."

"How awful," said Peggy.

"Peace of mind," said Philip.

They drank. Peggy wanted to know about Philip's travels in Europe, and he carefully selected the most attractive and adventurous episodes. He told her of his meeting with the anarchist underground outside Barcelona. He told her of his visit to Spandau Prison in Berlin, where he tried to see Hess and was briefly arrested by the Russians. He told her of the day he had interviewed Picasso on the Riviera.

"Damn you," she said.

He was startled. "For what?"

"For going to Europe with someone else." She set down her empty glass heavily. "I'm drunk, Philip. Don't pay any attention to what I say." She looked off. "Let's dance."

There were three couples on the small, shadowed floor, and the amplified music, soft and French, was *C'est* something or other. He supposed that he was drunk too.

She danced close to him, and the heat of her cheek on his, her hair, the fragrance of her perfume and flesh, stimulated him. Her thighs were against his, rubbing, challenging, as they glided across the floor. He felt excited, and the excitement was real. Her head moved slightly on his shoulder.

"You must want me very much."

"Very much," he said. "Right now."

"There's a motel here."

"I was afraid to suggest it."

"I want you just as much," she said.

They left the floor, arms linked, and walked to their table. She took up her shawl, and he left a bill for the waiter. They went outside.

The cold ocean air engulfed them, and he wanted the warmth of her naked body. She bent into him, against the wind, as his arm went around her, and they crossed the parking lot toward the red vacancy sign. At the door, he released her. "Wait here a minute," he said.

Inside the office, behind the counter, a lanky, elderly man was seated beneath a standing lamp, reading a magazine. He peered up over his glasses, as Philip came in.

"Yes, sir?" he said, rising.

"My wife and I have been driving from San Francisco," said Philip. "I think we've about had it."

"Too much for one day," said the elderly man, handing him a chained pen and a registration slip.

Philip hastily wrote in "Mr. and Mrs. Patrick Fleming," and filled in the address of a newspaperman friend in San Francisco, and then added his license plate number, changing one digit.

"That'll be twelve dollars for the night," said the elderly man. He handed Philip a key with a wooden marker attached. "Bungalow fourteen. It's all made up. We have room service from the restaurant."

"No, we're too tired."

"Need any help with your luggage?"

Philip shook his head. "We'll leave it in the car. Heading for Mexico before daylight. Good night."

"Good night."

Philip hurried out to Peggy, who was waiting, arms crossed against the wind. He held up the key triumphantly, then took her by the arm and started toward the bungalows. They found fourteen quickly, and Philip opened the door, turned up a lamp, then secured the door from the inside. The room was small but expensively furnished in hotel provincial. A large double bed, already uncovered for the night, dominated the center of the room.

Peggy kicked off her shoes, then circled the room, pulling the shades. Philip turned on the portable radio, then removed his coat and tie. A newscast came on the radio. Philip quickly worked the dial until he heard music.

Peggy was standing in the center of the room. She looked cute and small without her shoes.

"Aren't you going to take off your shoes?" she asked.

"I suppose I am."

"You always do that when you're drunk and in a motel."

He sat and pulled off his shoes. "Is that your experience?"

"It just feels right. . . . Now where were we? Oh, yes. Dancing."

She moved over to him, holding out her arms. He rose and drew her to him. She nestled close, her cheek on his chin. They danced in silence. He kissed her hair and ear, and slowly dropped his hand to her buttocks. He gently rolled her hips, and, in a moment, he was fully aroused.

She pulled herself free of him and gracefully lowered herself to her knees. She tugged at his hand. "Come on," she said. He went down to his knees. They embraced, kissing, then fell sideways, breaking the fall on his arm, then continuing to the rug.

They were stretched out, side by side, on the floor. Her arms were full around him as she kissed him, and finally his hand was on her thighs.

After a while, she said in a half-whisper, "No chastity belt tonight."

"It didn't matter. I had the key."

He rose, as she lay back with a sigh, and he lifted her dress and her half-slip to her hips. She was wearing a lace garter belt and nothing else. It held her stockings taut. Quickly, he removed the garter belt.

He could feel his heart quickening. He finished disrobing. She opened her eyes and looked at him. "Phil, I'm not —prepared."

"Neither am I."

"Well, you don't expect me to, do you?"

"Who the hell needs it—"

"I do." She sat up, unsmiling. "You're not the one who might get caught."

"Peggy, be reasonable, the odds are a thousand to one against it."

"That one's the one that bŏthers me."

"Look honey, I've got to have you, and that's all there is to it—"

He sat beside her, and pressed his lips against hers.

"Please."

"No."

"Don't spoil everything."

"No," she said weakly.

"I promise not to let you get in trouble," he said. "I promise."

"I don't know. . . ."

She sat, her naked legs drawn up tightly together, regarding him drunkenly. He waited, no longer touching her, but now fearing her decision.

"I'm a fool," she said suddenly. "All right, go ahead."

She lay back on the floor. He lifted himself wearily, knowing that it was too late, that the excitement was gone, that it would not return, and that he was sick of himself, thoroughly sick of himself.

"It's no use, Peggy," he said. "We missed the boat."

She opened her eyes. "Was it my fault? Did I talk it to death?"

"It's my fault. I don't know what's wrong. Come on, let's get out of here."

She had not wanted dinner, and they had driven back to Ridgewood Lane in silence. Now, at the door, he asked if he could come in.

"I'm too sleepy," she said. "And I've got a hangover. Will you take the sitter home?"

"Of course. I'll call you tomorrow."

"Sure."

"I'm sorry, Peggy."

She stared at him sympathetically, quickly kissed him, and went inside.

He waited in the car for the sitter. She was a chubby fifteen-year-old girl, carrying three fan magazines, and yawning. She directed him to her parents' home near the bottom of the hill. He waited until she was safely inside, and then drove home to The Briars.

Except for the night light that Helen always left on in the living room, the house was dark and still. In the kitchen, he had a glass of water. His mind was so filled with Peggy, so obsessed with the good and bad of it, mostly the bad of it, that he had to wrench his thinking to remember suddenly that he was supposed to have had dinner with Bill Markson.

He walked softly up the hallway, looked in on Danny, rumpled and doubled on his side, then returned down the hall and into the master bedroom. The lights were out. As the door creaked closed again, he could hear Helen stir.

He went to the bed. "Helen," he called softly, "honey, are you asleep?"

"Yes."

He undressed swiftly, throwing his clothes on the chair. He crawled across the bed to Helen, then lifted the blanket and slipped in beside her.

"Hello, honey," he said.

"Hello." She lay with her back to him.

"I want you," he said.

"It's so late—"

"I want you," he persisted.

She half-turned toward him, opening her eyes, and peering at him in the darkness. "I took a pill," she said, and there was a layer of thickness on her voice.

"This'll help the pill," he said.

"Let's wait till tomorrow."

"No." He pulled down a strap of her nightgown and kissed the exposed breast. Helen turned fully on her back, sleepily staring at him. He kissed the curve of her throat, knowing that this was her erogenous zone, and she sighed and placed her arms around him.

"I want you," he said.

She closed her eyes. "Yes," she said.

He threw back the blanket, and he went to her, without preliminary and with the uncurbed authority of ownership, and she accepted the fierce invasion with an outcry of pain.

"You're hurting me."

"Do you want me to wait?"

"No."

He resumed like a wild man. All that was pent up in him the long night, all that was held in, was now released.

How do you like me, Peggy? How do you like me?

"How do you like me, honey?"

"Shh. Don't talk."

5

Wednesday Night

"MR. FLEMING—Dr. McGrath will see you now," Miss Hanson, the blonde receptionist, was speaking to Philip, and several of the other waiting patients looked from her to Philip. He laid down his copy of *Fortune Magazine* and started into the doctor's suite.

"Sorry to have kept you this long," Miss Hanson added, as he passed her desk.

"It's all right," said Philip.

He had made the appointment earlier in the morning, on impulse, and he was not surprised that he had had to wait half an hour. Dr. Leo McGrath was much in demand. Though only in his early fifties, the doctor had already acquired an overflow practice, consisting largely of producers, directors, writers, and Beverly Hills matrons. This he had achieved, Philip had long ago decided, less for his competence as an internist than for an accident of manner. Dr. McGrath was tall, angular, and near-sighted. He wore a perpetually bemused expression, the absent air of one who has made too many promises. It gave him an appearance of profundity and assurance. He spoke distinctly, unhurriedly, and was devoted to quoting advanced medical research and speculation. He called patients by their first names, and he knew all that there was to know about hypertension.

Philip had been referred to Dr. McGrath several years before by a successful director, who spoke glowingly of McGrath as the reincarnation of Hippocrates. Philip was less sure of the doctor's superior medical wisdom. He doubted that, after a certain point, one doctor could know much more than another about salvaging the human anatomy. But there were some doctors who made you feel less frightened, less mortal, and Dr. McGrath was one of these. Philip always felt better when he left the doctor, and that was worth the ten or fifteen dollars.

He made his way through the corridor, past the small laboratory where the pretty nurse, Miss Radford, was giving a little girl a shot, and then past the closed doors of two examination rooms, and finally into the doctor's office. Dr. McGrath was not there. As usual, Philip examined the framed diplomas and certificates of healing on the walls, and then he studied the manila folder bearing his name on the doctor's desk. At last, he sat down to wait.

The decision to visit Dr. McGrath had come to him before breakfast. He had awakened with a tight band of pressure across his chest. This was not unfamiliar. A number of times before, he had seen the doctor about it and had learned it was tension, and afterward, the band had relaxed and gone away. This morning, when the old pressure recurred, Philip weighed the possibility of its being tension against a heart attack. Experience and instinct told him that it was the former, but he had wanted to believe that it was more serious. Somehow a heart attack would explain away to Peggy his poor performances of the last few nights. Too, it would resolve his immediate future and automatically release him from a situation with which he could not cope. At any rate, whatever it was, it was excuse enough to see Dr. McGrath. This was really the necessary thing, after all. The conviction had grown upon Philip, after the Kip Carster incident, that he must discuss his temporary impotence with someone authoritative. Perhaps, as he hoped, there was a minor physical deficiency. Perhaps, Dr. McGrath would prescribe some magical aphrodisiac.

Philip heard footsteps and turned. Dr. McGrath came through the door, lost in thought. He became aware of Philip. "Well, Philip—how've you been?"

"Okay—until this morning."

Dr. McGrath settled in his chair and opened Philip's folder. He looked up. "What's bothering you?"

Philip passed his hand over his chest.

Dr. McGrath nodded knowingly and inspected the notes in the folder. "Well, we've been through this before." He read off the symptoms. "Anything to add?"

"No, I think it's the same thing."

"Have you been taking the tranquilizers?"

"Off and on. They make me sleepy."

"It's probably tension. Are you working hard?"

"Yes."

Dr. McGrath rose. "Well, let's be on the safe side and make sure."

They went into the nearest examination room, and Philip stripped off his shirt. He hoisted himself on a table while Dr. McGrath listened to his chest and then to his back, and then took his blood pressure. After a while, they moved into the darkened cubicle where the doctor had his massive fluoroscope equipment. Philip stood rigid, the plate against his chest, while the doctor peered into it.

When they emerged, Dr. McGrath said, "So far, so good. You haven't had a cardiogram for six months. I think it might be a good idea."

"Whatever you say."

"I'll turn you over to Miss Radford, and then we'll see."

The session with the electrocardiograph machine was, as usual, boring, and, in the end, exhausting. Miss Radford chatted with him about movies that she had recently seen, as she attached the electrodes to his chest and legs. After this was done and the first cardiogram completed, she disappeared with it, then returned to take a second. Dr. McGrath usually insisted on a second taken after severe exercise. "Too many doctors," he liked to say, "only give you a cardiograph lying down. That's why it sometimes happens a patient will seem all right, then walk outside and drop dead. You've got to know the patient is also well under stress." To prepare for the second test, Philip had to climb hurriedly back and forth over prop steps, while Miss Radford timed him. When he finished, he was choking for breath. He lay down quickly on the table, and Miss Radford once more applied the electrodes. While the cardiograph scrawled its nervous history of his heart, he reclined on his back and reflected that this was a ridiculous, complicated prologue to a single question he wished to ask the doctor.

Presently, clothed again, he was back in Dr. McGrath's office listening to an interpretation of the cardiograms. His heart was fine. The chest pressure might be the result of a strained muscle, but more likely it was hypertension again. Dr. McGrath wrote out a prescription for a new tranquilizing drug.

Philip accepted the prescription, folded it, stuffed it into his shirt pocket. He made no move to leave.

"Just one more thing, doctor," he said. "Have you got a minute?"

"All the time in the world."

"Well, it's not got anything to do with all this. A friend of mine is having a problem. He wanted me to mention it— and if you think you can do anything, he'll come in."

Dr. McGrath waited, a bland, quizzical look on his face.

Philip posed the question in his head, revised it once, and then heard himself speak it. "He wants to know if anything can be done about sexual impotence?"

Not even a flicker of comment crossed Dr. McGrath's face. "It depends," he said. "Has he always been impotent?"

"No, no. He was fine. He's a married man with no problems. Then he took up with some girl on the side, and he hasn't been able to make love to her. He's tried several times. No luck. It's been going on for a week. He just doesn't know why."

Dr. McGrath shrugged. "It's hard for me to diagnose second-hand. There might be a dozen reasons for a temporary condition like that. It could be physiological. There might be a glandular disturbance or some genital disorder. Maybe he's been working too hard and is simply tired."

"As a matter of fact, he's been taking it easy. And he says he's well."

"Of course, he wouldn't know. He probably is well. Most conditions like that are emotional, anyway."

"What do you mean?"

Dr. McGrath unwrapped a package of Lifesavers, offered one to Philip, who shook his head, then took one for himself. "You said he's married and having an affair, didn't you? Well, the situation itself is tense. That could render him incapable. He may be inhibited in some way—or worried or angry. Maybe he's suffering from anxiety. Stekel thought this type of impotence comes from fear."

"He's not that kind of person."

Dr. McGrath looked up, peering keenly at Philip through his thick spectacles. "Are you sure?"

"Well, I—I don't know, actually." Under Dr. McGrath's close scrutiny, Philip felt himself redden. He tried to stare back. Dr. McGrath's squint was gone, and his face once again bland and uninquisitive. Its phlegmatic quality seemed to pass a special judgment, as if to say: all right, old man, you keep your subterfuge—it's childish, but we'll play the game—we'll observe the civilized conventions, if that makes it easier. For a moment, Philip was sure that Dr. McGrath knew the identity of the "friend," and in that moment Philip was tempted to reveal himself. But it was less degrading to appear foolish than unmanly.

Dr. McGrath was speaking. "Something's bothering your friend, Philip. Has he tried to have intercourse with his wife during this period?"

"Yes, he said he did."

"Well?"

"No problem. That was okay."

Dr. McGrath threw up his hands. "Then there's your answer, probably. He has success with his wife. He fails with another woman. That would indicate no physical problem. I'd say a hundred to one it's mental—psychic—"

Philip felt oppressed. "What do you suggest?"

Dr. McGrath sat up. "A psychiatrist—that's what I suggest."

After Philip left Dr. McGrath's office, he walked slowly through the medical building toward the parking lot in the rear. He still felt foolish. But what disturbed him more was Dr. McGrath's diagnosis. If a psychiatrist was the answer, then it was not an immediate answer. It solved nothing of his immediate problem. Moreover, the very act of visiting a psychiatrist repelled him. It was a concession, at last, that he was not a properly performing person. Always, in the back of his mind, he had felt a vague sense of inexplicable anxiety. He was anything but entirely happy. Yet, he performed. When he had to work, he worked without block. When he had to socialize, he was accepted and people thought him interesting. As to Helen, well, they were not at each other's throats. They did get along. If he conceded an inadequacy, an unhappiness, all this façade that had been constructed and that served would be torn down. He would be inviting another man to stick a huge eggbeater inside him and churn up and agitate all that was now in place and orderly. That it might one day, long after, fall into place better and make him happier, was not his concern now. Expediency was the issue. How would a psychiatrist help him with Peggy Degen this moment?

He had not resolved the question when he reached the building pharmacy near the rear exit. He glanced inside and saw a telephone booth near the counter. Whenever he was away from home any length of time, he usually telephoned home to learn if there were any messages. He had a secret and mystic belief, never fully articulated, even to himself, that someday there would be a message that would solve everything. He went inside the pharmacy and closed himself in the booth.

Though this was the day that Wanda, the buxom, smiling, colored day worker was in attendance and the day that Helen usually slept late, it was Helen who answered the phone.

"Where have you been all morning?" she wanted to know.

"Dr. McGrath's."

"What's the matter?" she asked quickly.

"The same old thing. I woke with a pain in my chest. So I drove over."

"What did he say?"

"I need love."

"Please, Phil—"

"Heart's perfect. It's just a tension thing. More pills. In fact, I feel better already."

"Well, thank God. I'm glad you called. Wanda took a couple of messages. Let me see if I can read them." There was a moment's silence. "Oh, yes. Nathaniel Horn. He wants to see you. He'll be in all morning. And then somebody named—it looks like Trubey. Does that make sense?"

Horace Trubey. What would he want? "Yes."

"Who's he?"

"The travel editor. You met him at that last party."

"I don't remember. Anyway, he left a number."

She gave it to him. He found a pencil and scribbled it on the wall. "By the way, Helen—"

"Yes?"

"What was the name of Danny's psychiatrist?"

"Dr. Robert Edling. Oh, I do hope you call him, Phil. He's expecting you to."

"I told you I would. What's his number?"

"One second—" She found it and gave it to him. He wrote it on the wall beneath Horace Trubey's number.

"When are you coming home?"

"I don't know. Probably after I see Nat."

"I'm taking Danny out after lunch. We're going swimming at Tina Barlow's."

"I'll probably see you before."

He hung up and considered the two telephone numbers he had written on the wall. At last, he dialed Dr. Robert Edling's number. He waited.

A young woman's voice answered. She repeated the telephone number.

"Dr. Edling, please."

"He's busy right now. Unless this is an emergency—?"

He wondered what, exactly, a psychiatrist would regard as an emergency. Now that he had gone ahead, he wanted to speak to Dr. Edling at once, see him at once. Was Peggy Degen an emergency?

"No," he said. "I just wanted to make an appointment, with him."

"If I can have your name and number, please, he'll call you."

He gave his name, carefully, and his home number. "I'm out now," he said. "Tell him he can get me after five."

"Very well. Thank you, Mr. Fleming."

He hung up, vaguely disappointed and suspended, and then dialed Horace Trubey.

A girl on the magazine switchboard answered, and his call was transferred to a secretary, and at last, he heard Horace Trubey's lively voice.

"This is Philip Fleming," he said.

"Well, hello, Phil. I'm sure glad you called. I was just leaving."

"How've you been?"

"Fine—fine. Just reading travel folders from Pakistan."

"I'd settle for that right now."

"Will you settle for a quick lunch?" asked Horace. "I have to be in Beverly Hills on some business. I have no lunch date, and I thought of you. You're not far—"

"I'm calling from Beverly Hills right now."

"Wonderful. But I won't be there for an hour—"

"That's all right. I have to see my agent first. Where shall we make it?"

"I have a cut-rate card for Panaro's."

"Then that's it."

"Is twelve o'clock all right? I know it's not smart—but I've got a one o'clock interview. I hope you don't mind gulping your food? I do want to see you."

"It's okay. Twelve o'clock."

As he headed toward his car, he wondered why Horace Trubey wanted to see him. Horace and Rachel were Peggy's friends. Was it something involving Peggy? But Horace would not know that he had the slightest interest in Peggy. Most likely, Horace just wanted to fill in an hour, and he had thought of Philip as the most accessible candidate. At any rate, Philip looked forward to the lunch. Since Peggy was the catalytic agent in their own relationship, they would speak of her. Today, more than ever, he wanted to discuss her with someone sympathetic. There was no definite reason for this, that he could yet understand. Yet it seemed urgent and important.

He drove slowly to South Beverly Drive, parked, placed a dime in the meter, and climbed the stairs to see Nathaniel Horn. Viola looked up from the typewriter, as he came in. He complimented her on her new hair-do and her dress, and she said that she thought that he had lost weight. He had not, but he did not want to disappoint her so he pretended that he was pleased. She buzzed Nathaniel Horn, then picked up the telephone and said that Mr. Fleming was here. She nodded to Philip.

He went inside. Nathaniel Horn lay back in his swivel chair. He was reading a red-bound studio script. He sat up, placed the script face down on his desk, and said cheerfully, "You look lousy."

"I wouldn't," said Philip, "if you'd make some money for me."

He stretched himself in the leather chair across from Horn, and they talked about the heavyweight title fight that was coming up, and about the latest scandal involving a well-known blonde actress who was having a rather public affair with a newly imported Italian actress.

After a while, Horn asked, "Any luck with Caroline Lamb?"

"None."

"Are you really trying, Phil?"

"What do you think? Hell, it's only been since Monday."

"Sure. But half your time is gone. Do you want to tell me what you've thought of?"

"I haven't thought of a damn thing."

"That doesn't sound like you." He studied Philip. "Is there something else on your mind—anything bothering you?"

You're damn right there is, Philip wanted to say. Instead, he said, "Oh, a few things have come up. Purely personal."

"Something that gets in the way of this?"

"I suppose."

"You don't want to talk about it?"

"No."

Horn was silent a moment. He stared at his Toledo letter opener, picked it up, drummed it slowly on the desk. He stopped drumming, looked up at Philip.

"Ritter called this morning."

"On the Western?"

"Today was the deadline."

Philip waited. Horn fiddled with the letter opener.

"I told him you were busy," Horn said.

"You *what*?"

"I said you couldn't take it."

Philip felt the old tightening band across his chest. "You mean you told him to shove it, without consulting me?"

"That's right."

He was furious with Horn. "Are you out of your mind?"

"Well—were you ready to take it?"

"Yes, you're damn right I was."

"Even with this Selby proposition still hanging fire?"

"Screw Selby. I'll never think of a third act to that Caroline Lamb thing. No one will. That's just a rainbow. Ritter is money in the bank. I've got a new house. I've got a family. What do you expect me to live on?"

Horn compressed his lips. Then, he spoke. "I was thinking of you, Phil. I don't want you to be buried alive."

"What's wrong working for Ritter? He's a name."

"He was." He paused. "He isn't now. And the picture is a dud—a low-budget dud, and we knew it. You'd get three months' salary. All right. But then what? Another low-budget, and another, and finally you're in television."

"So I'm in television. Is that a disgrace?"

"No, nobody'll cry for you. You'll still make five or six times as much as construction workers or clerks or accountants. That's not the point. You're you. You'll eat yourself up alive. You'll become a real psycho."

"At least, I won't be a hungry psycho."

"Phil, listen to me. I've seen them come and go. I've handled a hundred writer careers in this town. There's a point, for every man, when he reaches a crossroads. It happens, it just happens. I've seen it. I'm talking about this town. If you're an in-betweener, you don't stay that way. You gamble and maybe you go up and stay up. Or you play it safe, and you're a bum, a hack. Selby's your chance for a gamble. Show him this thing can be licked, and you're living abroad, subsidized, doing a prestige book, a prestige movie. Even if it doesn't come off, it's good for you. You've got to come out smelling good. But this Ritter thing—it's more of the same—only worse, because you're going downhill."

"Great—great. What if I don't make it with Selby?"

"You've got to make it."

"If I don't?"

"Well—" Horn threw up his hands. "You'll sweat a little, run behind in your bills, until I find you another low-budget picture or television. But you'll lick the Selby story if you put your mind to it."

"Don't give me that crap."

"I thought about it last night, Phil. I knew Ritter'd call this morning. I didn't want to consult you. I knew you'd play it safe, and that would be the worst thing. I wanted to make up your mind for you. I kept thinking, and then I thought of Prescott on Mexico. Ever read him?" He did not wait for Philip's answer. "I read him when I was in college. I'll never forget one part. Cortez was in Vera Cruz, I think, with his small band of armed hoodlums. He knew that they were badly outnumbered, that the odds were against them, that they'd never be any good as long as their ship was waiting in the harbor to take them home. So Cortez set fire to the ship. He burned it, Phil. There was no back door left, no escape, no way home to safety. The only safety was in going straight ahead and surviving by winning. And it worked. So, when Ritter called, I said no."

"Phil the Fiddler," said Philip.

"Who's that?"

"A book Horatio Alger wrote. Same sort of evangelistic tripe." Philip sat up. "Look, Nat, sometimes you burn your ship behind you and go straight ahead—and get the shit kicked out of you. They never tell that part of the story."

"It doesn't usually happen."

"The hell it doesn't. Maybe not in books. But for real. Don't give me any more of your sermons."

"I'm not sermonizing. What's my stake in this? I threw a sure ten per cent out the window. I did it because I'm thinking of you—not myself. I have your best interests at heart, and I don't care how it sounds."

"It sounds like it did before. Stupid. I can see Helen's face, when I tell her."

"She's not running as scared as you think."

"Oh, no?"

"Don't tell me she doesn't want the Selby deal?"

"It's romantic. Sure, she wants it. But when it doesn't work out and two months of bills pile up, she'll push the panic button. I'll hear 'Ritter' the rest of my life."

"Try to concentrate on Caroline Lamb, Phil. You've got until Friday."

"And if Friday comes, and I've got nothing?"

"Saturday morning then."

"And after that?"

"We'll worry about that later."

"Who in the hell invented agents, anyway?" he asked with dull anger.

Horn said nothing, and Philip went on. He went over the same ground again. Then they both did. It was like some pointless, wheeling domestic wrangle, and there was no right and no wrong. When Philip ran out of words, he sat tired and disgruntled. He glanced at his watch. It was five minutes after twelve. Suddenly, he remembered Horace Trubey. He rose quickly, and with little grace and no forgiveness, he left Nathaniel Horn and hurried down to his car.

He reached Panaro's in a few minutes, relinquished his car to the attendant in the lot, and hurried inside. The maître d' seemed to be expecting him, and led him through the crowded inner room where Horace, crew cut freshly shorn and a friendly smile on his face, was waiting with a drink. Philip greeted Horace, ordered a double scotch, and settled in the booth.

"I'm sorry to be late," Philip said. "I was just having a fight with my agent."

"You look upset," Horace said.

"Well, let's not spoil the meal. Did you order?"

Horace had ordered. Philip beckoned the waiter. He ordered a combination salad—his stomach was still an uncertain quantity—and then he proceeded to tell Horace a highly expurgated version of what had occurred with Nathaniel Horn.

When he had finished, he somehow expected sympathetic agreement. Instead, Horace shrugged and said, "It's none of my business, but I agree with your agent."

Philip blinked, genuinely surprised but not at all annoyed. He regarded his companion with new respect. "Why?" he managed to ask.

"First of all, he seems to be acting in your own best interests. There's obviously less in it for him this way. In the second place, if you don't do it now—then when?"

"I hate to gamble the security of the whole family on a longshot."

"I think you're rationalizing, Philip. I think you're just scared. You've been here too long. You're afraid to leave the mink-lined womb."

Philip considered this, and he knew at once that Horace was right. Horace was saying nothing that Nathaniel Horn had not said, but, somehow, it sounded more objective coming from Horace.

"I've known a lot of movie people," Horace continued. "They forget that you can live on less than forty or fifty thousand a year and be happy. I'm not being smug about it. I had a choice once. A partnership in a big public relations setup. I would have earned close to forty thousand a year. Rachel and I decided it cost too much. So now I make ten thousand a year, and I'm happy."

"Are you? I haven't heard many people say that."

"Completely happy. I'm doing exactly what I want. Plato said that's the key to a man's happiness."

"I suppose so," said Philip gloomily.

"When I heard you had a chance to go to Europe, I felt sure there'd be no question in your mind. I mean, just from the way you spoke the few times I met you."

"How did you know I had a chance to go to Europe?"

"I just heard it this morning. Rachel was talking to Peggy Degen on the phone. Peggy said she ran into you, and that you had a chance to go to London and Paris. I got quite excited about it. I always get excited when people I know are going abroad. I guess I want everyone to have a good time. It makes me feel better. So when I knew I had to be in Beverly—I though I'd call you."

"Well, now you know it's a longshot."

Philip explained the Selby deal, in detail, as the lunch was served and they ate.

When he had finished, Horace said, "Don't be so downbeat about it. Maybe you'll come up with something for Selby."

"Maybe. God knows. I want to."

"If it works—and this is one of the things I wanted to see you about—perhaps you can do something for our book."

"Like what?"

"Special features. You know—*In the Footsteps of Byron.* That sort of thing. In fact, you might stay over there a little longer and cover some assignments for us. We don't pay much. But it won't cost you much either—because you can free-load your way through the itinerary I give you."

"That's very kind of you, Horace."

"Nonsense. Self-interest, that's all. We find it difficult to get pieces from professional writers. My desk is cluttered with treatises from old ladies in Pasadena, who've been to Versailles and Capri—but professional writers who've talked to Picasso—far too few."

"How do you know I talked to Picasso?"

He thought a moment. "I guess Rachel heard that from Peggy, too."

"Well, we'll see. I'll let you know what happens about the trip." He finished his coffee, then inquired casually,

"Have you and Rachel known Peggy Degen very long?"

"Ages. Ever since she married Bernie Degen. I knew Bernie in New York. We were in the same publicity outfit for about a year—until he left to become a literary agent."

"She seems an awfully nice girl."

"She is. Bright, and no malice."

"And sensible," Philip added. "For a pretty girl, I mean."

"Sensible, yes," said Horace. "About the pretty part, I can't say. When you've known a person so long, you come to regard them with brotherly-sisterly affection. Anything else would seem improper."

"She's darn good-looking," Philip said firmly. He was anxious to prolong the conversation. "Do you think she'll ever marry again?"

"Of course. Peggy's one of those girls who needs someone. Not that she's not self-sufficient. She's managed very well since Bernie's death. But she needs someone. Certain girls have to be married."

"I guess that won't be a problem."

"I don't think so. There's a nice fellow who's been seeing her. I think he's serious. His name's Jake Cahill. In fact, he just got back into town this morning. We're going to see him next week."

Philip remembered the name, Jake Cahill. Traveling economist. The earnest one. And suddenly, he envied him. For he could be serious about Peggy. He could say anything, promise anything, and mean it. The Trubeys would be seeing Jake Cahill next week. That meant, probably, that Cahill would be with Peggy. They would be together. And where would he be? He felt excluded, the outsider, and he wanted desperately to belong, to be unencumbered and Peggy's man. The serious one.

He glanced at Horace, who was winding his watch. He speculated on Horace's reaction, if he were suddenly to blurt out the truth. What if he told Horace that he was in love with Peggy Degen? What if he told Horace that he had lain side by side with Peggy, nude, on her bed? What if he told Horace what had happened between them—or rather, what had not happened—and that this, more than anything, was disrupting his chance to go to Europe? How would Horace react? At once, it seemed remarkable to Philip how little, how very little, anyone knew of anyone else. No matter how long you were acquainted with another person, how intimately you talked, there was still so little that you actually knew or could guess. No man revealed everything, or even half of everything, to anyone. Every man had his private areas, like those blank unexplored sections on old maps. Or was there a special breed of men now—superseding witch doctor and priest—who knew everything? A breed of men like Dr. Robert Edling. He wondered.

He became aware that Horace Trubey was signing the check for the waiter. He tried to intercede and make it Dutch Treat, but Horace brushed him off with the usual something about an expense account. When the waiter had left, he thanked Horace. "I hate to stop this now," Horace said, pushing the table away from them. "But I've got that damn interview. I wish we could get together for a long evening, Philip."

"We will. I want you to see our new place. I'll have Helen call Rachel."

Horace was standing. Philip slid off the seat and joined him. "I hope you get to Europe," Horace said, as they started out. "Will you let me know?"

"I'll let you know."

Driving home, hardly aware of the traffic or the landmarks, he thought of Peggy Degen. With Jake Cahill in town, he realized that much of her time would now be occupied. He would have less and less justification for expecting her to arrange to see him whenever he called. Cahill had something specific to offer her. Cahill was a symbol of permanence and security; he represented a future. What could Philip offer that was half so attractive? He tried to sort out attractive arguments. There was only one. He loved her. He had said it, and tried to demonstrate it, over and over. But then, of course, Jake Cahill loved her too. Still, that was not the crucial point. The point was: whom did Peggy love? He did not know the extent of her relationship with Cahill, or how she felt about him. But Philip did know how she felt about one Philip Fleming. She had demonstrated that clearly, not in words but in performance. She had been willing to give herself to him at once. She was not the kind of woman who would give herself purely out of physical need. It was her response to his love. Her own love offer. That she felt for him this strongly was his own strength and advantage in my competition against Jake Cahill.

Suddenly, he found the complex speculation disagreeable. Why was it necessary to weigh what he could offer Peggy against what Cahill could offer? Why did he have to worry the point? Elsewhere—in France, say—this speculation would be ridiculous. There a married man would not measure his inability to wed a mistress, against a rival who could do so. There a married man would find it sufficient and plausible that his mistress loved him and had proved it. There a married man would not be surprised that a mistress was satisfied with illicit love alone. Hell, the gift of love was enough. How many times did any human being receive it in a lifetime? But he was not in France, and he was not a Frenchman. He was an American, and he was equipped with guilts and hesitations inherited from an elderly couple in the Midwest, who would have been astonished by all this. Not astonished—shocked.

As he turned for home, he remembered a fragment of conversation with Peggy the night before. Something that she had said had made their relationship finite, and he had objected. She had been extremely practical. How could he continue to maintain a double life by night? How could he continue seeing her without Helen knowing? He remembered that he had not faced it. The conquest of Peggy held enough problems, without permitting reality to enter into it. Yet, and this was really what disturbed him, was she trying to tell him that their relationship would end soon, not because of Helen, but because of Jake Cahill? She must have known that Cahill was returning to the city today. It must have been uppermost in her mind. Still, that could not have been important either. For an hour later, she had submitted herself to him on the floor of the adjacent motel.

Philip had reached the garage at the rear of his new house. He drove into it, turned the ignition, and started up the narrow side walk to the service porch. Wanda was leaning against the drier, smoking. He greeted her absently, and went into the kitchen. No one was there. Helen and Danny must be in one of the bedrooms. He moved out of the kitchen, through the entry hall. And at once, he was aware that there was someone in the living room.

He halted and stared in bewilderment and disbelief. Peggy Degen was seated on the sofa, a picture book in her lap, reading to her son Steve.

She did not see him at first, and he stood stock-still, gazing at her, his mind spinning. Peggy Degen in his house. It was incredible. Why was she here? Helen had sent for her. That was the first explanation that entered his mind. Helen had become suspicious, and had had him followed, or somehow heard that he had been seeing her, and Helen had sent for her. This was a showdown. But that was absurd. That was movies. Helen would not send for her, and if she did, Peggy would not come. Besides, the whole atmosphere of Peggy's presence was too relaxed. She was on the sofa, reading a picture book to her son.

He started into the living room. "Peggy."

She looked up, not at all surprised. "Hello, Phil. Helen didn't think you'd get home before we left."

He crossed to the chair next to the sofa, his eyes on her all the time, and sat down. She saw his face. "Surprised?"

"You're damn right," he said.

They both ignored Steve, who blinked, looking from one to the other with no comprehension, but with a child's reaction to the urgency in their modulated voices.

"What are you doing here?" he went on.

"We're going to go swimming," she said cryptically.

"You know what I mean."

"When I had the party last Saturday, Helen mentioned something about taking your boy swimming a couple of times a week. I said I did that with Steve. She invited me to call her whenever I felt like a swim. So I did."

"But why?"

"I just wanted to."

He was not satisfied. "Has it got to do with us?"

"Maybe. I don't know." She glanced at Steve. "Do you remember Mr. Fleming, Steve? He sold us our house."

Steve looked blankly at Philip and said nothing.

"Have you met Danny?" Philip asked the boy.

He nodded. Peggy said, "Oh, yes. I think they'll get along. You have a very attractive son."

"Thank you."

He tried to understand the reason behind Peggy's visit. It was as if now, suddenly, she felt it necessary to know more about him. Perhaps, it was this same need that had motivated his agreement to see Horace Trubey for lunch and had driven him to question Horace about Peggy. Both he and Peggy had arrived at some decisive moment in their relationship. Both he and Peggy wished to be more fully informed, before proceeding further. That was the answer, he decided. But proceeding further to what, he wondered.

"You have a lovely home," she was saying.

"Palatial is the word."

"The back yard seems like an extra room." Banality came curiously from her. She was awkward, and he knew it. "Is that your office out there?" she asked.

"Yes."

She was wearing a hip-length, starched piqué beach coat, and it fell open to reveal the pink, candy-striped two-piece swimming suit beneath. The suit covered very little. The strip of cloth across her breasts was adequate, but the strip below her waist, laced at the sides, was not. Her whole appearance was provocative, and he felt desire.

She saw that he was studying her, and she blushed. He said quickly, "Where are you going swimming?"

"I don't know. Your wife said something about some friend having a pool."

He heard footsteps in the hall and rose quickly. Helen, wearing the aquamarine swimming suit that made the flesh bulge at her thighs, hurried in, trailed by Danny.

"Phil—when did you get back?" She went to him and kissed him. He wished that she had not. He withdrew from her and rumpled Danny's hair.

"How are you, Danny boy?"

"I was sorting my bubble gum cards. Do I have to go swimming?"

"Of course. You want to be an Olympic star one day, don't you? Look at Steve. He doesn't mind swimming." He turned to Helen, who was apologizing to Peggy for the delay. "Where you going?" he asked.

"The Barlows," said Helen. "We should have been there ten minutes ago."

He did not want Peggy alone with Helen, unsupervised, all the way to Bel-Air. Peggy might ask questions about him. And Helen might be derogatory about him in her usual manner. There was only one solution.

"Look, why don't I drive you both to the Barlows?" he asked.

"It's not necessary," Helen said.

"I have to go to the Beverly Hills library. I'll drop you off—and pick you up whenever you say."

"Well, if you're really going into town."

"I think I'd better."

"Do they have a good Byron collection?" Peggy asked Philip.

"A few items I don't have," Philip said.

Helen looked at Peggy with surprise. "How did you know he was researching Byron?"

Philip's heart stood still. Peggy answered easily, "Why, Philip was just sitting here telling me about the project."

Helen nodded and began to herd Danny toward the kitchen. "Let's go."

Peggy's eyes met Philip's in brief apology as she passed him. He watched her long, bare legs beneath the beachcoat, as she led Steve into the kitchen, and he wanted to be alone with her. Never before had he felt so resentful of Helen.

At the garage, the others waited while he backed the car out. Danny and Steve joined him in the front seat. Peggy and Helen sat in back. They drove to Bel-Air.

During the ride, the talk in the back seat, for the most, was neutral. Helen did most of the talking. They discussed the children, schooling, Ridgewood Lane, recipes, and recreation. On the subject of recreation, swimming was mentioned. Helen described the Barlow pool, and then she briefed Peggy on Tina Barlow.

"That's why Philip is driving us over there," he heard Helen say.

"Because of Mrs. Barlow?" That was Peggy's voice.

"She's got a letch on Philip. She makes no bones about it. She compliments him, and he dissolves."

He gritted his teeth. With the proper implements at hand, he would have enjoyed garroting Helen. He peered into the rear-view mirror. Peggy was staring at the back of his head with a small, set smile.

"Is that true, Philip?" Peggy was asking. "Do you feel weak in the knees when she compliments you?"

"Why not?" said Philip, trying to mask the anger in his voice. "My wife never does. I'm love-starved."

"She's got a crush on him," said Helen. "She acts like a five-year-old when he's around."

"Oh, cut that rot," said Philip.

"You'll see," Helen said to Peggy.

Helen went on to discuss Sam Barlow's dental chain. Peggy listened with the same set smile. Philip drove the rest of the way, silent and sulking.

At the Barlows, he helped Peggy and Helen out. He thought of leaving at once, but he knew that Peggy would note that. He followed the others to the door. Helen pressed the doorbell. They waited. The door opened, revealing Tina in a polka dot halter and white shorts. She inclined her head, indicated the room behind, and said cheerfully, "Welcome to Muscles Beach."

Helen hastily introduced Peggy, and Tina acknowledged it heartily, and stepped aside to let them in. Tina reserved the full glow of her smile for Philip. The long dimple made an attractive crevice in her right cheek.

"You didn't tell me today was my birthday," she said to Helen, taking Philip's hand.

"What?" said Helen from the center of the living room, confused.

Tina circled an arm around Philip's waist. "You didn't have to bring gifts. The pool's for free."

Helen glanced at Peggy, but she was looking at Philip mockingly. He felt sheepish and stiff.

"What's the occasion?" Tina asked Philip.

"Chauffeur's day off," said Philip. "So I drove them."

Tina pouted. "Not me?"

Philip suffered. "Well, you, of course. The other was a subterfuge. My wife's canny, you know."

"Oh, I know," said Tina. She turned to Helen and Peggy. "The pool's all yours. The kids are already in it. I'll go up and change. Just be a minute."

Philip edged toward the door. "Well, I'd better be getting along. When do you want to be picked up, Helen?"

"Four o'clock," said Helen.

Tina looked pleadingly at Philip. "Can't you stay a little while? I want you to see my new suit."

"Next time."

"Remember," said Tina, and she hurried off.

Helen went out to the rear, shepherding Danny and Steve before her. Peggy was about to follow, when Philip caught up with her. He took her arm.

"Peggy—"

She waited. "I've got to see you," he whispered.

"Think you can clear it with Tina?"

"Stop it. What about—"

"Not now," she said firmly. "Not here."

She hurried out after Helen. Philip remained standing, knowing that he must leave, but reluctant to leave. He walked slowly into the bar, and stood at the screen door, gazing out at the pool. The Barlow children were cavorting in the deep end. Helen had gone down the steps into the shallow end, and lifted Steve into the water, and was trying to urge Danny to come in. Peggy was seated on the lounge, taking off her red-gold sandals. Now she rose and removed her beach coat. The two-piece suit was skintight. In his mind, he fondled the excitement of the image. He watched Peggy stride nakedly to the diving board. It struck him with amusement at how chastely concerned women were with their protective garments—full dresses and petticoats and undergarments—and how anxious they were to cover their knees when they crossed their legs. Yet, how simply and naturally, once joined to the cult of sun and water, they exposed themselves in swim suits. Peggy had reached the edge of the diving board. She balanced a moment, the perfect profile of poise and grace, and then she left the board, arcing high and then straightening, slicing into the water clean as an arrow. Philip, a clumsy swimmer at best, was impressed as she shot to the surface, and, arms glistening, stroked to the side of the pool. He felt, again, a surge of pride that she had submitted to him. He turned and walked out to the car.

It took him twenty-five minutes to reach the library. Once in the monastic reading room, his half-dozen reference biographies piled before him, he tried to wrench his mind around to Caroline Lamb. The process was difficult. Peggy's white, supple body intruded. The gnawing shame of his failure, which he had tried to repress through the day, loomed with her body to jeer at him. He had failed with Peggy, yet he had not failed with Helen. Dr. McGrath had regarded that as significant, as indicating that his impotence was psychic. Did this imply that he would fail with any woman other than his wife? Or was it just Peggy, just Peggy herself? Suddenly, it seemed important to know the truth. But how would he ever know? In his decade of marriage, he had made no advance toward another woman, except this one fiasco with Peggy. He reviewed some of the women—a new studio secretary, someone's date at a dinner party, a woman at the next table in a bar—that he had once regarded as possibilities. Then sleek red-hair and a dimple and overflowing breasts filled his mind. Tina. He had had sex fantasies often, pre-Peggy, about Tina Barlow. But they were wispy indulgences, and not serious. Now, he thought of her seriously. At once, abruptly, he pushed it from his mind. His problem was Peggy. No other woman would solve Peggy. Or would she? Would an affair, a single infidelity, with another woman break this thing that made him helpless with the one person he desired more than any other? Again, he pushed it from his mind. He picked up one of the books that lay before him. With grim determination, he began to read.

It took him almost an hour to reach a point where he would concentrate fully on the life and miseries of Caroline Lamb. When he had tired of scanning the biographies, he sat back and tried to think how he might end the story for Selby. Two years before her death, Caroline Lamb had been separated from William Lamb. Yet, on her deathbed, Caroline had whispered, "Send for William. He is the only person who has never failed me." And William, faithful as ever, had come to her. Was this ill-treated husband the key to Caroline's story? Could he have taken Caroline on a last desperate honeymoon to Italy? And there a meeting with Byron, which would resolve Caroline's story and send her back happily to her husband? It had not happened, of course, and this would be the grossest distortion of history, yet this was for fiction and this was a way. But if such a liberty might be taken, then why not similarly use Teresa Guiccioli, the last of Byron's mistresses? After Byron's death, she had visited England to meet Byron's friends and his sister, and to visit his haunts. What, then, if Caroline had still been alive, and the Guiccioli had met her, and somehow laid the ghost of Byron that was shattering Caroline's last years along with her marriage? This was another distortion, and it repelled Philip.

But he was thinking now, and he sat at the library table and let his mind wander to Brocket Hall. Here, Caroline, surrounded by drink and drugs and pages, had entertained an attractive young neighbor, Edward Bulwer, who would later become renowned as the author of *The Last Days of Pompeii*. With him, she had tried to recreate the long dead Byron affair, much to her husband's distress, and she had failed. Would young Bulwer, appearing in the last third of the novel as the reincarnation of Byron, give the tragic tale the unity and sustained interest that it needed? Caroline had given Bulwer the ring that Byron had once worn. Was this sufficient? Philip held to the thought, examining it, projecting it, twisting and turning it every possible way. Should he try it on Nathaniel Horn? At once, he knew that he would not. It was simply not good enough. None of the ideas were. Caroline's story still ended with Byron's departure for Italy. Nothing that he had yet conceived kept it alive. There must be something better, some fact, some invention, that would integrate heroine, husband, and lover in the climax. But what?

For a moment, he emerged from the strange, timeless recess of creativity and was aware of the table, and the books, and the reading room itself. He looked down at his watch. It was a quarter to four. He tried to remember when it was that he was supposed to pick up Helen and Peggy, and then he remembered that it was four. He dragged himself back to the present, and hurried out of the library.

He drove swiftly to Bel-Air, all the while considering the various unlikely subjects that Helen, Peggy, and Tina might have discussed. He wondered if Peggy and Tina had discussed him, and if Helen, by chance overhearing this, had disparaged him.

When he reached the Barlow house and rang the doorbell, Helen and Peggy, and the boys, were already waiting in the entry hall. Helen was in her damp swim suit, Peggy was wearing the provocative beach coat, and Tina came hurrying in from the kitchen, where she had been writing down the address of a bakery that Helen had requested. Tina was wearing a white blouse and blue skirt and she was barefooted, and Philip realized that this was the first time he had seen her wearing more than a swimming suit or shorts in almost a year. He had to admit that she looked good. But in quite a different way from Peggy. His eyes met Peggy's. She was exquisite.

"We thought you'd never get here," Helen was saying to Philip.

"I got lost in research."

"Any luck?" Helen asked.

"Well, I had a few ideas." He turned to Peggy. "All set?"

Helen and Peggy, leading the boys, went past him toward the car. He turned to say good-by to Tina, but she was silently summoning him with her finger. He went into the living room.

"I thought you were going to come by for a swim," she said in an undertone.

"I didn't think you meant it."

"What do you want—an engraved invitation?"

"I'd love to drop by."

"Then, why don't you?"

"All right. Name it."

She pretended to think. She looked at him. "What about tomorrow?"

"Tomorrow's perfect."

"Two-thirty?"

He nodded. "You know," he said, "my intentions are strictly dishonorable."

Tina smiled. The dimple cut her cheek. "I hope so," she said.

He took her hand. "See you," he said. She closed her eyes and offered her lips. He kissed her briefly, too briefly to receive any sensation from it, then released her hand and hurried out.

Helen in the front seat at the open window, was watching him narrowly as he made his way around the car and slid behind the wheel. Peggy was in the rear with Steve and Danny. She had given them a package of gum, and they were busy sharing it. He drove down the hill toward Sunset Boulevard.

"What did Tina want with you?" Helen asked.

"She and Sam have been hoping to get together with us for dinner. Go out somewhere. We were trying to settle a date. We finally agreed that she would phone you and work it out."

"She had all afternoon to ask me."

"That's Tina," he said.

They rolled through the growing traffic toward home. The further west they drove, the cooler it became. It felt refreshing and Philip inhaled the pungent, clean smell of the grass and eucalyptus trees that crowded the twisting highway on either side.

Once, half turning his head, he inquired, "How was it this afternoon?" The question was meant for Peggy, but Helen answered.

"Relaxing, I suppose. Though I must admit, I sometimes find Tina a strain."

"In what way?" he wanted to know.

"If you asked her for an opinion of Eisenhower, she'd probably think you were talking about a new gadget for your crankcase. She's just interested in gossip." Helen moved on the seat. "What did you think, Peggy?"

"I didn't really have a chance to talk to her," said Peggy. "She is attractive."

"If you like that type," said Helen, glancing at Philip. "I just think there's too much of her, in every way."

"What does that mean?" Philip asked.

"I don't know. I can't explain," said Helen. She looked at Philip. "Do you think she chases with other men?"

"Of course not," said Philip indignantly.

"Well, I think so," said Helen.

Philip looked up at his rear-view mirror. Peggy had opened her beach coat and her legs were crossed. "She sounded quite devoted to her husband," she said.

"Talk is cheap," Helen said. "Have you ever seen him? He looks like a hog that's going to burst any minute."

"I don't think looks are important," Peggy persisted. "He may be the nicest person on earth."

"He is," said Philip firmly, in full alliance with Peggy.

Helen backtracked slightly. "I'm not arguing about that. I'm just saying that she's the kind who might look else-where."

Philip was thoroughly irritated. "If you don't like her," he said to Helen, "why do you see her?"

Helen did her familiar about-face. "Can't I be bitchy once in a while?" she asked. "It's good for you. It opens up the pores. Sure, I like her. All I resent is the way she talks about you. She talks about you more than she does about Sam. Did you notice, Peggy?"

Peggy nodded. "I heard her say Philip was the most interesting man she's ever met. I quite agree with her."

Helen wrinkled her nose at Peggy. "You should live with him," she said.

When they reached the house, Philip parked in the circular driveway, about ten yards behind Peggy's convertible. They all got out of the car to gather for a moment before the house.

Peggy extended her hand to Helen. "It was an enjoyable afternoon. Thank you very much."

Helen took her hand. "Whenever you'd like to do it again, call me. Only next time, we'll go to the beach."

"Fine," said Peggy. She took Steve's arm and turned to Philip. "Thanks for the transportation."

They started for her convertible. Philip quickly followed them, hoping Helen would go into the house, hoping for a moment with Peggy, but Helen came right along. Irked with Helen, Philip opened the front door. He hoisted Steve inside and then helped Peggy in behind the wheel. He tried to catch her eye. She busied herself with her keys and the hand brake.

She started the motor, then looked up. "Well—good-by."

Philip tried to tell her with his eyes and face that he wanted to see her tonight. She failed to read his plea, or, more likely refused to interpret it.

"See you soon," said Helen.

"Good-by," said Philip.

Peggy drove out of the driveway and was soon out of sight. Philip watched as long as he could, and then, utterly frustrated, he followed Helen and Danny into the house. Their return brought Wanda in from the kitchen.

"Mistah Fleming," she said. "There was just now a call for you. I got it wrote down."

Philip went into the kitchen. On the pad next to the telephone was the name Edling and a telephone number. Philip had almost forgotten. Quickly, he dialed the number. It was the message service again. Philip told the girl that Dr. Robert Edling had just called him and that he was returning the call. The girl asked him to wait a moment.

He waited impatiently. There was loud clicking on the other end of the line, and a man's voice, very distant, came on.

"Hello. Dr. Edling here."

"This is Philip Fleming. I phoned you this morning."

"Oh, yes, of course. I'm glad you called. I'd been hoping to hear from you." The voice was surprisingly soft. You could take it in your hand and squeeze it, and it would come out on either side.

"My wife said you wanted to see me about Danny. I'm free tomorrow."

"Tomorrow—tomorrow—" said Dr. Edling. "One moment, let me see—"

Philip waited. Dr. Edling's voice came on again. "How would eleven-thirty in the morning be?"

"Sounds okay by me."

"Tomorrow morning, then. I'll look forward to meeting you, Mr. Fleming."

After he had hung up, Philip remained standing a moment, staring past Wanda, who was cooking. He tried to speculate on how he would switch the conversation with Edling from Danny to Peggy Degen—no mean transition—and then he decided that he would have to play it by ear.

He wandered into the living room. It was empty. He continued up the hall, looked briefly into the study where Danny was changing the television channels, then went into their bedroom. He heard Helen puttering in the bathroom. He walked to the door.

"Helen?" he said through the door.

She opened it slightly. "Yes?"

"I just spoke to your Dr. Edling. I'm going to see him tomorrow."

"I'm glad. You won't be sorry."

"No. I guess not."

He dug pipe and pouch out of his pocket and began to fill the pipe. "How'd you like her?" he asked casually.

"Who?"

"The Degen girl." This pleased him. The off-hand, casual note.

"Very pleasant," she said. "I'd like to see her again. She's pretty, don't you think?"

"I hadn't noticed," he said.

"I think the man that marries her will be darn lucky."

Yes, he said to himself, yes, indeed. He lit his pipe and walked slowly to the window overlooking the back yard, and he wondered how it would be if it were Peggy Fleming in the bathroom, and he waiting here, and the back yard, their yard.

It was Wednesday night and this was a good television night. The three of them sat in the study, their attention focused on the screen. The rerun of a once successful horror film was unfolding, with its crowded cast of ghouls, monsters, insane doctors, and damsels in distress. Danny hunched in the leather chair, mesmerized. Helen sewed placidly, as she half-watched the screen. Philip was bored and restless.

On the screen, the coffin had finally been opened, and the corpse inside it was revealed to be shrunken to the size of a doll, and now the commercial came on. Philip shifted in his seat. The station break came on. It was eight-thirty. Another commercial began.

Philip twisted toward Helen. "I think I'll take a drive out to the ocean," he said.

Helen looked up at him with a frown.

"I think I'm on to something with Caroline Lamb," he said quickly. "I'd like to figure it out by myself. Maybe the fresh air'll help."

"Must you go out every night?"

"Just a drive. I'll be back before the picture is over."

"A family should be together at least once a week," Helen said.

"We were together all afternoon."

"Well, suit yourself."

He got to his feet. "I won't be long."

He found his jacket in the dining room and went out to the car. He backed it quickly into the street, and then pointed it east toward Ridgewood Lane. Passing the telephone booth at the filling station, he wondered if he should stop and telephone her first. He decided against that. He was uncertain of her mood, since the motel fiasco, and the afternoon had told him nothing. He did not want to be denied. He had no plan or defined purpose. He wanted to consummate their affair—this desire was a part of him now as much as the limbs of his body—but he was not sure that he wished to attempt it this night. Somehow, tomorrow held a special magic promise, and he wanted to wait until tomorrow. He would see Dr. Edling. This might provide the formula. And he had not forgotten Tina Barlow. He would see her, too. This might give him the needed confidence.

He drove on through the cool night. What did he want of Peggy, anyway? He still could not define it. Yet, in some curious way, he sensed that they were being drawn closer together and toward a decision that each of them must make. Ignoring the incident at the motel the night before, the earlier part of the evening had been wonderful fun. She had been the perfect companion. He could not recall when he had enjoyed a woman's company more. He remembered that while they had been drinking, he had regarded her not as someone who was passing briefly through his life, but as someone who would remain there permanently. It was difficult for him to conceive of a single day in the future, without her. It was this that had impelled him to question Horace Trubey about her. In fact, if it were possible, he would have tried to question every person who knew her. He could not know enough about Peggy. He wanted to know a lifetime of her, within a short week. If only it were she who was going to Europe with him on the Selby deal, he felt certain that he would have resolved the Caroline Lamb story, at once.

At the same time, and this aspect of it he weighed carefully, she seemed to be displaying a special and more serious interest in him. It was as if the transitory element of their relationship had finally been cast aside. At last night's meeting, she had been interested in him beyond mere physical attraction. She had wanted to know about his work and his life before they had met. And the circumstances of her visit this afternoon. Surely, she could have no real interest in Helen or in spending an afternoon swimming with Helen. No, there was something else and more. It was as if she were investigating him to be sure, to know, to be positive that she could invest all of her self in him.

It was this that he wished to explore tonight. He would sit with her, across from her, and drink a little and smoke his pipe and talk it out. He would talk, and then she would talk. They would find the common root, the one depth where both were joined, and then joined, they would decide what could be done and what must be done. If, after that, he would go to her, take her in his arms, with their mutual awareness of a new understanding, he was sure that she would submit, and that he might successfully make love to her at last.

Involuntarily, half-concentrating on the road, he frowned at his last thought. Was his entire plan to have a serious talk with her only another self-deceit, a subterfuge to get at the essential thing, a means to get to her body once more? Why had the last intruded itself upon him? Why was it always and only the consummation that mattered, and little else? He was determined that his evening's destination would not be the love act. He was going to see Peggy to talk to her. This would be the kind of conversation they had not yet had. It would determine what lay ahead. There was time enough for the other.

Almost unaware of the manual move, he had made the turn north off Sunset, and was climbing up Ridgewood Lane. As he slowed before the house, he saw the living room lamps were on. He parked. Peggy's convertible was in the garage, and there were no other cars around. So far, so good. She was alone.

He went to the door and pressed the doorbell. He listened for her footsteps, and heard them. They seemed oddly heavy. The door swung open, and an overweight fifteen-year-old in abominable blue jeans stood staring at him. He recognized her, just as she remembered him.

"Oh—hello," she said.

She was the sitter from down the hill. He had driven her home late last night.

"How are you?" he said. "Is Mrs. Degen in?"

"She went out to dinner at six-thirty. I'm sitting with Steve."

"I see. Did she—did she go out with some man?"

"He picked her up. I was introduced." She knitted her brow. "I think—Mr. Caham or Caman—"

"Cahill?"

"That's him!"

"Did she say when she'd be back?"

"Early was all she said. Would you like the number of the restaurant where they went? She always leaves a number in case Steve gets sick or something."

"No," said Philip.

"Who should I say was here?"

"Nobody—nobody," he said quickly. "I just happened to be passing by. It's nothing important."

"Okay."

He turned away, and she closed the door. He returned to the car, thinking hard. If he had any sense, he would head for home. But he hated the idea of enduring another night of unfinished business, of incompleteness. He eased into the car and started it. The sitter had said that she would be home early. It might be worth waiting a little while. If it became too late, he could always tell Helen that he had had a flat tire at the beach and that the automobile club had been a long time in coming. He shifted the gear into reverse and backed up along the curb, scraping it several times, until he was four houses away and safe. He held his wrist to the dashboard. It was nine-fifteen. She had gone to an early dinner. She would certainly be back soon. He turned on the car radio, spun the dial until he had the baseball game, and then lit his pipe and listened without hearing a word.

Once, at ten minutes to ten, he heard an automobile approach. He lowered himself in the seat hastily and waited. The car coughed past and away. He straightened, turned the game on a little louder, and waited. He found that he was looking at his watch every five minutes. It made the time move at a miserably slow pace. When it was ten-fifteen, he decided that he would make ten-thirty his absolute deadline. This was foolish. He was acting like some crazy, love-struck high school boy. The sports announcer's voice and the singing beer commercials grated on his nerves. He turned the radio off. He put a match to his pipe and smoked and waited.

Suddenly, there was the sound of another automobile. He peered into the rear-view mirror. The car was entering Ridgewood Lane. He slid low in the seat and was very still. Slowly, the car came past, and then the engine was cut. He did not dare to rise and look. He remained huddled below the windshield. He heard a car door slam, up ahead, and then indistinct voices. He lifted himself slowly in the seat. Even at this distance, and in the darkness, he was sure that he recognized Peggy. There was a man with her, no taller than she, and Philip could only make out that he appeared stout. He had her by the arm and led her up the walk. After a moment, they disappeared into the house.

Philip straightened up fully behind the wheel. He was unaccountably annoyed. He felt cheated. He had expected that Jake Cahill would bring her to the door, kiss her on the cheek, and depart. She had had a long day. She must be dog-tired. What was he doing, going inside? Perhaps, she had been polite and asked him in for a moment. Maybe for a drink. One for the road. Then he would depart, and Peggy would be alone. Philip decided to wait another fifteen minutes.

The minutes crawled by on tortoise legs. When fifteen had gone, and then twenty-five, Philip was beside himself. He could stand no more. He must know if Cahill was readying to leave or if he was digging in for a long session.

He left the car, unsure of precisely where he was going or what he was going to do. He went up the street to Cahill's club coupé—the latest model, he observed sourly—and then he stared at the living room window. He remembered that the sitter had not left. She has probably in the kitchen, waiting for Cahill to drive her home. How long would he keep that poor young girl waiting?

He circled Cahill's coupé to the lawn. The venetian blinds were not fully drawn, yet they screened the activity in the living room. If he were closer, he might know if Cahill was preparing to leave or not. He stepped over the hedge, and advanced across the grass until he was alongside the house. He edged toward the window, then crouched and peered between the blinds.

Cahill was standing at the hi-fi, his back to the window.

He seemed to be placing a stack of records on the turntable. Peggy was seated cross-legged on the floor, beside the coffee table. She was peeling through an album. There were drinks on the coffee table. Without looking up, she reached for a glass and sipped the drink, as she continued to leaf through the album. The baby sitter was nowhere in sight. Cahill had the stack in place now and started the turntable. From his uncomfortable position, Philip judged that it would take an hour or two to play those records. Cahill was far from ready to go home. Squatting beside the window, Philip tried to decide what to do. Should he go boldly to the door and knock and join them? Should he call it quits and go home? He straightened, trying to decide—when suddenly he heard the purr of the automobile motor, and the shocking bright spotlight hit him in the face.

Instinctively, he threw his arm up across his eyes. The spotlight moved down to his chest. He squinted over it and saw that it was aimed from a black and white sedan, idling in the middle of the street. At first, he thought it was a taxi, and then the light blinked out, and the sedan door opened, and he knew that it was a squad car.

A tall, uniformed policeman, hand on his leather holster, stood beside the car. He signaled with his hand. "Come here."

Philip felt the sudden perspiration on his brow and the dryness of his lips as he made his way across the lawn on leaden legs. The policeman met him at the curb, and gestured him to the car. The driver inside, a husky, red-faced officer, peered out at him.

The lanky young policeman beside him spoke curtly. "Turn around."

Philip turned around, his back to the policeman, who rapidly frisked him, patting his jacket at the chest, the pockets, his trousers at the side and behind. "Okay," the policeman said. Philip turned to face him.

"What do you think you're doing there, buddy?" he asked. "Ever hear the law about Peeping Toms?"

The whole thing had happened so fast, that Philip had not had time to gather his wits. Now, at once, his mind was electric, alert to the danger. If he were arrested, right here, for peeking or prowling, it would expose him to Helen. There would be no adequate explanation. Immediately, he realized that it would not get to that. He would tell his story and be taken into the house and brought before Peggy. She would clear him. But the humiliation would destroy him. And how would Peggy ever explain him to Cahill? He looked up at the tanned young policeman. To hell with Cahill. His own future was at stake.

"It was nothing at all," he heard himself say. "My—my girl lives there. She was out, and I was waiting for her to come home. I told the sitter I'd be out here waiting. Another fellow brought her home and I kept waiting for him to leave. I wanted to see her alone."

"So what were you doing under the window?"

"I wanted to see if he was getting ready to leave—or if I should give up and go."

"Lemme see your wallet."

He fumbled for his wallet and handed it to the policeman. He waited, guilty and nervous, as the policeman flashed a light on it and studied his driver's license and several other cards. The policeman looked up. "Says here you're married."

He thought his heart would beat his chest open. "Yes."

"So what are you doing with a girl?"

"I sold this house to her. We're friends."

The policeman looked at the driver and shook his head. "Geez, these crummy Romeos."

Philip felt himself trembling. He wanted to kill the man. He bit his lip and said nothing.

The husky driver leaned across the seat. "You," he said to Philip. "Maybe you were waiting out here to lay into the other guy."

"I don't even know him," said Philip. "Anyway, he's bigger than I am. I tell you, I was just waiting to see her alone. I wanted to see if I should stay or go."

The tall policeman looked in at the driver. The driver nodded almost imperceptibly. The tall policeman said to Philip, "Where's your car?"

Philip pointed behind him.

The tall policeman handed him his wallet. "Beat it," he said.

Philip bobbed his head gratefully and hastened to his car. He got inside and started it. The policeman watched him, then stepped into the squad car and slammed the door. The squad car roared away.

Philip sat limply behind the wheel. He had hardly enough strength to turn it. At last, he did so. He made his turn, backed up, and headed down toward town. Not until he reached Sunset Boulevard, did the trembling cease.

What a person will go through, he thought. Why?

But he knew why. And he knew that tomorrow he would be back.

6

Thursday Night

HE SAT STIFFLY in the chair watching Dr. Edling speak
into the telephone. He did not hear the precise words that
Dr. Edling spoke, because he was outwardly inattentive and
entirely self-absorbed. The telephone had rung jarringly a few
minutes before, and Dr. Edling had been extremely apologetic. Even as he held the telephone in his hand, he had
explained that his message service was only permitted to interrupt him with an emergency. Philip had accepted this
explanation with a generous nod, for he actually welcomed
the break in their conversation. He wanted a moment to
regroup his thoughts and find a way to transfer the discussion from Danny to Peggy Degen.

Dr. Edling was continuing on the telephone. Philip tuned
him in momentarily. Apparently the subject being discussed
was a young high school girl who had gone amok and
destroyed her room. The call was from her mother. Philip
deduced that the girl was a new patient. Dr. Edling was
trying to reassure the mother. Philip listened a moment
longer and then tuned it out. Peggy, he thought. How in
the hell was he going to get to Peggy Degen?

He blinked down at his wrist watch. Almost half an
hour had passed since he had first entered the office and

begun to discuss his son. He calculated. A psychiatric session was supposed to last fifty minutes and not an hour. He guessed that the extra ten minutes was allowed to give the analyst time to go to the bathroom or adjust his antenna to the incoming patient. Well, thirty of the fifty minutes were gone, and that left twenty to the subject of impotency. He realized that he would have to get right to it. But how?

He stared at Dr. Robert Edling. The limitations of time suggested the direct approach. Doctor, Danny aside for a moment, I've got a problem. That would do it and twenty minutes might suffice. Did he dare? For one thing, Dr. Edling was Helen's discovery. For another, Dr. Edling might be secretly amused. How could he confide so humiliating a secret to a total stranger? Yet it appeared the only logical thing to do.

Originally, all through the morning, while he waited for the appointed hour of eleven-thirty, and even during his drive to Dr. Edling's office, he had weighed and polished one approach. He would handle the analyst, as he had handled his internist. He would employ the same fictitious, face-saving friend he had used to obtain information from Dr. McGrath. But, from the moment he had walked toward Dr. Edling and shaken hands with him, his carefully devised approach had seemed embarrassingly transparent and juvenile.

He had come to the appointment half an hour early, with a mingled feeling of fear and resentment. He resented the idea of baring himself to another man who was no more than his equal. He resented being placed in a position of needing help. He was afraid of the witch doctor's magic. Afraid of it, and yet anxious and hopeful for it.

He had found Dr. Edling's office at the end of the corridor, on the first floor of the medical building, and gone into the tiny reception room expecting a nurse but finding none. Disconcerted and increasingly apprehensive, he had sat turning the pages of the inevitable *Fortune* and *New Yorker* and waiting. Once, he thought that he heard muffled voices through the door to the adjoining room, and he listened hard, but he heard nothing. He had been waiting ten minutes, when Dr. Edling finally appeared.

Dr. Edling was a small, deeply tanned man. He was not entirely bald, but he would be soon. Wisps of hair covered his lightly freckled head, and the increasing baldness gave him the appearance of being high-domed and wise. His eyes, behind scholarly, rimless spectacles, were direct and friendly. He wore a bow tie, which promised a certain nattiness, but his trousers were surprisingly baggy, and the over-all effect was of one rumpled and slouched. When he greeted Philip and firmly took his hand, his voice was as soft as it had been on the telephone. His movements, as he followed Philip into the large office and motioned him to a chair and took his own place in a cushioned seat between the brown sofa and the table, were hushed and respectful. Later, after they had conversed a while, Philip decided that Dr. Edling's modulated speech was an attention getter. When he spoke, you leaned forward and listened intently to catch every word. But even later than that, when they had conversed yet longer, Philip decided that the modulated speech might be more than an attention getter. It might be a way of not frightening the frightened, of allaying, of soothing, of making it clear that everything was, really, not so unusual, and abnormal, and hopeless after all.

Once seated, Philip had eyed the enemy couch with its fresh doily only briefly, and then not looked at it again, though never fully unaware of it. He had faced Dr. Edling, trying to appear relaxed and easy, and asked if he might smoke. Dr. Edling, examining several file cards, had assured him that he did not mind. Philip was certain that these cards contained notes taken from the earlier meetings with Danny and Helen. He wondered, with fleeting anger, what Helen had said against him, and determined to refute in a subtle way her familiar charges.

Dr. Edling looked up and began to speak of Danny at once. He spoke of Danny with genuine affection. He spoke of him as an exceptional, promising, and winning child, and Philip felt warmly proud and complimented. "Danny can grow up to be anything he wants to be," Dr. Edling had said. And then, he had added with a smile, "Even a psychiatrist." Then, gradually, as Dr. Edling continued, so gradually that the intrusion of the fact was almost painless, Philip was made to know that his son was not fulfilling his potential, and that he was unhappy. He had clung to Dr. Edling because he wanted and needed a father. He had resisted visiting the homes of friends or going to camp or to school, because he was afraid and insecure and did not know if his parents would be waiting when he returned. And so it went, in this vein, on and on. Nothing that Dr. Edling said was exactly new to Philip. All, at one time or another, he had sensed or understood. But he realized, listening, that he had been incapable of acting upon it. Yet, somehow, this old knowledge presented by Dr. Edling suddenly seemed new and illuminating.

Impatient as ever, Philip wanted easy answers. Seeking them, he interrupted. Dr. Edling promised no quick panacea. He would have to know Danny better. He would have to know more about Helen and Philip. "On the basis of one visit each, I can't make a profound recommendation for help," he had said. "After a few more visits, I'll be better able to make a diagnosis and suggest a treatment program—that is, if I find one necessary." Going on again, he had mentioned the absolute necessity of a solid family bond and of the need for a consistent relationship with Danny.

He had begun to question Philip, almost casually it seemed, about his own attitudes toward Danny and his activities with his son. At once defensive, Philip was prepared to trot out the best of it. He perceived then, that Dr. Edling would expect an expurgated version. And so, with a blunt frankness and honesty that is never really frank or honest or beneath the studied and conscious level, Philip paraded a series of self-deprecating anecdotes. Dr. Edling seemed neither shocked nor intrigued. Philip decided that he had better balance the picture. He banished Caligula and became the understanding and admirable Marcus Aurelius. He had gone on for several minutes this way, when the telephone call had abruptly halted him.

Now waiting for the resumption of the interview, he still felt vaguely disturbed in his confused role as the father of a troubled child. Yet, in the presence of Dr. Edling, he felt safe about that aspect of his life. He sensed that beyond the corner, there was a way out. It was something that could be handled in the near future. The predicament with Peggy Degen was more immediate and more serious. This was a dark thing that had, in less than a week, become an obsession. It had ruined all rationality, destroyed all normal activity, and it threatened to make him impotent not only as a sex-capable man but as a complete human being. He was not sure of the exact symptoms of a nervous breakdown. Whatever they were, he felt positive that he was swiftly approaching that kind of emotional earthquake.

He was suddenly aware that Dr. Edling had hung up and was observing him. Quickly, he removed the pipe from his mouth and emptied the bowl in the standing tray beside him. He found his tobacco and began to refill the pipe.

"I'm sorry about the call," said Dr. Edling. "You were telling me about the first time you took Danny to a baseball game."

"Oh, yes," Philip said. "It was great." He felt tired and unconvinced about Danny and himself. "He'd never shown any interest in baseball, but I took him anyway. The two of us. I explained things, and there was a foul ball once, and popcorn and dogs, the whole bit. He didn't understand a damn thing, but he really enjoyed himself."

"Maybe he didn't have to understand it. Maybe he just enjoyed being with you."

"I suppose that was it. Anyway, we had a great time. I try to take him once a month. It's always wonderful."

Dr. Edling did not speak for a moment. He stared down at the file cards on the table. Then he looked up. "I am sure it is wonderful, Mr. Fleming. But only your words tell me that—not your face."

"What do you mean?"

"You are telling me what a great time you have with your son at the baseball games. That should bring a smile to your face, some sort of happiness. Yet it doesn't. Your face was troubled when you spoke. It was exactly that way before. You were telling me how much you wanted a boy, how happy you were to have one, and about all the fun that first Christmas. Your words were joyous—but I must tell you, your expression was, well, depressed."

Philip felt the defensive tension rise. "I wasn't aware."

"No, of course not. Let me explain something, Mr. Fleming. You are extremely intelligent. You are a writer. In some ways, we are in the same profession. So I can be more open with you, explain more to you. When you go to your internist, you go to discuss physical matters. When you come to an analyst, you come to discuss feelings. Usually, when patients find it in them to visit us, their feelings are near the surface. When a patient addresses us, we are quick to notice discrepancies between content and affect. Do you understand?"

"I'm not sure."

"What you say does not match how you look when you say it. You are telling me things that should bring satisfaction, something pleasing that reflects in your face. Yet they don't. Instead, I see anxiety. I say to myself, something is bothering him, he seems unhappy. Then, I ask myself, what could it be?" He looked levelly at Philip. "Perhaps you'd like to tell me, Mr. Fleming?"

Shrewd little bastard, Philip said to himself. This was the opening, of course. Plunge and get it over with. Peggy Degen. She was at the tip of his tongue. He need only speak her name and wait for magic. Yet, inexplicably, he could not do it.

"It's just something personal," he said. "It's got nothing to do with my son."

"I should think most everything personal in your life might have to do with your son?"

Prying old lecher, Philip thought. He's coaxing me now. He's being clever with me. All the goddamn books he has read. Treat them this way, treat them that. Nurse them along easily, don't bruise them, wean it out of them. Slowly, slowly.

Pretentious bastard, he thought. He knows it all, and he knows he knows it all, but he is giving me the humble act. Who was the character in Dickens? So humble you wanted to vomit.

He felt the nausea in his throat and clenched the pipe stem between his teeth. He touched the pipe and realized that it was cold. He dug into his pocket for a match and lit it. He knew that his hand was shaking, and he was furious.

Oh, the hell with it, he thought suddenly. What difference what I tell him? What do I care? Who is he? I'll never see him again, anyway. Screw him. He doesn't mean a thing. Why am I making so much of it?

Suddenly he thought: shock him, shock that little bastard right out of his tight little pants. Give him a jolt in the ass. Pour it to him. Let him have it and watch his face.

He sucked on his pipe and exhaled a cloud of smoke, and at once he felt himself sag. He felt it, and he knew that Dr. Edling saw it. The anger and bitterness were still there, but they were no longer directed at the man across from him. They were turned inward, at the proper target, and at once all his pitiful façade of self-esteem was punctured, and he felt deflated and helpless. He wanted magic. To hell with shame, humiliation, pride. Magic. Instant magic.

"As a matter of fact, you put your finger on it," he said at last. "I'm very upset."

Dr. Edling said nothing.

"I visited my regular doctor yesterday," Philip went on haltingly. "Dr. McGrath. He's an internist—"

"Yes, I know. What was the matter?"

Philip touched his chest. "I had pains here. He put me through the mill. My heart checked out okay. He said it was tension." Philip hesitated, then continued. "Afterward we talked a while. I asked him for some advice for a friend of mine. I told him my friend—he's married—was having an affair with another woman. Only, he had some trouble. He was—well, he just couldn't get an—he couldn't make love. Dr. McGrath thought it might be something physical, until

I told him my friend was able to sleep with his own wife okay. Then, Dr. McGrath said he thought it was mental and my friend should see a psychiatrist." Philip looked at the couch a moment, then directly at Dr. Edling. "I guess you know there was no friend. I was talking about myself."

"No, I didn't know that."

"I was going to try the same with you, but I figured you'd know it, and I'd look like a fool." He heaved a sigh. "So there it is. Me."

"Well, I'm certainly glad you weren't secretive. There's nothing to be ashamed of. Temporary impotence isn't that uncommon."

"I think it is," said Philip. Now that it was out he was determined to flagellate and debase himself.

"I assure you it isn't. It's not surprising you were having cardiac difficulty. Emotional problems very often have physical symptoms."

"My heart's the least of it," said Philip impatiently. "The whole thing's become an obsession. I'm all mixed up. I can't think straight. It's driving me nuts."

"I can well imagine," said Dr. Edling sympathetically. "Do you want to tell me something about it?"

Here we go, thought Philip. He remembered a dinner party where they had all sat around discussing the reasons why men undertook their various jobs and careers. What made a man become a surgeon and cut into human flesh? They had decided the choice of the surgeon was rooted in sadism. Behind the oath of Hippocrates and the legend of Healer, stood De Sade. The scalpel was his release and satisfaction. And the psychiatrist? He was the curious tailor branded Peeping Tom at Coventry. Every analyst was subconsciously gratifying the pleasures of a voyeur. For him, every patient was the nude Godiva. To surreptitiously view the forbidden, this was his release and satisfaction. It had all seemed clever and bright and superior at the party. But, now, Philip did not care about all that.

He heard his voice, and the words, and felt too detached to interrupt himself. "It started last Sunday night," he was saying. "Well, actually before, on Saturday night. There was a party, and we were having this little flirtation. Then she invited me over—or maybe I invited myself—I don't remember—anyway, we made a date for the next night. That was Sunday. Last Sunday."

He halted momentarily to organize the sequence of events. He heard Dr. Edling speak. "Had you ever done this sort of thing before?"

"Never," said Philip quickly. "I never cheated on Helen once. I suppose that's abnormal, too."

Dr. Edling remained silent.

Philip resumed. "I can't say any special thing led to it. Maybe I was just unhappy and bored. I suppose Helen told you we haven't been getting along so hot. Nothing critical, but just steady bickering and disagreeing. And then Danny. Well, you know all that. My work didn't help either, I suppose. I haven't been enjoying it—and it's been like losing your way in a maze—how do you get out? Especially, if you don't know where you're going. Anyway, our old house was for sale, and she came in, and there she was. I felt like a school kid. I haven't gone for anyone this way since I've grown up. She was young, pretty, bright—and she said she loved me." He looked eagerly at Dr. Edling for understanding. Dr. Edling nodded tolerantly. Philip wanted to be positive that he understood. "I mean, here's the perfect girl, and she wants me—I'm somebody—she makes me feel like a man."

"You don't feel you got that from your wife?"

"Hell, no. Helen's the original emasculator. She's been paring away at me for years. I don't suppose I knew how much, until Peggy came along."

He suddenly stopped. He realized that he had mentioned Peggy by name for the first time. He studied Dr. Edling's face for a reaction to this slip, but there was none. He felt a certain disloyalty in having uttered her name without permission. Peggy and he had a secret, shared a private life, and now he was dragging it into the open before a stranger and exposing her by name to this stranger. But it was done, and it was for her sake as well as his own, so no need to feel coy or guilty about it.

He glimpsed the time. There were fourteen minutes left. He would have to make giant steps in his exposition. He looked up. "Anyway, I had this date with Peggy. I went over. We drank and talked and necked a little. I wanted her, but I think I was a little scared. I don't know why. But it got to the point where she just stood up and asked me if I wanted to sleep with her—just like that. Well, I did, and I said so. Ten minutes later, we were in bed. But when the time came, I just couldn't. Nothing happened. No matter how hard I tried, it was no dice. She took it pretty well, but I can't say I did. I've been a wreck ever since."

"Was that the only occasion you tried to make love to her?"

Philip hated this. "No. I tried the next night and the night after that. I haven't tried since."

"But you've had intercourse with your wife since?"

"That's right. After I struck out the third time with Peggy, I came home and went with Helen. I suppose it wasn't right. But I had to."

"And no problem there?"

"None."

"Has this kind of thing—this impotence—ever occurred in your marriage—with your wife?"

He thought about it. "Maybe a couple of times. It's hard to remember. Sure, it's happened two or three times, when I've been tired or loaded. But normally I'm okay."

"Is your wife a fairly aggressive sex partner? I mean—does she actively stimulate you—try to arouse you—?"

"I don't know. Sometimes. Why?"

"Well, it's quite involved. Let me put it this way. Many men—a surprising number—are fairly passive in bed. You might say they're looking for someone to mother them. They have a tendency toward impotency. An aggressive wife may often overcome this by stimulating them, making them feel secure, masculine, big."

"I'm not sure Helen does that for me. Anyway we get along well enough. I've had no real problem with her."

"I suppose not. After all, she *is* your legal wife. What you do with her is proper and acceptable."

"What is that supposed to mean?"

"I'll go into that in a moment," said Dr. Edling. "I just want to follow through with our discussion. This young woman you've been having an affair with—is she fairly aggressive in love play?"

Philip considered this. At last, he shook his head. "I don't think so—not the way you mean. Of course, in a sense she invited me to sleep with her—and she's been willing enough, God knows—but once we're in there, it's mostly up to me. You think that has anything to do with it?"

"Not really," said Dr. Edling.

"What is the matter then?"

"I'm afraid I can't answer that yet, Mr. Fleming. I know you are in an unhappy predicament—and impatient to solve it. But it may take a little time. Maybe this temporary impotence is just that and no more—temporary—a single accident, an isolated disturbance, that will right itself and go away, and you will go on to perform as normally as you ever have. On the other hand, it could be something more profound. I don't know which—and I won't know, until I'm better acquainted with your problems."

An old dim memory crossed Philip's mind. He had awakened in the middle of the night, or so it seemed, and called out for his mother, and then for his father, and neither had replied. Frightened, he had left the bed to hunt through the dark and vacant house. He could find neither of them anywhere. He had stood in the middle of the living room, terrified, wetting his pajamas, shivering and whimpering—until they returned from the porch across the street, where they had been visiting with neighbors.

He stared at Dr. Edling. "You mean there's nothing you can tell me now?"

"Nothing specific about your case—because I don't know your case. I can and will tell you the basic causes of the kind of impotency you have described. Perhaps, they will give you a better understanding of what might be troubling you. In subsequent visits, I hope we can explore this a little more fully, and perhaps fasten on one cause."

"But I have to know now."

"You mean you intend to continue with this affair?"

"I've got to."

Dr. Edling sat very still. Only his fingers moved, slowly tapping the file cards on the table. "You know that this can have grave consequences for your family and yourself?"

"I love this girl, Doctor. At least, I think I do."

"Well—"

"I have to sleep with her. That's all I care about right now."

Somehow, Philip expected Dr. Edling's face to display censure. Instead, it revealed only concern. "If you feel you must—" he began.

"Yes, damnit, I must," said Philip. "You were going to tell me the causes—"

Dr. Edling shifted in his chair. "Very well," he said at last. There was almost a hint of regret in his voice. "I should say one of the primary causes of impotency is guilt—guilt over having an extramarital affair—guilty over submitting to an unacceptable impulse. You know and I know that society in general frowns on infidelity in marriage. It goes on, of course, but we know it is considered a bad thing, a wrong thing, an act that meets with open disapproval and must be performed in secrecy." He sat more erect now, leaning toward Philip. "All men are beset by countless impulses not acceptable to their environment. Some are sexual impulses. Others are aggressive impulses. If you are tempted by them, you feel guilty. For example, if you have a brother, you are expected to like him. If you secretly hate him, that's an aggressive impulse you are ashamed of, and it makes you feel guilty. So it is with sex. You have a wife, a family, a home, a position in the community. You are depended upon as a provider. All this is understood and acceptable. Then, suddenly there is an unacceptable impulse. You meet another woman, and you want to sleep with her. If you can shake this impulse, and go on, it speaks well for your maturity. If you can't, if you are tempted by it, well, it may mean you are in for a certain amount of pressure and tension. You are doing something wrong, but nevertheless you go ahead. But now, way deep down, you feel guilty. You are transgressing on family, home, station, your role as provider. But you are obsessed, so still you continue. Your guilt rides your desire. You suffer anxiety. And, at the moment of intercourse, this anxiety born of guilt renders you temporarily impotent."

Philip had followed the primer recital with complete absorption. It seemed so simple an explanation and so natural. In a curious way, he no longer felt threatened.

"Do you think that's what happened to me?" he asked.

"Possibly. I don't know."

"But that's not the only explanation?"

"Oh, no. There are many more. I'm just trying to point out a few basic ones. Another cause for impotency can be one's attitude toward sex. A large number of persons regard the sexual act as something you speak of behind your hand —as something nasty, wrong, dirty."

"I'm sure I don't feel that way."

"Don't be so certain. You may not actually know how you really feel. At any rate, this attitude toward the sexual act creates an aggressive male, one who desires to hurt his partner. This can create temporary impotence."

"I don't understand," said Philip.

Dr. Edling blinked at the ceiling, then returned his gaze to Philip. "Let me illustrate with an analogy. You are a soldier in the front line with your buddy. Your buddy wants to make a charge on a machine gun nest. You think it is unwise. He starts to go ahead. You reach out your right arm to stop him, and miss him. He goes ahead and is instantly killed. Had you stopped him with your right arm, he might be alive. Soon after, your right arm becomes paralyzed. The cause, of course, is psychic. Your right arm is the offending arm—the same arm with which you once, as a youngster, wanted to punch your teacher or slug your father, but dared not. Do you understand that much?"

Philip nodded, faintly annoyed, but then sat back, for there was no condescension in Dr. Edling's tone.

"In the same way, you may have an offending organ," Dr. Edling continued. "As a youngster you were forced to be too good, too clean, forced not to fight and warned that masturbation was a sin. Your aggressiveness was inhibited. As you grew to maturity, you realized that your reproductive organ represented all masculinity, virility. You wished to use your ability to make love aggressively, to prove yourself. When you had intercourse with your wife, you fancied that you were hurting her. This made you feel confused and guilty. For, the ability to love should be used for pleasure, yet you were using it destructively, with aggressive intent. The offending organ worried you. So you tried to repress its aggressive intent, tried to inhibit it. As a result, you were temporarily impotent."

"That doesn't make sense," said Philip.

"It should. Perhaps I explained it too hastily. I assure you, this cause of sexual impotence can manifest itself in many other ways. One who suffers this way may also suffer in his social life and career. He may become a person who never makes his will known, who dares not to do certain things, who is indecisive at critical moments. It's all one and the same thing."

Philip felt suddenly let down. He was too tired to protest or comment. Dr. Edling watched him.

"We often find," said Dr. Edling softly, "that the various forms of impotency go hand in hand with depression. A man who suffers impotency, usually has poor interpersonal relationships. He may be charming and affable on the outside, but that is only superficial. Beneath it all, he is lonely, depressed, unable to make proper contacts with people— and that includes sexual contacts—you know, he can't even perform as a man, so that he may have a normal bond with a woman."

"I wasn't depressed until I came in here," said Philip.

"I didn't mean to upset you further," said Dr. Edling. "I was only trying to clear the air. I wanted you to know there are perfectly understandable reasons for temporary impotence, and they can be treated."

"Well, that's something."

"You've been disturbed, but I think you should know that this may be more related to previous elements in your life than to this one incident. You've told me a little, of course.

The very fact that you are having an extramarital affair tells me something, and the fact that it has failed tells me more."

He glanced at his watch and rose. "Be assured, Mr. Fleming, that what has happened to you is not unique. Right now, it has obsessed you, but it is a passing thing. You can overcome it. I would suggest a few more meetings. I'm sure we can get to the root of this."

Philip was on his feet. He felt unenlightened and disappointed. "Well, I—I'll have to work this out."

"However you wish."

"Let me work it out and call you. We'll get together."

"Fine. I'll expect to hear from you."

"Okay. Thanks, doctor." He started to the door, then turned, and smiled sheepishly at Dr. Edling. "I—I'm sorry we didn't talk much about my son."

"On the contrary," said Dr. Edling. "We talked a good deal—about your son."

The telephone booth in the parking lot was occupied by a matronly woman with a floral arrangement on her hat. Philip waited, puffing at his pipe, trying to remember what Dr. Edling had told him and trying to organize it in some useful way. But everything he had just heard seemed to elude him. One catch phrase danced in his mind: the offending organ. You're damn right, he thought.

The woman squeezed out of the booth, cast him an apologetic glance, and waddled off. He went into the scented booth and dialed home.

Danny answered in a high-pitched, distant voice. With some difficulty, Philip managed to identify himself. Danny wanted to know when he would be home. He promised that he would be home soon. Danny pressed for an exact time. Mercifully, Helen took over the phone.

"Did you see Dr. Edling?" she asked with what he thought was unnecessary anxiety.

"Just finished."

"Well? Don't you think he's awfully nice?"

"Remarkably human for a psychiatrist," said Philip a little sourly. "We got along fine."

"Did you talk about—?" She hesitated. Obviously, Danny was at her feet.

"At great length," said Philip. "He gave me the whole picture."

"Are you going to see him again?"

At once, he was irritated. "Are you?" he snapped.

"Certainly."

"Then, I will too." He knew he was reacting childishly, and he was sorry. He made an effort at being reasonable. "He explained that he wanted to see us along with Danny. He thinks he can straighten him out faster that way."

"I'm glad."

"Were there any calls?" he asked.

"Nathaniel Horn wants you to call."

"Did he say why?"

"It was his girl. She just left the message."

"All right. I'd better see him."

"When will you be home?"

He remembered his date with Tina Barlow. "I don't know. I'll grab a bite around here and then dig in at the library."

"Try to be on time for dinner."

"I will."

After hanging up, he considered calling Horn. He decided that he preferred to see him. He wanted to consume the time before his meeting with Tina. He consulted his wrist watch. It was ten minutes to one. Horn usually left the office for lunch at one. If he hurried, he might catch him.

He drove as rapidly as he could, through the crowded shopping traffic, to South Beverly Drive. He circled the block once seeking a parking slot, and, at last, he found one. He hurried up the stairs to Horn's office.

Horn, a briefcase under his arm, was already in the corridor on his way to lunch.

"Phil—I've been trying to get hold of you—"

"I know. I was tied up."

Horn took him by the arm and propelled him back to the top of the staircase. "I wanted to talk to you a bit—but I'm already late—I've got a luncheon appointment with a New York playwright—his first week here."

They started down the stairs.

"Could we make it for right after lunch?" Horn asked.

"I'll be busy."

"Okay. There's nothing much, really." They had reached the foot of the staircase. "Where's your car?"

Philip pointed it out. Horn walked with him to the car.

"Alexander Selby called," Horn said.

"Yes?"

"He seems anxious about the Caroline Lamb project, which is all to the good. He reminded me that tomorrow is the deadline he had set with you. He has to pick up the option on a play over the weekend or drop it and settle for Caroline Lamb. He wanted to know if you had anything yet."

"What did you tell him?"

"What could I tell him? I said yes, you had several good ideas, but you were trying to follow them through. I think I convinced him that you'd have something."

"Oh—good," said Philip acidly.

"He kept trying to pin me down. I tried to keep him off, but he insisted on a meeting tomorrow. I made it as late as possible. Four in the afternoon, at the studio." He looked at Philip worriedly. "You must have something you can tell him?"

Philip felt oppressed, as if everything, everyone, was crowding him to a brink. "I don't know. I thought about it yesterday, Nat—I gave it some real time in the library— but I'm not sure I came up with anything workable."

"Not even one idea? You don't need more—just one little thought, approach, to bait him, make him take the hook—"

"I thought of bringing Teresa Guiccioli to London after Byron's death. She actually visited England much later, after Caroline Lamb was dead too. But I'd keep Caroline alive. Make it a historic convenience. The two of them meet— Byron's first important mistress and his last—and, somehow, the Guiccioli helps resolve Caroline's story." He searched Horn's professionally phlegmatic listener's face. "What do you think?"

Horn was silent a moment. "It's clever," he said at last, "but I don't think it's strong enough. Byron isn't really in it for the finish. And you have to cheat. It's not true."

"This is a novel," said Philip defensively.

"I know. But the end is so important, I think it should be true. You can embroider—but the fact must be there. It would give the whole thing more impact."

Philip shrugged. "Well, that's all I've got."

"If it's the best you have by tomorrow, then we'll go in with it, of course. Who knows? But you've still got more than twenty-four hours. I wish you'd keep after it."

"Well, I thought I'd go to the library after lunch. Maybe if I start reading again—"

"Try it, Phil. If there's anything you want to bounce off me tonight, just phone. I'll be in all evening." He shifted his briefcase to the other arm. "I'd better run now. Don't forget —four tomorrow. I'll be in the studio reception waiting. I think we better hit Selby together."

Philip nodded unhappily. "All right," he said.

He watched Horn depart, then started for his car when he realized that he had not had lunch yet. He looked up the block, and then across the street. His gaze held on the sign

PORTER'S BAR AND GRILL. He remembered having a drink and sandwich there several times with Horn. He waited for a break in the traffic, then crossed hurriedly to the opposite side and entered the confined restaurant.

When his eyes became accustomed to the dim interior, he saw that the few tables near the long mahogany bar, and those in the next room beyond, were occupied. The bar was only half filled. Porter, the squat proprietor, approached him, menu in hand. He nodded at Philip uncertainly, with half recognition.

"One?" he asked.

"Yes," said Philip.

"Be about fifteen minutes."

"No hurry. I'll have a drink."

Philip made his way to the end of the bar where there were three vacant red-leather stools. He lifted himself on the middle one and ordered a scotch and water.

He surveyed the tables and observed the customers without interest. When the drink came, he downed half of it in one gulp. Immediately refreshed, he tried to focus backward to the meeting with Dr. Edling. The image of Peggy on the bed intruded, and suddenly he wished that she had been with him in the psychiatrist's office. Somehow, he imagined, the sane analytical explanation of impotency would have erased a part of his humiliation and again given him stature in Peggy's eyes. The subconscious guilt over an extramarital affair would have made reasonable sense to her. Still, goddamnit, what did it all amount to anyway? All that Freudian patter could not, and would not, in a million years obscure the stark simple fact of failure. Peggy had bared herself, opened herself, to the promise of his masculinity, and he had not been able to deliver. This was the naked fiasco. No amount of verbiage about guilts and repression could camouflage his non-performance. To all intents and purposes, Dr. Edling had been a waste. Philip was still on his own—to prove himself or carry the burden of the fiasco to the grave.

Bringing the glass to his mouth again, drinking, he could not free himself from the oppressive thought that the resolution of his problem was in his own hands. Why was he always seeking a crutch? But then, he supposed, most men always did. How else to account for the success of a man like Dr. James Graham, that London medical quack of the 1780s? Philip tried to remember why he even knew of Dr. Graham, and at once he recalled that he had been doing research for a screenplay set in the eighteenth century and had stumbled upon Graham and briefly pursued him. Gradually now, the facts came back to him. Dr. Graham had opened a Temple of Health and Hymen. The main feature of his ornate establishment was the "Holy of Holies," a huge bed that had been built at a cost of sixty thousand pounds. It stood on six glass legs, and was concealed behind perfumed blue curtains. There were incense, and soothing music, and vari-colored lights. For a fee of one hundred pounds, a faltering male might have use of the bed for a single night, and in it receive electromagnetic charges that were guaranteed to enhance his virility. In the newspapers of the day, this place of rest and revival—and hope—was advertised as "The Celestial Bed."

These facts had once amused Philip, but now they seemed less quaint and humorous. He recalled that Dr. Graham's fraud had actually been helpful to men and women alike. Apparently, the confidence that it had inspired often overcame sexual blocks. If there existed such a rejuvenating bed today, Philip reflected, he would probably, in his utter despair, partake of its promise. But no such wonder bed existed—and his success or failure must take place on the ordinary bed that was Peggy's own. Perhaps, symbolically, her bed was a berth of judgment, a matted field that he had selected to prove that he was more than he had ever been. It was, indeed, his celestial bed—to disillusion or revive him for the remainder of his days.

He hunched on the bar, his mood black, but with one thin shaft of hope penetrating. There had been three successive fiascoes with Peggy, yet there had been no problem in his one attempt with Helen. Still, Dr. Edling had hinted that a wife was proof of nothing. With a wife, he felt secure. It was the area beyond marriage that was forbidding. And then, for the first time since he had sat down at the bar, he remembered Tina Barlow. This excited him. She desired him. There could be no question about that. And he wanted her. He wanted Peggy more. But in a purely carnal sense, he wanted Tina as much. This was the challenge he needed. A successful affair with Tina might wipe out all his inhibitions about an extramarital affair. From Tina, he could return to Peggy with perfect confidence.

He began to fantasy an affair with Tina, and then, at once, it seemed improbable. Peggy was one thing. He was in love with her. She was a separate world away from Helen. But Tina was Helen's friend. He, himself, had great affection for Sam Barlow. Their lives were socially interlocked with telephone calls, afternoon swims with the children, dinner parties. Moreover, he had no real love for Tina. If he seduced her, he would be performing as a stallion and little else. And what would it lead to? And what if he failed and had to continue seeing her? Failure with Tina was unthinkable. But, then, the idea of having intercourse with her, the wife of a friend, a friend herself, was also unthinkable. What kind of a son of a bitch was he, anyway?

He downed his drink, ordered another, and went to the wall telephone in the alcove beside the checkroom. He had agreed to visit Tina at two-thirty. Probably, she was inviting him to no more than an extended flirtation. She would be too sane and calculating to risk losing the stability of security and station for a momentary physical adventure. She might pet and provoke—she was a teaser—but she was not an adventuress. Yet, perhaps she was. Who could really tell about any woman? In any case, it was too immoral and too involving to take the chance. He would telephone her immediately and cancel out. He would spend the afternoon in the cloistered library, where he belonged. He dialed the Barlow number.

Tina answered. Her voice was huskier and sexier than he had remembered. "Where are you, Philip? I thought you'd be here already?"

He held up his wrist watch. It was almost two-thirty. "I was detained," he said uncertainly.

"Well, come over and relax. The pool is perfect. I'm just wandering around—waiting. I even sent the children out. Just so we can drink in peace. What'll you have to drink? I'll get it ready while you're driving over."

"Scotch," he said, "plain scotch. I'll be over in ten minutes."

"Do you love me?"

"Passionately," he said.

He replaced the receiver on the hook, returned to the bar, and quickly finished his second drink. So I'm a son of a bitch, he thought finally. He laid two bills on the bar and hastily left.

The drive to Bel-Air took fifteen minutes. Only once, on the way, did he speculate erotically on Tina Barlow. He wondered if she would be wearing the skintight blue swimming suit with the skirt above the crotch and the buttocks bursting free. If she did, he disclaimed all responsibility for what occurred thereafter. Enough was enough.

He parked before her entrance, then went to the door and rang the bell. In a moment, it opened. She stood clothed in a full white terrycloth bathrobe, holding a dark amber drink. The red hair was combed back tightly as usual, and her large innocent eyes and sensuous mouth were smiling.

"You see," she said, offering the drink, "I'm determined to make you happy."

"Hello, Tina." He accepted the glass and kissed her on the lips. Her lips were alive, but he pulled away.

She smiled up at him, and the long dimple folded across her right cheek. "Did you bring your trunks?"

"Oh, yes—I almost forgot. Here, hold this."

He handed her the glass, grabbed up trunks and towel from the rear seat of his car, and returned to her. She gave him his drink again, circled his waist with one arm, and they went inside.

"Well, it took a long time to get you to visit me," she said.

He looked around. "Are we really alone?"

"No man is an island, but we are." She found her gin and tonic on the piano. "I'm a practiced courtesan, you know. I do this all the time. No problem."

"Where's Sam?" he asked casually.

"In Pomona or some damn place. A dental meeting. He won't be back until dinner."

"How can he leave you alone like this?"

"Shouldn't he?"

"I wouldn't."

She linked her arm in his. "You're different. You want me."

"I sure do," he said lightly.

"Let's get some sun."

They went out to the pool and settled on a striped padded divan. They drank. He felt the overpowering effects from his scotch at once, and he realized that she had given him two or three shots.

"You must think me a dreadful hussy," she was saying.

"I do, of course. Why do you ask?"

"Compromising you like this."

"I'm delighted. I wouldn't have had the courage to ask myself over."

"I never see you alone," she said seriously. "There's always the goddamn kids or Sam or Helen. I've had a crush on you since the day we first met."

"Make that mutual."

"I thought it would be fun just to be alone—together— like in all those novels."

"I'm having a good time already."

"So am I."

She finished her drink, set it down on the patio and stood up. "Why don't you change?"

He nodded but did not rise. She opened the belt of her

terrycloth robe and wriggled out of it. The blue swim suit seemed to be bursting. He was sure it must be a size or more too small. She lifted her arms and waved her hands. "How do I look?"

The skirt was pulled high, drawn boldly back and above her loins. She dropped her hands to her hips. "Well—say something?"

"What did Odysseus say when he sailed past the isle of the Sirens?"

"What did he say?"

"He was speechless. I dare you to bend down."

She bent forward toward him. The great, bulging pink breasts strained against the suit. He quickly rose, placing his hands on either side of her breasts, feeling the mounds of flesh give beneath his fingers, and he straightened her. "I've just proved Newton was wrong," he said.

She contemplated him, then kissed his neck. "Go ahead and change," she whispered.

He walked slowly to the nearest of the two white cabanas, looking back only once as she secured her rubber bathing cap and began to lower herself into the pool. He entered the cool, small cubicle, closed the door behind him, and began to undress. He tried to conjure up a picture of himself with Tina, but he could not make the picture clear. He told himself that she was a teaser. He simply could not imagine her going all the way. He stepped into his trunks, pulled them up, and emerged into the sunlight.

She was on her back in the water. "Come on," she called. "It's wonderful."

He trotted to the pool's edge and executed a shallow dive. He slid under the surface, and bobbed up, and then in a few overhand strokes he was beside her. They floated in the water. She turned her pink and glistening face toward him.

"I'm drunk," she said. "Did you know I'm drunk?"

"On one?"

"I had a couple before you came. Are you drunk?"

"High . . . How do you feel?"

"Winging. Wing-dinging. Why doesn't everyone feel this way?"

She was off, and he followed. They went forth and back a couple of times, and then they rolled a beach ball into the pool and batted it around. After a while, they were exhausted by the game, and again they floated.

Finally, she did a breast stroke to the ladder, climbed out of the water, and stood beside the pool, dripping. She unbuckled her rubber cap, jerked it off and cast it aside, then loosened her red hair and shook it free as he came up the ladder before her. She was soaked through, and this made her suit transparent. He lifted his eyes to the upper expanse of breasts above the suit. And then he saw that she was watching him. Well, he thought, if you're going to be a son of a bitch, this is the moment.

Quickly, he closed the single step that separated them, took her in his arms, and pressed his lips to hers. She did not resist. She closed her eyes and kissed him back. He reached for her shoulder strap and pulled it down her arm, and he knew that when he stepped away one breast would be naked. He stepped away, but she snatched at the strap and held it and pulled it back into place.

He almost smiled and felt strangely reassured. He was right. She was a teaser and nothing more. Somehow, he suddenly felt relaxed.

His mood was gay. "Let's get dressed and have another drink," he said.

She did not reply. Her eyes fixed on him, and her face was serious.

He leaned forward and kissed her lips quickly. She did not respond. "See you in a minute," he said.

He strode to the cabana, his wet feet leaving fading prints on the hot cement, and he did not look back. Inside the cool, shadowy enclosure again, he stood motionless thinking about Tina. It would have been sensational, he thought. But it had not been worth forcing, and he felt very right. Their relationship would go on now, as always—the provocations, the flirting, the teasing, the half-promises never to be fulfilled. And yet that seemed as it should be. Alone in the cabana, the thought of making love to her seemed a wild juvenile fancy. As a reality, it might have been memorable, something to cherish and relive long after, and it might have been useful in his pursuit of Peggy. But the reality was nonexistent, and the flirtation was enough. He would change, and they would drink and pet, and he would go home.

He unbuttoned his wet trunks, pushed them down his legs, then kicked them into a corner of the cabana. Naked and dripping, he reached for the towel and began to dry his face. He heard the doorknob behind him turn. He wheeled around as the door opened. For a second, there was sunlight, and then Tina slid through it, shutting the door behind her and leaning back against it. She was still in her wet suit. Her face was tense. She forced a half-smile, regarding him wordlessly, then letting her eyes drop down his body.

"I wanted to see you like this—I had to—"

He stared back at her with disbelief.

She moved toward him the few steps, and flattened against him, arms around his wet back. He kissed her ear and her cheek and her neck. Her probing hands glided down his back, caressing, and then around his thighs, moving in gentle circles. Her breath was short now. "Love me, Philip—love—"

With effort—all movement beyond the essential movement was an effort now—he reached behind her and unzipped her suit. It seemed to erupt free under the release. He grasped her shoulder straps and pulled them down over her arms. Her magnificent breasts spilled out, rounded and firm, the nipples crimson and erect. He dragged her down on the bunk, and buried his face in her breasts, kissing them at last, kissing them endlessly. She was whimpering softly now, almost tearfully it seemed. "Don't—don't—please stop—"

He shoved her back hard on the bunk, still covering her bosom with his lips as she continued to make small inarticulate sounds. He reached down to her waist, taking hold of the soggy roll of swim suit, and pulling the suit off her expansive hips and down her legs. It was like peeling adhesive. He threw the suit to the cabana floor. She tried to rise as he returned to her, but he held her firm. For a moment she resisted, and then she gave and sank back.

"Philip—Philip—Philip," she called weakly.

"You're beautiful," he murmured.

"Philip—now—now—hurry—"

At last they were joined in a close straining embrace. The agitation created by his wet body slapping against hers aroused him more and more. She had ceased making sounds, but lay laboring for breath, eyes shut, face turning from side to side.

"Wait a minute, Philip—let me rest—just a minute—"

"Yes—"

He slowed and gradually full consciousness was restored. He leaned down to find her lips. They continued imperceptibly as they kissed.

Her eyes were wide. "Philip—you know—" She closed her eyes a moment and her body shivered with animal pleasure, and then she opened her eyes again. "You know—I never did this before—I—I never cheated on him."

He said nothing. She sought his eyes. "You don't believe me, do you?"

He nodded. "I believe you."

She smiled. "I'm not sorry."

They clasped each other in a frenzy now. He could feel her breath on his chin and her choked whisper, "I'm a bitch—a terrible bitch."

He was losing restraint as he groped for a foreign

thought, and then his mind held on Peggy, the image of Peggy on her bed, caressing him, looking at him with be-wilderment and hope, and he wanted to cry out—

See me now . . . see, I'm a man . . .

He felt her arch beneath, clamping him, clenching his shoulders.

Peggy . . . Peggy . . . look at me . . .

Turning for home, drained and restored, he realized that he had not smoked in an hour, and he automatically reached for his pipe. He placed the stem between his teeth and dug into his coat pocket for the leather tobacco pouch. The pocket was empty. It was always there, and this confused him. Quickly, he felt through his other pockets. The pouch was in none of them. He slowed the car and examined the seat beside him and the floorboard. The pouch was nowhere in sight.

And then, as he began to puzzle about it, knowing he had smoked in Dr. Edling's office and after, he suddenly remembered. He had left the leather pouch on the unfinished table, next to the bunk, in the cabana. He had quite forgotten that he had placed it there when they had sat on the bunk afterward, nude and dry and spent, arms around each other, silently smoking. He had lit her cigarette and then filled his pipe and dropped the pouch on the table. They had talked a little about what they had done, the fun of it, the morality of it, and then about their mates and the whole point and purpose of their lives, and finally she had reminded him it was getting late. She had kissed him good-by and hurried nakedly across the patio to the bedroom. He had dressed rather quickly and departed. He had completely forgotten the leather pouch.

At once, he thought to stop at the filling station and use the telephone booth to call Tina. But he knew that it was almost dinnertime. Sam would probably be home. Any phone call from him—for Tina and not for Sam—would be in-explicable. He knew that he could not risk it.

Guiding the car into the garage, he prayed that Tina would locate the pouch first. For now he remembered, too, that it had his initials stamped in gold on its side.

Inside the kitchen, he found Helen busily absorbed in laying out a cheese tray. He kissed her on the cheek, "Hiya, ever-lovin'?" he asked cheerfully.

"How are you, stranger? Any luck today?"

"Luck?"

"You said you were going to the library on Caroline Lamb."

"Yes," he said quickly. "Had my nose in books all afternoon. A few leads, but I'm not sure."

"What did Nathaniel Horn want?"

"We have a date with Selby tomorrow afternoon."

"What are you going to tell him?"

"Whatever I have by then."

"I keep thinking of Europe. It'd be a pity to miss it."

"Don't pressure me."

"I'm not. I'm just saying."

"Where's Danny?" he asked.

"Televisioning."

She finished the cheese tray. He became fully aware of it. "That's dinner?"

"No, silly. Poker night."

"You mean all the girls are coming here?"

"Well, Betty couldn't have it. So I thought since most of the girls haven't seen the house, even if it a mess, this was a good excuse. So I made it here."

"You've just lost me," he said, taking a piece of cheese. He nibbled at it.

"You're not going out again?"

"I sure am. You want me to hang around and talk Spock and the last sale at Saks?"

"You could spend some time with your son."

"I spent all morning with my son."

"You liked Dr. Edling, didn't you?"

"My favorite Jivaro," he said cheerfully.

"What's that?"

"Head shrinker."

"Fun-ny."

He picked up the afternoon paper and opened it elaborately. "I'm going to a movie tonight, that's what I'm going to do. I'm going to eat popcorn and fall asleep and let the missus gamble home and savings away."

It was Thursday night, and he was driving up Ridgewood Lane.

He saw the new coupé at once. It was parked several yards beyond Peggy's driveway. His irritation was immediate. He had purposely left home early, insisting that the main feature went on at seven-thirty, but inwardly determined to corner Peggy before she could go out. Cahill had arrived earlier.

He drew his car to a halt and turned off the ignition. Well, this time, he decided, he was not waiting outside or peeking into windows. He was going right inside, where he belonged. He would face this Cahill, outsit him if need be, and have his private talk with Peggy. He was less positive than he had been the night before as to what he would say to Peggy. But he felt confident that when he was done, this Cahill would be out of the picture for good.

He opened the car door, stepped outside and turned toward the house. Even as he did so, he saw Peggy emerge from the house, followed by Cahill. It was unexpected, and he remained behind his car, gaping at them as they made their way down the brick walk. He viewed Peggy in a kind of hypnotic trance. He had never seen her more beautiful. In the moment of seeing her fully, under the white pool of street light, seeing her with that provocative Italian bob, and a mandarin jacket over her dark evening gown, all other women, Tina, Helen, all he had ever known, were obliterated. This was his woman.

She was waiting for Cahill, when he moved into the open and she saw him. She did not hide her surprise. "Why, Philip—"

"Hello, Peggy."

He went straight to her while Cahill joined them. Disconcerted, Peggy waved her hand at Cahill and then at Philip. "Mr. Cahill—this is Mr. Fleming." She turned to Cahill. "He's the gentleman that sold me the house."

"How do you do?" said Jake Cahill offering his hand.

"How are you?" asked Philip, not caring, but shaking his hand.

He had a close look at Cahill now. He was pleased to see that Cahill was shorter than himself—certainly too short for Peggy—but disappointed to find that he was less stout than stocky. His hair was cut in the college manner, his shell glasses gave him a scholarly, owlish appearance, and a stubby briar pipe stuck out of his perfectly round, boyish face.

Philip instinctively resented the ostentatious pipe Cahill was smoking, and facing Peggy, aware now that she wore an orchid corsage, he resented her corny acceptance of the flower.

"Were you coming to see me?" she was inquiring, all innocence.

He wanted to slug her. He wanted to kiss her.

"I was just in the neighborhood. There were a couple things I promised to tell you about the house."

"I'm sorry. We were just rushing off to a—a première."

"Well, mine can wait," he said curtly.

He was about to turn away, when suddenly he took her arm. "Oh, there was just one thing I wanted to tell you right away." He glanced up at Cahill, who was placidly billowing smoke. "Do you mind? It'll just be a moment—a little money matter—"

Quickly, he walked Peggy off toward his own car. When they were out of earshot, he halted, facing her. He saw that Cahill was not even watching them. He was tamping out his pipe on the heel of his hand.

"Peggy," he whispered, "I've been trying to see you—"

"I've been busy."

"So I see," he said bitterly. "I waited out here half of last night for that goon to go home."

"I didn't know. You shouldn't have. It's foolish."

"It's not foolish. I'm in love with you."

She looked worriedly toward Cahill. "Please, Phil—"

"I mean it. I've got to talk to you alone. A serious talk."

She made no promise. She moved her hand in a half-gesture toward Cahill. "I can't keep him waiting. He's an old friend—"

"I know all about him. What time will you be back?"

"I don't know. We're going out for supper after. Please, Phil, don't be difficult."

"You mean you don't give a damn about me?"

"You know I do," she whispered desperately. "But now's no time for all this. I—I'll talk to you."

She turned sharply on her heel and returned to Cahill. He watched a moment as Cahill helped her into the front seat. Then, he went around his own car and got inside. He waited while Cahill eased in beside Peggy, started the coupé, then made a tight U-turn. Philip started his engine, and pretended to let it warm up, as he observed them passing him. He saw Peggy sitting upright across from Cahill. She did not turn to meet his gaze or wave. She kept her eyes straight ahead. He peered up in the rear-view mirror until they were out of sight.

He hated Cahill with all the hate that he could muster. And he hated Peggy.

But he loved her. He loved her with an intensity and a passion that he had never realized he could invest in another creature. He loved her possessively, jealously, totally. He wanted her in bed beside him, all his own, beyond the claim and reach of anyone else on earth but himself. And yet, rationally, he knew that he could not have her unless he was prepared, once and for all, to face the ultimate decision. He had not faced it before.

Now, at last, as he shifted the car from neutral to drive, he began to think of Helen . . . Helen and Peggy . . . Peggy . . . and then at last, without rhyme or reason, that ridiculous phrase of this morning . . . the offending organ.

7

Friday Night

WHEN THE TELEPHONE RANG, some sixth sense told him that he should answer it.

Philip had spent the entire morning in the study, trying to concentrate on Caroline Lamb, and failing, and now he was seated in the kitchen waiting for lunch. He had just turned to the sports section of the morning paper, and Helen, at the stove, had finished transferring his macaroni from a casserole to a plate, when the telephone sounded.

He pushed his chair back, preparing to rise, when Helen crossed over and set the plate before him. "Here, eat this while it's hot. I'll get the phone."

Had he risen a moment before, with some real intention to take the call, he might have had it. But he felt enervated by the events of the day before and in no mood for pointless social talk with any friend who might be calling. He wanted and expected Helen to take the telephone, and yet there was that nagging instinctive warning inside that she should not.

The telephone rang a third time, and by then Helen had the receiver off the hook and to her ear.

"Hello?"

He waited, fork poised over his plate, watching Helen's face with curiosity.

Her face lit up. "Sam! Well, this is a surprise. What are you doing home in the middle of the day?"

Fear gripped at Philip's stomach. Sam meant Sam Barlow. The goddamn tobacco pouch. Philip knew that he should have warned Tina somehow. Sam probably took his early morning dip before going off to work—he had mentioned once that he always had a morning swim, even in the winter since the pool was heated—and then he retired to the cabana to dry off, and there he found the pouch. That would explain why he was still home at noon. Probably interrogating Tina.

"He's right here having lunch—" Helen was saying.

Philip waited tensely, as Helen listened.

"All right. I'll pass the message on," she said into the telephone.

Philip lowered his fork to the table. He waited for the inevitable. Helen was bobbing her head at the mouthpiece, without any visible reaction.

"Tobacco pouch," she repeated. "One second—" She looked over the telephone at Philip. "Did you leave a tobacco pouch at the Barlows?"

Before Philip could reply—and how could he reply, without knowing what Tina had said to Sam?—he heard Sam's voice, tinny and filtered, speaking to Helen, probably assuring her that it was indeed Philip's pouch, that it bore his initials, that it had been on the unfinished table next to the bunk in the cabana.

"Well—I guess he left it there last Sunday," Philip heard Helen say.

His eyes were on Helen's face. For the first time, it betrayed confusion. Philip knew, without having to overhear the phone conversation, that Sam Barlow was insisting that the pouch had not been there before yesterday.

"It wasn't? I—I don't understand."

He'll make you understand, thought Philip grimly.

"Tina said what?" Helen's expression changed from confusion to incredulity. "He visited her yesterday? But he couldn't have. He was working all—"

She glanced past the mouthpiece at Philip, who pretended utter ignorance of what they were discussing. He could hear Sam's tinny voice, louder than before. The words were a jumble. Then; Helen again.

"If Tina said so—but I'm so upset. I can't believe—"

Sam was interrupting her once more. There apparently was no question as to what he believed.

"Sam, do you know what you're implying—?"

She listened, and the color was on her cheeks.

"Of course, he's your friend—"

Philip knew that he could not just remain seated, the bland and unmoved observer. He was being batted forth and back across the wire like a badminton bird. He scraped the chair back and came around the table.

"What in the hell is he bending your ear about?" he demanded of Helen.

She turned her back on him. "Let me speak to him—I'll talk to him—" she said into the telephone.

He thought that he could hear Sam's voice. There was something about not wanting to see Philip any more, and something about mailing the pouch.

"Yes, mail it," Helen said. Her voice had gone flat.

Philip was directly behind Helen, and he could now hear Sam's voice clearly through the receiver at her ear.

"You just tell your husband," Sam was saying, "if I ever find him around Tina again, I'll break his neck. Good-by."

The distant received slammed on the hook. Helen hung up slowly. Philip touched her arm.

She swung around, her eyes blazing, her face livid. "Let go of me!"

"Now wait a minute—"

"You dirty, filthy thing!"

"Helen, for Chrissakes, wait a minute—you get a phone call, and you're ready to blow your stack—at least listen to what I have to say."

"What have you got to say? That you weren't there?"

"I stopped by—I stopped by for five minutes on the way home from the library."

"Sure—sure—and you had tea in that clothes closet—in the cabana—you talked about the weather—"

"I changed in the cabana. We went for a swim. She'd invited me over a dozen times for a swim. I felt tired and hot—"

"I bet you were hot."

"What kind of rotten mind have you got anyway? Is that all you can think about? Can't a man see a woman for a few minutes—have a swim—talk a little—come home—without laying her?"

"Oh, sure—I can see it—a nice, placid intellectual little conversation—that little whore tries to crawl into the pants of every man she meets—and you're no better—panting after that cheap bitch in heat—"

"Helen, listen—"

"Don't give me any more of your fancy talk. You make me sick!"

She pushed past him, and ran out of the kitchen toward the bedroom. He knew that there was nothing to be gained in letting her calm down. This was a crisis, and it had to be met. Somehow, he did not find it entirely disagreeable. Perhaps he had wanted a crisis, a cause, a reason, this prelude to Peggy.

He walked out of the kitchen and into the corridor. Danny appeared out of his room.

"Dad—"

"Later, Danny. I'm busy."

He went swiftly past the boy and into the bedroom. Helen was seated on the side of the bed working a Kleenex in her hands. Philip closed the door behind him and approached her. He looked down at her silently. She looked up at him, her face hurt and angry, and her eyes red.

"Look, Helen," he began, "you're way off base. If you'll be reasonable, if you'll just listen to me a minute, you'll see—"

"I see plenty now," she said. "I see everything."

"What's that supposed to mean?"

"The other day when we were waiting in the car—going into the house with her alone—arranging this meeting—what a fool I've been."

That was, indeed, the moment he and Tina had arranged their assignation. Philip felt warm and uncomfortable.

"I told you she only wanted to arrange a dinner date," he said.

"Sure she did. With you. In the cabana." Her lips tightened until they seemed bloodless. "And all the rest of this week. Every night out. I've got to see Selby—I've got to see Horn—Bill Markson—the movies—oh, yes, I bet—"

"Talk to them and find out for yourself."

"I'm sure you've arranged everything."

"So now I've been with Tina every night this week. And what was Sam doing? Sitting and enjoying the circus?"

"Sam's a fool—just like I've been—"

"Well, you are—for thinking what you're thinking."

He tried to sound injured and put upon. In a way, he told himself, it was unfair. A tobacco pouch in the cabana. And now she was attributing the entire week to Tina. How incredible it was, he thought. She had everything right but with the wrong girl. He tried to imagine her reaction if she learned that the girl was really Peggy Degen. He was sure that she would be stunned. He was almost tempted to tell her.

"What makes you so positive I've been having an affair with Tina?" he asked.

"Because she's so easy—she's a nympho—and you men are all alike. You'll put it in anywhere, just to feed your rotten ego."

"You're being crude, Helen."

"And you're no good. You're just dirty no good. When I think of the nights I've waited for you to come to me in bed. I thought it was the drinking. But now no wonder—with that Tina—that professional hooker—"

"Jesus, if you could hear yourself—"

"If you'd only stand there like a man and admit it—maybe I could understand—"

"All right," he said. "I admit it. I put her down in that cabana and I laid her. She's great. I loved it. We both loved it. I did it twice, and I did it the night before, and the night before that. Now, that's what you want, isn't it?"

She jumped to her feet and swung at him. He grabbed her arm, deflecting the blow, and wrenched her arm downward until she cried with pain. She tried to tear free. He held tight. At last, he released her.

She stood across from him, staring at him like a wounded animal, breathing in short gasps.

"I hate you," she said. "I really hate you."

"Don't you want to save something for Dr. Wolf?"

"I'll save it for the divorce court—"

He felt almost exhilarated. "Is that what you want?"

She said nothing.

"Well—is it?" he pressed.

"Get out of here," she said. "Get out of this house right now. I don't want to see your face around here. I despise you."

He turned and walked swiftly to the bedroom door. Opening it, he hesitated a split second, and then he continued out, banging it shut behind him. He heard her muffled sob. He went past the study, hardly glancing at Danny inside, snatched up his coat from the dining room chair, and hurried to the car.

He did not know exactly where he was driving, or to what end, except that the car was pointed in the general direction of Ridgewood Lane. Approaching the corner filling station, he realized that he should telephone Tina. His affection for her, since she gave herself to him, was greater than ever. His own negligence and stupidity had placed her in a hopelessly compromising position. As for himself, he was not sorry or even disturbed by the aftereffect. But for Tina, he felt genuine concern.

He guided his car into the station and drew up before the row of pumps. He left instructions to fill the tank and then walked to the glass telephone booth. He closed himself inside it, deposited his coin, and dialed. Waiting, he wondered if Sam was still there. He pitied Tina. If Sam answered, he would simply hang up.

It was Tina who answered.

"Tina? This is Phil—"

"My partner in crime." She sounded neither bloodied nor bowed, but rather tired bright.

"Are you alone?"

"Now that's a question," she said. "I'm alone when I'm alone or with Sam. No, don't worry. He just zipped up his trousers and left. And sans shotgun."

"I'm sorry about that damn tobacco pouch—"

"This ought to make you give up smoking."

"You sound cheerful," he said with surprise.

"Oh, I am—I am. I was weeping in a corner when Sam called Helen. I was proud of him. Real sterling. But poor guy, he doesn't know that dialogue went out with *East Lynne*. Well, tell me, what happened?"

"Murder. Helen went wild. It was like wrestling ten samurai."

"You mean she threw things?"

"Practically. She insists we've been in the sack together all week."

"Why do I miss all the fun? I bet she really raked you over."

"She did."

"What did she call me?"

"This is a public phone, Tina."

"So now we're old lovers."

"I'm afraid so."

"Suits me."

He was forced to smile. "Me, too. I always thought you were lovely. Now, I know it."

She chuckled. There was pleasure in it. "Keep that up, and I'll invite you right over."

"Fearless Tina."

"Where are you calling from?"

"A booth at the corner. Helen threw me out."

"No kidding?"

"What about you?" he asked.

"Well, when Sam found the pouch, he just went apoplectic. I couldn't talk to him. He charged in and made that call. But afterward, I got to reason with him. He's a very mild person, you know. He hates trouble. I made him feel real bad—said he was playing kangaroo court—lynch mob —not giving me a fair trial—condemning me on the flimsiest of circumstantial evidence. I invoked the Age of Reason, God, Children. Sam's very puritan you know. So am I, I think. Wives just don't do things like that. Just like mothers don't. Infidelity belongs in a rental library. By the time I was through he was apologizing."

"And that was it?" Philip asked with wonder.

Tina laughed. "Not quite. I knew mere words wouldn't last out the day. Reconciliation, true love, have to be dramatized. We fell on each other, and, well, there was some emotional grappling—and, need I remind you, I'm size thirty-six—"

"I'd have wagered they were forty-two."

"Now, stop it, Philip, or you'll have to come over. Anyway, we wound up in the bedroom—and except for the fact that I feel beat up—"

"I'm impressed with Sam."

"I'm referring to you, dope. Except for general dehabilitation, my domestic life is again on an even keel. All is forgiven. He went off to work, promising to phone Helen again. He wants to apologize. He's going to tell her he behaved badly, and that Tina behaved in a sisterly fashion to Philip, and let's be friends."

Philip had been listening with true awe. This was the female incarnate. Of course, you had to have the natural equipment to go with the feline mentality, but Tina had it all.

"You're a miracle, Tina."

"That I am. Now go and make up with Helen. No, better wait until Sam softens her up."

"We'll see."

"What do you mean?"

"We had a bad fight. I want to think about it."

"Well—if you move out, let me know your address, and I'll move in."

He smiled. She was irrepressible. I'll notify you of any change of address," he said. And then he added. "You're the only genuine redhead I've ever loved."

She was pleased. "You writers. You notice everything. Good-by."

"Good-by, Tina," he said, and hung up.

Returning to his car, he saw that the filling station clock read a quarter to three. He signed for his gas, and then he drove off. He was no sooner on Sunset Boulevard again than he remembered his four o'clock meeting with Alexander Selby. He realized that he was in no shape for the meeting. The brief mood of gaiety provoked by his crazy conversation with Tina had by now evaporated. The bitterness of the fight with Helen was what remained. Yet, it was not the bitterness of it alone, but the release it had offered. He had been discharged by Helen. He was, for the first time in a decade, a free agent. For this hour, and those immediately ahead, he was liberated of all family ties and obligations. Perhaps, there was a residue of guilt, but he was less conscious of guilt than any time during all the previous week. As a free agent, he could think as he wished and plan whatever he desired, without the handcuff of responsibility. All the day ahead was his own, and the night. And, possibly, too, the years. It was as if he had suddenly been showered with a hundred gifts. They could be opened slowly, each to be enjoyed and savored by itself, and still there would be others. The day ahead held much promise. He wanted to use it well. Peggy was the whole point and purpose of the day, of course, and he wanted to plan, seriously plan, how he would perform with her and what he would say to her. With this at his fingertips, Alexander Selby was an intrusion. Caroline Lamb seemed a faded and musty creature, a scholarly corpse buried in books. Peggy Degen was the major part of his living life now. She dwelt in a real house on a street named Ridgewood Lane and could be reached in a given number of minutes. And Peggy was a real person who could be touched by the hands that held the steering wheel. The image of Peggy, naked on the bed, was clearer than ever. Her arms were outstretched to him. She wanted him, and he needed her. Caroline Lamb was a phantom. Let her sleep.

He drove to Beverly Hills, parked before the familiar building, and climbed the stairs two at a time. The outer door to Nathaniel Horn's office was open, as usual. Viola was typing. He entered noiselessly and tickled the back of her neck. She squealed, and swiveled toward him.

"It's you—"

"Couldn't you tell by the touch?" he asked. He peered into the inner office. "Where's Nat?"

"Making the rounds," said Viola. "Sa-ay, aren't you supposed to be meeting him at—?"

Philip held up his hands. "I can't. I'm tied up. It's an emergency. Can you get hold of Nat?"

The telephone rang. "He calls in." She lifted the receiver. "Hold on, this might be him."

It was Horn. Philip stood by impatiently while Viola read Horn several cryptic messages over the phone. Then she reported Philip's presence and handed the receiver over to him.

"What are you doing there?" Horn wanted to know. "We've got a date—"

"I know, I know. Listen, Nat, I can't make it—"

"You can't what? You've got to."

"No. I can't. Something's come up. It's important."

Horn's voice did not disguise his displeasure. "What can be more important than this?"

Philip wished that he could tell him. Horn might even understand. Instead, he said, "It's personal. I can't explain on the phone. Someday, maybe I'll tell you."

"Phil—Selby isn't the kind of guy you push around—what'll I tell him?"

"Tell him I'm having a baby—having menstrual cramps—anything. Tell him I'm sick."

"He's under pressure, Phil. He may get disgusted, blow you off."

"I can't help it."

"You mean whatever you're doing is that important?"

"Yes."

"Well, you know what's best for you. All right, I'd better call him right away."

"Maybe you can make it for Monday."

"He won't sit still for that. You know he's got to make a decision this weekend. You're sure you can't make it? We can see that it's a short meeting."

"I'm sorry, Nat. No."

Horn's voice was resigned. "I'll see what I can do. But no promises. Let me have Viola again."

Philip returned the receiver to Viola, waved good-by, and went down the stairs to his car. He stood aimlessly beside the parking meter a moment, not sure what he should do next. At last, he decided to telephone Peggy. The liquor store, three doors down, had a blue telephone sign above the window. He went inside. The proprietor was busy with several customers. Philip located the open telephone on the far wall. He deposited a coin and dialed Peggy. Waiting, he reviewed what he would say to her. He would impress her with the urgency and importance of their evening together.

The phone buzzed and buzzed. There was no reply. Worried that he had dialed the wrong number, he hung up, retrieved the coin, and tried once more. Again, the persistent buzzing. And still no answer. She was not home, and that was that. He would try again, later. Leaving the liquor store, he realized that he had not eaten since breakfast. He wondered where he should go, and then he knew.

He drove the half-dozen blocks to Santa Monica Boulevard, then turned in and eased the car into the first parking slot he saw. He strolled slowly to the Pegasus Book Shop, not sure what he wanted of Dora Stafford, certain only that he wanted to speak and hear Peggy's name. He squinted past the gaudy window display. He saw the high mop of brown hair bent over a stack of books on the counter beside the cash register. He went inside. A bell tinkled overhead as he entered.

Dora Stafford looked up. "Speak of the devil," she said. "I know you write. I didn't know you read."

"Hello, Dora. I was just passing—"

"Too many people do that. That's what's wrong with the book business."

"I promise to buy a book, next time—maybe two. I had to skip lunch and thought I'd better make up for it. Can I treat you to coffee?"

She studied him. "You look like you got caught in a Bendix. Have you been drinking?"

"Not especially."

"All right," she said at last, "Lonelyhearts Limited stands convened." She shouted over her shoulder, "Irwin!"

"Yeh?" he piped back from the stockroom.

"I'm going out to get drunk! Mind the register!" She took Philip by the arm. "Come on," she said. "Let's talk about ships, and shoes, and sealing wax—and maybe Peggy Degen."

They went to the corner and took the booth nearest the door. He ordered a hamburger plain and a Coke, and she ordered coffee black.

"Why that crack about Peggy?" he asked.

"Because I'm sure you want to ask me about her—or maybe just talk about her."

He was forced to smile. "Mother Shipton," he said.

"Don't give me any of that classical crap. I talk to Peggy every day. She finally admitted you took her to dinner."

"Is that all?"

"Is there more?"

He grinned. "We danced close, and afterward, I held her hand."

"In a pig's eye."

"You don't seem to have much faith in your friend's resistance. She's not exactly a pushover."

"She's a girl. She has what a great assortment of boys like. She's normal. So maybe she likes what they like."

He remembered that he was a free agent. "I've got it bad for her," he said. "I admit it."

"You don't sound happy about it."

"I've also got a yellowing marriage license."

Dora Stafford nodded. "I can see where that might present a problem."

The hamburger, Coke, and coffee appeared. He took a bite of the hamburger, and then devoted himself to it. He had forgotten how hungry he was. After he had finished, he reached for the pipe in his pocket, and then remembered that he was pouchless. He borrowed a cigarette from Dora Stafford, lit hers and then his own.

"I thought I might see Peggy today," he said. "I called. She wasn't home."

"No. I spoke to her at noon. She went shopping. She'll be back around dinner."

"I tried to see her the last couple of nights. She had company."

"I know—I know—Junior Veblen the Economist."

"I met him last night."

"A real foul ball, isn't he?"

"I don't know. We just shook hands."

"I shouldn't knock him. But for me, he's from Creepsville. Dull and the square root of square. Peggy says he's much more than that, only shy and inhibited."

"Is she serious about him?"

"How would I know?" said Dora Stafford. "Ask her."

"I intend to."

"Look, I'll give you a free diagnosis. The Stafford Special for today. I'd say Peggy has round heels when she looks at you. I'd say she goes for you all the way. You got the class and the speed, but in my book that boy Cahill stays the odds-on favorite. 'Cause he's got one thing old Fleming hasn't got. Eligibility."

"She wouldn't marry somebody she doesn't care for."

"What grade are you in—sophomore? What's that got to do with what? Besides, who says she doesn't care for him? Sure she cares for him. She's got the hots for you, but she cares for him." Dora Stafford lit a fresh cigarette off her old one. "Look, my naive friend, you've had the Stafford Special, and now you shall have the Stafford Theory. Marriages are not made in heaven. There is not one man meant for every woman on earth. There's a type of man. A woman falls for a type, a vast category. In a woman's lifetime, there are a hundred men with whom she might be as happy as with the one she finally nails down. If she misses one love, well, wait, here comes another. Too late to get Fleming, so settle for Cahill. The babies will be just as healthy, and the marriage will be just as miserable or wonderful in either case. It always makes me ill to read in the papers about some lovesick kid killing herself over a guy. If she had only waited one more year. The facts of life, my friend. Our divine Peggy loves you, but she likes Cahill and ten others. What can you do for her? Make her a mistress. Pay the rent for some pad on a back street. What can he do for her? Make her a wife. You pays your money, and you takes your pick. You may make a run on it, but the future book says Cahill." She paused and stared at Philip. "That is, if all remains *status quo*. Does it?"

"I don't know what you mean."

She smiled. "Sure, you know what I mean." She wriggled out of the booth and stood up. Now, take me to my leader."

He returned Dora Stafford to the store. He was pleased that he had seen her. Not only was her no-nonsense personality stimulating, but her diagnosis and point of view seemed to fortify what was in his own mind. He walked to the corner drugstore and purchased a can of tobacco. He was about to telephone Peggy again, when he recalled that Dora Stafford had said that she was out shopping and would not be home until dinner. He walked back to the car, opening the tobacco tin and filling his pipe.

In the car, he glanced at his wrist watch. It was ten minutes after four. Peggy would not be home for another hour or two. Then, he must allow at least one more hour. He wanted dinner and Steve out of the way. He wanted to stage their meeting perfectly. At the same time, he did not want to be too late. She might be going out, and he would miss her and wind up in some motel, alone and brooding and with nothing resolved.

He drove to Wilshire Boulevard. He wanted to pass the three hours quickly, and he had an idea how to accomplish this. He left his car in the parking lot next to the ornate theater with the spiral tower, and went to the box office. He bought a loge ticket. The forecourt of the theater was empty, populated only by great masses of bearded Biblical figures charging down at him from multicolored billboards. The picture was exactly what he wanted. It was short on dialogue and long on spectacle. It was called *Armageddon*, and it had been advertised as costing upward to five million dollars. Its running time was three and a half hours. Philip recollected having read a thumbnail synopsis of it in some magazine review. The final epic battle between the goods and the bads, before the Day of Judgment, had been brought on by the swarthy prince of one tribe pilfering a blonde maiden from another tribe. Philip was sure that Homer had not been given collaboration credit with the Book of Revelations. The last mammoth slaughter had been shot in the Near East using thousands of underpriced extras, and the film had been highly praised in the reviews except for the ending. In the last scene, a stalwart lieutenant and several of the goods were allowed to survive, along with the pilfered maiden, and all faced the Last Judgment with perfect confidence.

My colleagues, Philip reflected bitterly as he found an aisle seat near the back of the theater. All of us in a costly nursery, with blank strips of celluloid and fat crayons. When his eyes had become accustomed to the interior of the theater, he saw that there were only a few dozen customers scattered about in front of him. On the grossly elongated screen, in all colors of the rainbow, fuzzy-helmeted tribesmen were tramping up an incline toward battle. The music was loud and ominous and intrusive, but there was no dialogue.

Philip sank deeper in his soft leather chair, until the seat in front almost blotted out the screen, and then lit his pipe and tried to think. Helen came to his mind at once. He tried to imagine what she was doing at this hour. Most likely, she was lying inert on the bed, wallowing in self-pity, while Danny rattled helplessly around the house. It was Helen who had spoken of divorce. It was not the first time one of them had used the word. But it had always been followed by quick forgiveness and reconciliation. This time, the provocation and the vehemence had been greater than ever before, and Philip realized that he had not encouraged reconciliation.

He tried to imagine a state of divorce. They had been married ten years, and that made it all the more difficult. A union of a year or two or three could be quickly dissolved. One emerged with a bad taste and a bruised ego, but perhaps no more. But cutting away ten years involved a major operation and considerable pain. It would upset Helen's parents and his own. It would shove Danny deeper into the abyss. And who would get custody of their friends?

He tried to project Helen as a divorcee. Would she marry again or would she devote her middle years to pity and hate and Danny? She was still young and attractive, and there would always be a few men who enjoyed her company. She might marry one of these. And himself?

He thought of Peggy Degen and tried to recast her as Peggy Fleming. His friends would like her, and he liked her friends. Dora Stafford and Horace Trubey were real finds. Where would they live? What would they do? They would not remain in Los Angeles. He could not imagine dwelling in the vicinity of an embittered and vindictive Helen. Too, Peggy could not possibly be satisfied to see him remain a spiritless motion picture or television writer. They would go abroad, of course. Even with a limited income, and alimony, they might manage that. They would live in one of those picturesque old three-storied houses in a village outside Paris, and they would commute. He would find occasional work abroad. He would even write books and become celebrated. They would put Steve in the American school. Perhaps, he could even send for Danny. They would have plenty of help. Manpower was still cheap there. They would travel with the sun, and they would make love. He would be alive at last.

He could not, he found, project Peggy into Helen's role as wife. He could not envision a day-to-day routine with Peggy. He could picture himself in bed with her in the morning. He could picture himself making love to her in the afternoon. He could picture them going to bed early in the evening. Beyond that, his imagination refused to serve him.

He sank deeper in the loge, permitting the image of Peggy to fill his mind. He regarded her possessively, with pleasurable lassitude. The music from the screen was distant and romantic. He wondered what was on the screen. His eyes were heavy. After a while, he ceased to think consciously.

When he awoke, it was to the sounds of whispered conversation of people who were being seated behind him, and to thunder from the screen. He remained still a moment, and realized that he had fallen asleep. He sat up quickly. His back ached. He bent close to his wrist watch and saw that it was twenty minutes after seven. Shocked with the lateness of the hour, he rose hastily. The expanse of colored screen loomed before him. A chesty young man in armor and rawhide, somewhat the worse for wear, had dropped his spear to lift a sobbing maiden from a field of corpses. Philip turned his back on the screen and went outside.

Night had come. The theater lights were on. There was a cluster of people around the box office. A newsboy hawked the evening paper. Traffic hummed busily on the boulevard. Friday night. Decision.

He hastened to his car.

Seven successive nights, he thought, as he wheeled his car into Ridgewood Lane and drove toward her house. Seven nights, he thought, since she moved into the house, and he had come to see her. A week of nights that had transformed his life.

It was suddenly incredible to Philip that it had been only one week. To fall in love so completely with a person that he had not known existed the month before, to consider uprooting and reshaping his life because of a relative stranger, was something that seemed, or would have seemed, implausible on paper. Yet it had happened. How? How had it happened? Of course, he knew the creaking bromide about love at first sight, but this was more than the mere emotion of adoration, this was the wrenching of a decade of marriage.

Reflecting upon it, it seemed to Philip quite normal. The answer was that Peggy, when she had appeared in his doorway that first Friday noon, had been no stranger at all. He had been acquainted with her, at least with someone remarkably like her, for many years. The explanation was the statement Dora Stafford had made a few hours before. Stafford's Theory, she had jokingly called it. There was not a single person born for every person, not a mate prepared in heaven for each marriage, but rather there was a type of person and a category of mate. And this was the actual point, he supposed. For every male on earth, there was a type of woman who arrested and aroused him. There was a certain countenance unspecific, a body, a manner, a personality, defined yet general. The favored Ideal existed. Sometimes, he saw her, unexpectedly but not surprisingly, on a motion picture film, and she was the leading lady or the most casual backdrop extra, or he saw her posing artificially in a Sicilian plaza for a fashion magazine layout or kneeling in Bermuda shorts at a staged picnic in a glossy picture magazine, or he saw her on a windy corner waiting to cross with the light as he drew up at the intersection. She was many women, and one, and he knew her well, for he had known her since puberty. He knew her from fleeting visits in his night dreams and his daydreams, but he knew her—and when she walked into his living room with a friend and a realtor, she was no stranger. Only in this way he told himself, the all-consuming experience of the week gone by was understandable and probable.

Approaching the house that he had never quite left, he was gratified to see that the coupé was not parked before it and that her convertible was still in the garage. He switched off his motor and squinted toward the living room. The blinds were drawn, but the room was brightly lit.

He quit the car and hurried across the brick walk. He rang the bell and waited. The inner feeling of excitement and resolution, that had been growing all through the day, was still there. He did not hear her footsteps. He rang the bell again, several times. Then he heard the running feet. Behind the door they halted, but the door did not open.

"Who is it?" It was Peggy's voice, stifled by the wood between them.

"Philip," he called back.

The door opened. She was hastily securing the belt of a long, sheer white negligee. The room lights behind melted the folds of the negligee from her and what was left was her marvelously curving, slender body.

She made no move to invite him in. "What are you doing here?" she asked. There was a nervous edge to her voice.

"I tried to phone you. Then I saw Dora, and she said you were out. I told you last night—I had to see you."

"Not tonight, Phil," she said. "I just can't. I have a date in an hour. I was just putting my face on."

"It can't wait," he said doggedly. "It's important."

She stared at him with indecision.

"Really important, Peggy," he persisted. There was desperate urgency in his voice now. "I've got to talk to you about us."

"All right. But just for a minute."

She opened the door wider. He went inside. He waited near the coffee table as she closed the door, then came to him, tightening her belt.

He sat on the sofa. She sat on the edge of the chair across from him, her knees together, her hands folded on her knees. For a moment, he beheld her, saying nothing, simply adoring the delicate fragile face beneath the gamin bob.

"It'll take more than a minute," he said at last.

"Phil, I've told you—"

"Why don't you hear what I have to say, first?"

She sighed and nodded with resignation. "All right," she said.

The moment was here, the culmination of a week of secret hopes and dreams and fantasies. He felt like a child with a wondrous gift to give. He looked directly at her. She sat in prim repose, a faintly perplexed wrinkle on her brow.

"Helen's giving me a divorce," he said. "I want to marry you."

He had tried, earlier, to anticipate her reaction. Her face would burst into a joyous smile of fulfillment. She would fling herself into his arms, giving herself to him completely, gratefully, whispering of her love and their love.

Instead, her face revealed surprise and then distress. "No, Phil," she said almost inaudibly.

He was bewildered. "Did you understand what I said?"

She nodded.

He leaped to his feet. "Damn it. Peggy, I want to marry you."

She rose, a hand at her temple, shaken, as he went to her and took her by the arms. "We had it out at noon," he said. "Divorce was the final thing we talked about. Then I walked out. I've been waiting all day to tell you."

"Did you tell her about me?" she asked quickly.

"Why, no. You didn't come up. She doesn't know about you. The whole thing was about something else. It has nothing to do with you. I told you right from the start, we weren't getting along."

"You've had these fights before, Phil—"

"Not like this one."

"Did you bring up the divorce?"

"She did," he said truthfully.

"But you didn't talk it over. You were just fighting."

"There's nothing to talk over, Peggy. I've wanted it since the moment I laid eyes on you. I want to marry you. I want to live with you. Isn't that what you've wanted?"

"I never asked you to get a divorce."

"I didn't say you did. But we love each other. It had to come to this."

She shook her head. "I—I don't know what to say."

"Say you're happy."

"Phil, I—" She did not finish it. Another thought occurred to her. "What time is it?" She took his arm and turned his wrist watch toward her. She dropped his arm. "I'd better call him."

"Who?"

"Jake was taking me to dinner." Her eyes met his. "I think we'd better talk this over. It's going to take more than a minute."

"Whatever you say. I just want to be with you."

She started for the bedroom hallway, and then halted, flustered. "Let me think. I've got to know what to say."

"Say there's a man here to marry you," he said lightly.

She stood thinking. He suddenly remembered Steve. "Where's Steve?" he asked.

"I farmed him out with friends overnight. We were going down to Laguna for dinner. Well, I'll think of something."

She started toward the bedroom.

"Mind if I have a drink?" he called.

"Make me one too. Double."

He went into the kitchen, took the bottle of scotch off the shelf, and then two glasses. He removed a tray of cubes from the refrigerator, broke it open, and dropped two cubes in each glass. He did not limit the scotch as he poured. He filled each glass half full, then added water, and started with the drinks toward the bedroom.

He could hear her indistinctly on the telephone, as he approached. He went into the bedroom. There was one large lamp on. She stood in the shadowy portion of the room, on the opposite side of the bed, next to the unlit lamp on the bedstand.

"No, really, Jake," she was saying, "that's not necessary. I'm sure it's just a twenty-four hour virus. I'll be fresh as a daisy tomorrow. I've just taken a pill, and I'm going right to sleep."

She listened, and Philip remained in the doorway with the drinks.

"You are a dear," she said. "I'll call you the first thing in the morning."

She listened again. Philip felt no jealousy. He was in a superior position and above all that.

"Me too," she said into the receiver. "Good night, Jake."

She settled the receiver on the hook. Philip came into the room and joined her. She turned and accepted the drink. Her face was troubled.

"To us," he said, lifting the glass.

She nodded, halfheartedly imitating his gesture, and then they drank.

"Good," he said, wagging the glass. "Now, you said we were going to talk."

"Let's finish our drinks first," she said.

They drank steadily, silently. She placed her empty glass on the table. He set his glass beside hers.

He looked at her curiously. "Something's bothering you," he said.

"Yes," she said. "Sit down, Phil." She patted the bed beside them. "Sit down here. Right here."

He lowered himself to the bed, and watched, puzzled, as she took several nervous steps before him and then sat on the bed a few feet from him, half facing him.

"Phil," she said, "before we go into anything, I want you to know this—I love you very much—really very much."

He leaned over to kiss her, but she held him off.

"No, wait—"

He resumed his former position, but apprehension was forming like a fist in his stomach.

"I think I wanted you to say that you could marry me—that you would marry me—more than anything in the world. But, at the same time, I was afraid of it," She hesitated. "I've got to be honest with you. I—I can't marry you."

The bald statement, the flat rejection, was so unexpected, that at first he was not certain that he had heard her correctly.

"What are you saying?" he asked. "What do you mean, you can't marry me? Why can't you?"

"It's not that I can't—I mean I won't—that's a better way of putting it—I won't."

"Peggy, do you know what you're saying?"

"I've thought about it all week. When I finally knew that it couldn't be—and believe me, that was hard—I did what I was going to do before I met you." She looked up. "I told Jake Cahill I'd marry him."

He did not conceal his disbelief. "Jake Cahill?"

"We'd been sort of going together. You knew that. Dora told me that she once told you—"

"I know—I know—but you're telling me you love me—you're telling me you wanted to marry me—and at the same time, you say you're going to marry someone else."

"Because it's the only thing that makes sense."

"How does it make sense?" he asked angrily. "You've been sitting here talking and not saying a word of sense."

"Let me explain—please, Phil."

He waited. He could feel his arms trembling.

"I don't want to break up someone's marriage," she said.

"But you wouldn't be. It was no good when you came along."

"It's lasted a long time. And it'll go on, no matter what fights you have. And there's Danny. And Helen was telling me that you'll have another, sooner or later. I don't want to be in the position of breaking up a family. We'd probably live here. How would it be? The two of them—you've known so long—just a short drive away. And me trying to live up to Helen—"

"You're ten times what Helen is."

"I don't know. In my heart, I think I could make you a better wife, love you more, give you what you need—but this way it would be too hard. Anytime anything went wrong with us, I would remind myself that you left them for this, you left what you were used to, what you had built, you'd broken the whole pattern for me. I have a million faults, Phil. You'd see them, eventually—and you'd start comparing—wondering—"

"That's not true, Peggy. I love you too much."

"Now. But ten years more? Would you look at me then, and the son who isn't your own, and then think of the son who is your own and—" She broke off, her eyes imploring. "Look, Phil, if you'd been divorced and alone when we met —or if we had met ten years ago—I know it would have been different. We'd have married and been happy and unhappy, but happier than most, with our own children and life built around us. But this way, it would be no good."

"Peggy, I've written this lousy renunciation scene a hundred times, and I've never believed it, and I still don't. You're cluttering the whole goddamn thing. It's clean and simple, believe me. I love you. You love me. We add it up and it reads marriage. That's the sum total. There's nothing else."

"There are my feelings. There's the way I feel, react, worry. I take that with me wherever I go. I'd be taking it into a marriage with you. And I couldn't."

"So you're going off and marry some guy you don't give a damn about. Do you think that's fair to him or to me?"

"That's not true—what you're saying isn't true. I like Jake very much. Maybe I love him. I don't know. We understand each other. It would be uncomplicated and peaceful—and I'd live with a quiet conscience—"

The vision of Peggy with Jake Cahill was incomprehensible. "You really mean you could undress in front of him and go to bed with him?"

"Of course. If he's my husband. He's attractive in many

ways. And he loves me." She paused, and then she added. "Besides, there's more to marriage and love than sleeping together."

The trembling, a chill, had spread to his chest, and he folded his arms over his chest to cover it. He looked at her, and he felt exhausted and hopeless. He saw that she was watching him. He saw compassion for his hurt, and he despised it.

"Phil," she said, "don't look like that."

"I burned my bridges for you," he said and knew that he sounded foolishly dramatic.

"You haven't," she said. "You'll manage with Helen. You always have."

"No," he said inconsolably.

She seemed about to say something more, and then she hesitated. She watched him, and suddenly she decided to say it. "There's another thing. I know you'll deny it, but—I think maybe you love Helen more than you'll admit—and me less—"

"You're out of your mind." His entire body was quivering with the chill.

"I—I don't know how to put it," she said. "I think you love me, yes—I thought so when I went to bed with you, but—the way it happened, I mean what happened—maybe that made more of me, of the whole thing, than you really meant. You wanted to sleep with me. That became the whole thing. That became the obsession. I still think it is. I think you like me—but I think this obsession means more to you than I do—I mean me, as a separate thing."

He could hardly find his voice now. He was choked. "You're going to marry him?" he said.

She looked at him with concern. "Next week," she said.

He closed his eyes, his arms wrapped across his chest, and he rocked slowly on the edge of the bed. "I want you," he said almost to himself. "I want you so much—that's all I want—"

And then he felt the hot tears on his cheeks, and he could contain it no longer, the defeat and the frustration, the loneliness. He began to cry, trying to choke down the wracking sobs, and failing. He wept uncontrollably, and then through the blinding tears he saw her. She was before him. Her arms were around him.

"Don't, Phil—please don't—"

He was beyond shame and pride. He continued to choke and sob. She drew him to her breasts, and held him closely. "Here, baby," she said softly, "be my baby."

With one hand inside her negligee she unfastened her brassiere, and then she removed it and dropped it to the floor. She directed his wet face to her naked breasts. She cupped one breast in her hand and pressed his head to it until his lips touched the soft nipple.

"I want you—want you," he said brokenly.

"You have me, darling. I'm all yours. I want you too. Come here, lie down—lie on the bed—let me lie with you."

He sank down on the bed, hardly moving, or helping, as she unbuttoned his shirt, and then pulled off his shoes, and then his trousers. His sobbing had ceased. He lay breathless and opened his burning eyes. She was standing over him. She had thrown off her negligee. She knelt on the bed over him, looking down at him with the smile of love, and her small breasts hung over him. He reached up and took one in each hand.

"They're yours," she said. "You can do whatever you want. I love you."

He circled his arms around her back and drew her down on top of him. They rolled to their sides, hugging, enfolded. He passed a hand down the unyielding arch of her spine and then across the satiny texture of her thighs. His breathing was difficult, and he felt his desire grow. He moaned softly.

"Don't wait," he heard her whisper.

"Darling—"

"Come to me—please—"

She turned on her back. For a moment, above her, looking down at her, seeing her smiling up at him, arms outstretched, he knew that the image so long held, so persistent and yet elusive, was now a reality. His chest and torso were aflame. His mouth found her mouth, and as it did, he felt the searing contact with the warm lips below. And, at last, as if magnetized, they were united, merged, coupled into one being, flesh inside flesh.

It was beyond his most erotic fancies. For him, it was a towering on the pinnacle of sensation. What she lacked in expertness she possessed, and beyond, in spontaneous passion. For her, it was a soaring. Thus transported, her unrestrained response created the tempo and the rhythm of their mating. Her nails raked the hard flesh of his back, and her eyes were shut and her face drawn in the pained mask of pleasure. And his giving, and taking, begun with control, was now driven to an unchecked fury.

They went on and on, beyond the former limitations of his masculinity and humiliations and defeats, beyond the hungry yearning of her emotional and physical needs.

Together and together, in the lofty place, in and beyond the blazing torch, together and together, in the high away, Corybant and Cybele and the orgiastic dance.

Suddenly, she stiffened beneath him and she half-lifted herself from the bed in an agonizing tremor, and it was then that he clutched her in the final paroxysm of release and liberation. . . .

Languidly, he noted the time. It was a quarter to eleven. He looked at Peggy. She was sleeping on her side, her undraped back curved in repose. He was dressed, except for his shoes. He sat on the chair, pulled on his shoes, laced and tied them.

They had lain together a long time after, side by side, cushioned by contentment, his hand covering hers, neither one speaking. They had spoken only once.

"Peggy," he had said, "Are you going to marry him?"

She had said, "Yes."

"Am I ever going to see you again?"

"No. She needs you."

"I love you, Peggy."

She had turned on her side. "I love you, too."

"Good night," he had said.

"Good-by," she had said.

He rose from the chair and looked down at her. He moved the blanket to her shoulders. Then, he bent and kissed her cheek. She did not stir.

He extinguished the large lamp near the door, and went into the hall. He walked to the kitchen. He thought that he might have a nightcap. Once in the kitchen, he had no desire for liquor. He took a glass from the shelf and filled it with water from the faucet. Then, glass in hand, he moved to the strange dinette table and looked out the window on the familiar beaded crisscross of lights far below. It was a clear night, and the view was overwhelmingly romantic. He sipped the water and continued to look out the window.

The figure of a young woman materialized in his mind. He recognized her immediately. Caroline Lamb. The difference was that for the first time he saw her clearly as a person, alive and vivacious, and as real as any woman he had ever known. The graceful movements of her slender body, the way she inclined her head, the fragile, beautiful face and the smile, all were familiar to him, and he thought that they were familiar because the resemblance was to that of a young woman he had just loved.

He emptied the water into the sink, set the glass down, and went outside. He stood on the brick walk, soaking in the crisp air and gazing at the city below. The night around was still except for the crickets. He started for his car. Never before had he known such peace.

Suddenly, he was aware of the cool wheel beneath his fingers, and the pressure of his foot on the brake, and the traffic light beyond the windshield that shone red. He glanced at the intersection, at the landmarks in the shadows, and it took him several moments to orient himself.

He realized that he had been driving along Sunset Boulevard for twenty minutes, and, until now, he had felt no sensation of those minutes or of his passage through the city and its hills. Since leaving Peggy's house, he could not recall a single face, vehicle, building, tree. It was as if he had been suspended in a timeless vacuum, propelled forward by a foreign body, with all senses shut off. He had been in perfect balance on the frictionless fulcrum of nothingness, weighted down by no pain of the past, no apprehension of the future, no lingering residue of the pleasure so recent and intense.

It was strange, he reflected, strange to be drained of all feeling after the buffeting and miseries of the seven days gone by, after the dark depths of those days and the dizzying heights of exultation that he had known little more than a few hours ago. Yet, it was a fact. He could not recollect a single impression, caught by eyes or mind's eye, since turning off Ridgewood Lane.

Beyond his curved windshield, the red light blinked off, and the green light glared brightly. He tugged at the hand shift, and the machine carried him forward.

But perhaps it was not so strange, he continued to reflect. Twenty lost minutes were as none compared to the seven days behind him. For, in a way, not quite the same way, but in a way, they had been lost, too. Except for the activities of Peggy and himself, and a few other indistinct events in the background, he could not account for anything else that had occurred during the week. From every corner of the city, the nation, the world, great media of communication, newspapers, magazines, television, radio, had been transmitting tidings of import and interest. Surely somewhere, foreign ministers had conversed in stilted, guarded words of destruction or survival; surely somewhere, men had died by violence and lived by heroism; surely somewhere, floods had raged, and lovers scandalized, and sums of gold had been gained and lost—but to all of this, Philip had been blind and deaf. For a week, he had lived on a planet inhabited by two, and on this planet no other life existed.

It was less strange than amazing, he decided, that this most momentous week in his memory would play no part in his public history. To him, the week had been the summary of his being, it had been everything, yet to others it would have no actuality. No one on all the earth knew or would know of the crucial days except he and Peggy—and not even she knew or understood its significance to him. He would grow into the years ahead, have more anniversaries, children, friends, acquaintances; he would become famous or respected or frustrated; he would add achievement to achievement and failure to failure, and earn money and spend it, and become grandparent and sage or old fool; he would love, and he would disappear, and no one would know of this one crucial week in his story.

Was it possible that this happened to other men, too? If so, history was a fraud, and those who were diggers into the past were indulging in the idiot's play of simpletons. Was it possible that the most decisive days in the lives of Jesus, Mohammed, Socrates, Kant, Darwin, Napoleon, Goethe, Freud, Marx, Tolstoi were not to be found in their writings or writings about them? Was it possible that even those whose lives had been so thoroughly illuminated by themselves and others—Samuel Johnson, Rousseau, Lincoln, Lord Byron—had carried their most vital secrets to their graves?

Philip tried to imagine another who might have had a week such as his, not a week of the same obsession but a week of equal meaning that must be kept hidden in the heart. He could think only of Byron. Had Byron possessed his half-sister Augusta Leigh and committed incest? Byron had known and Augusta had known, but no one else would ever know. And certainly Byron, like others before and since, like Philip himself, had participated in a private life secreted from all witnesses. Had not the dying poet, during the late afternoon of an Easter Sunday in Greece, summoned his valet Fletcher and gasped, "It is now nearly over. I must tell you all without losing a moment"? And had not Fletcher kneeled to him and listened and found Byron's last confession "quite unintelligible"? What had Byron wanted to reveal before the end? Would his words have affected other lives—the lives of Lady Byron, his daughter Ada, Augusta Leigh, Caroline Lamb? They were never to know. Yet . . . All at once, again, Philip became aware of the present, the reality of the car he was driving, the tight grip his hands had on the wheel, and the absolute realization—as satisfying as the consummation of love—that creative inspiration had come, and that what had been unsolved all the week past was solved all at once.

The surge of inner excitement that he felt was supplanted quickly by the calm of total victory. If no one knew Byron's secret history, the content of his last confession, then he, Philip Fleming, would be the first to know. For now he had the arrogance of the artist who, breathing alive the wraiths of fancy, is briefly God. The week of bitter bafflement, the night of despair and ecstasy, the lovely young woman on a bed in a house on Ridgewood Lane, had served this moment—had given him Lady Caroline Lamb, fulfilled.

From the car window he could see that he was entering The Briars, minutes from his house, and he could see the familiar filling station and the public telephone booth. The station was darkened, and the street before it empty. Philip turned sharply off Sunset, drove into the station, parked beside the closed pumps, and almost ran to the booth. He could not remember Nathaniel Horn's home telephone number. Impatiently, he dialed information, and then he called Horn.

"Hello?" Horn's voice sounded worried.

"Nat? Did I wake you?"

"Is that you, Phil? I always get scared when the phone rings late. No, of course you didn't wake me. I was just playing gin with my wife."

"Did you call Selby today?"

"Yes, of course." He voice quickened. "Have you got something?"

"Well—what did Selby say?"

"He bought the explanation about your being indisposed. He said he'll see you anytime tomorrow at his place."

"All right. Make the date. Nat, I've got it—"

"The third act?"

"It's good. It's better than everything else. I just got it, so I haven't had time to think it out. No details. But listen. Remember when Byron died in Missolonghi? He was in a delirium. His old valet, William Fletcher, was with him. Byron muttered his last words to Fletcher. He had some important things to say to him, about his sister, his wife, his child, things he wanted Fletcher to take back to England with him. Fletcher begged to get pen and paper and write it all down, but Byron was failing and wouldn't let him. Byron tried to pass on these vital words, but he was too sick, and he kept muttering. Fletcher couldn't hear or understand most of it. Well, here's the crux of it. For all we know, Byron might have given Fletcher a crucial message to take to Caroline Lamb, among others. It's possible, you know. Are you listening?"

"Every word."

"Okay, Byron dies. And his legacy, his last words, are in his valet's head. Fletcher sails from Greece with Byron's body. All true. Now, Fletcher is in London. Byron is buried. Fletcher must deliver those last cryptic words. But here is Caroline, alive and at a crisis in her life, as she actually was at the time. Perhaps, she's about to give herself to young Bulwer or somebody and destroy her last hopes of reunion with her husband and a life of decency. Something like that. Lo, Fletcher appears. He delivers Byron's deathbed words. Somehow, this legacy from the grave resolves Caroline, enables her to make the right decision. Or better, maybe Fletcher never clearly heard what Byron wanted him to pass along to Caroline. But Fletcher's no fool. He sees what's up with Caroline. So he fills in, invents, makes up Byron's last message—and thus helps Byron resolve, save, his first mistress."

He was out of breath. He waited.

He could detect the excitement in Horn's voice. "It's great, Phil. Just great. Absolutely perfect. It's true and it's creative, and Selby will be out of his mind. You can apply for the passport right now. I knew you'd do it—"

Philip felt too tired to continue. "Okay. I'm calling from a public booth, and I want to get going. Set me up with Selby, and I'll tell it."

"I feel like calling him right now and telling it myself. All right. I'll make the appointment. I'll get back to you in the morning. But you're in—I assure you."

He got into the car, backed out of the station, and headed west. In minutes, he was home. He parked in the garage beside Helen's coupé, squeezed out, and pulled the garage door shut.

For a moment, staring at the shrubbery alongside the house, inhaling the wonderfully fresh salt air, he thought of Peggy Degen. He looked up at the sky with its endless splash of stars, and he tried to evoke the familiar image of Peggy. Almost forcibly, he brought it into his mind, but, try as he would, it refused to come into focus. At last, he let it go.

He walked to the side entrance, unlocked it with his key, and went through the service porch into the kitchen. The lights were on, but the kitchen was empty. He went into the living room.

Helen was seated on the sofa, her legs drawn under her,

staring blankly ahead. She had not heard him, and was not aware of him, and then she saw him. She uncurled and jumped to her feet.

"Phil!" she cried.

She ran to him. He held out his arms, and she came into them, holding onto him as if she would never let him go.

"Oh, where have you been, Phil? I called everywhere. I was ready to call the police. I was going out of my mind. I thought something happened to you."

He smiled. "Nothing happened."

"I behaved terribly, and I apologize. I began to realize that after you left, and then Sam called, and I knew I had jumped to conclusions. I guess I'm just jealous. Will you forgive me?"

"There's nothing to forgive," he said.

She clung to him, and he kept her in his arms. The thought that he had held earlier in the week came back to him. In the movies, in most escape fiction, you come to the moment of decision, and once the right decision was made, then it resolved all the other things in your life. Well, maybe, he thought. But he supposed it would not really turn out that way. The book for Selby would not be all fun. It would be grinding work. And this thing that had happened to him, the entire nightmare and marvel of the week past, it might happen to him again, for there was this need in him, this unacceptable impulse. And Danny, that would be a long road, and there would be much to understand and learn. And Helen here in his arms. It might be better. It just might. But each was the product of a childhood long past, the product of those two old people and that place each remembers as being big because he was small, and there would always be that to live with. No, he thought, it's not all wrapped up in a pretty package and resolved. But, somehow, it did not seem quite so hopeless as before. The gnawing thing that had been with him all the long week, the faceless anxiety, it was gone. In this way he felt freer than he had felt in years. And he felt assured. About what, he did not know. Nor did he care. Just assured, and that was good.

He pulled away from Helen.

"I'm hungry," he said. "Whip me up a couple of eggs. I've got a lot to tell you."

She started into the kitchen, and after a moment, he followed her.

Don't Miss These Bestsellers
Available for the First Time in Paperback in SIGNET Editions

THE KING   by Morton Cooper

The daring novel about a crooner from the Bronx who rockets to the top of the show business world and turns to national politics in an attempt to give meaning to his sordid life. "It should be printed on asbestos paper," said *The American News of Books*.   (#Q3367—95¢)

THE MASTER AND MARGARITA by Mikhail Bulgakov

The *only* complete, unexpurgated paperback edition of the controversial, highly acclaimed Russian novel, called "a classic of 20th century fiction" by *The New York Times*. A ribald, uproarious epic of modern Moscow.
(#Q3397—95¢)

THE GROUCHO LETTERS   by Groucho Marx

At the drop of a cigar-ash, the irrepressible Groucho writes letters—to Howard Hughes, *Confidential* Magazine, T. S. Eliot, Harry Truman. No person is too big, no subject too sacred for the rapier-wit of Groucho. In print, as on the screen, he has the last word.
(#T3395—75¢)

TREBLINKA   by Jean-Francois Steiner

An international bestseller published in nine countries, the powerful story of a group of Jewish prisoners who led a successful rebellion against their Nazi captors in a model death camp during World War II.   (#Q3445—95¢)

THE MISSION   by Hans Habe

An international bestseller, the shocking novel, based on fact, about a man commissioned by Hitler to sell the German Jews to the nations of the world at $250 a head.   (#Q3176—95¢)

THOSE WHO LOVE   by Irving Stone

The bestselling love story of Abigail and John Adams, two people whose devotion to each other was equalled only by their patriotic passion for freedom. By the author of *The Agony and the Ecstasy*.
(#W3080—$1.50)

IN COLD BLOOD   by Truman Capote

The highly acclaimed bestselling study of the brutal and senseless murder of an entire family, the police investigation that followed, and the capture, trial, and execution of the two young murderers. "A masterpiece."—*New York Times Book Review*. A Columbia Picture starring Scott Wilson and Robert Blake.   (#Y3040—$1.25)

THE DELTA FACTOR   by Mickey Spillane

Spillane's toughest, most resourceful hero yet, Morgan the Raider, makes his debut in a fast-moving thriller in which he pulls a forty million dollar heist, escapes from prison and is recruited by the Feds for a vital mission.
(#P3377—60¢)

THE GRADUATE   by Charles Webb

The highly praised first novel about the misadventures of a brilliant young post-graduate who revolts against his solid-gold future. Now an Embassy Picture starring Anne Bancroft and Dustin Hoffman, and directed by Mike Nichols.
(#P3167—60¢)

HOPSCOTCH   by Julio Cortazar

From love in a Paris flat to a madhouse in Buenos Aires, a novel that gets to the core of life, love, and death. "The most brilliant novel in years,"—*New Republic*. By the author of *Blow-Up*.
(#Q3329—95¢)

BABYHIP   by Patricia Welles

Alternately sophisticated, coarse, dreamy, seductive, childish and bored, the sixteen-year-old heroine of this entertaining novel sums up the defiance, the off-beat humor, and the flamboyant originality of her flipped-out generation.
(#Q3465—95¢)

DOWN THESE MEAN STREETS   by Piri Thomas

A powerful autobiography, unanimously praised by the critics, this is the story of one man's journey from childhood to maturity in the violent world of Spanish Harlem.
(#Q3471—95¢)

THE SWEET RIDE   by William Murray

Everything swings in this novel about a rootless, restless new breed of youth who want nothing more than a "sweet ride" on alcohol, on drugs, in bed, but mostly on the pounding surf. Coming soon as a Twentieth Century-Fox motion picture, produced by Joseph Pasternak and starring Michael Wilding, Tony Franciosa, Bob Denver, Michael Sarrazin and Jacqueline Bisset. (#T3228—75¢)

TO OUR READERS: If your dealer does not have the SIGNET and MENTOR books you want, you may order them by mail enclosing the list price plus 10¢ a copy to cover mailing. (New York City residents add 5% Sales Tax. Other New York State residents add 2% plus any local sales or use taxes.) Please order books by book number and title. If you would like our free catalog, please request it by postcard only. The New American Library, Inc. P. O. Box 1478, Church Street Station, New York, N.Y. 10008.